Also by Ron Schwab

Sioux Sunrise
Paint the Hills Red
Grit
Cut Nose

The Lockes
Last Will
Medicine Wheel
Hell's Fire

The Law Wranglers
Deal with the Devil
Mouth of Hell
The Last Hunt
Summer's Child
Peyote Spirits

The Coyote Saga
Night of the Coyote
Return of the Coyote
Twilight of the Coyote

Cut Nose

Ron Schwab

Uplands Press
OMAHA, NEBRASKA

Uplands Press
4922 Cass St
Omaha, NE 68106
www.uplandspress.com

Publisher's Note: This is a work of fiction. Names, characters, places, and incidents are a product of the author's imagination. Locales and public names are sometimes used for atmospheric purposes. Any resemblance to actual people, living or dead, or to businesses, companies, events, institutions, or locales is completely coincidental.

Ordering Information:
Quantity sales. Special discounts are available on quantity purchases by corporations, associations, and others. For details, contact the "Special Sales Department" at the address above.

Cut Nose / Ron Schwab -- 1st ed.

ISBN 978-1943421398

To the defenders of liberty, wherever they may be.

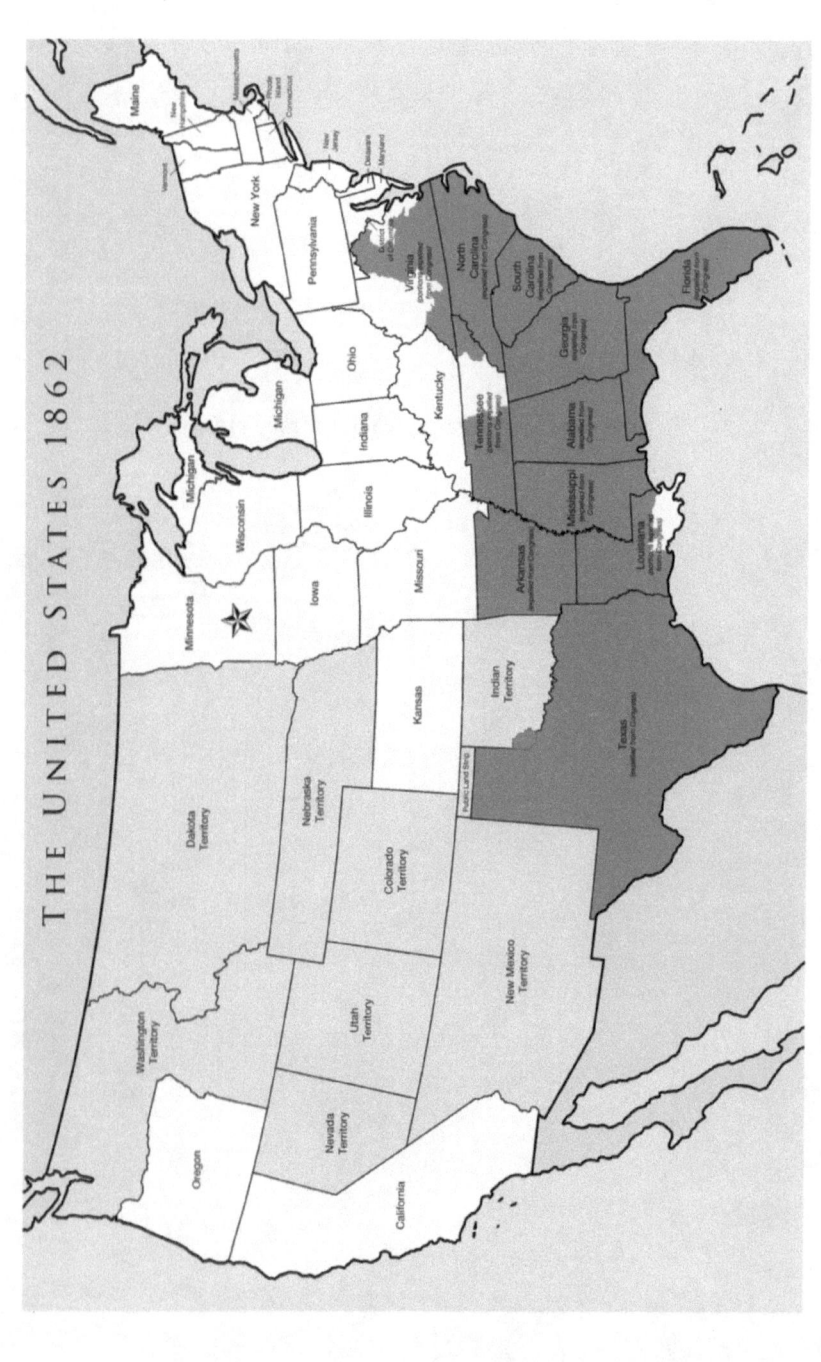

THE UNITED STATES 1862

SW MINNESOTA 1862

Fort Abercrombie

DAKOTA
TERRITORY

Red River of the North

Mississippi River

Dakota Reservation

Minnesota River

St. Paul

Fort Snelling

Hutchinson

Shakopee

Upper Agency
(Yellow Medicine)

Birch Coulee

Henderson

Lower Agency
(Redwood)

Fort Ridgley

New Ulm

St. Peter

Mankato

IOWA

Cut Nose

Part I

The Uprising

Chapter 1

WILL NILSSON SAT in a straight-back chair in the waiting area of the post commandant's office at Fort Snelling, an Army post lying southwest of St. Paul in the new state of Minnesota. The former territory had acquired statehood on May 11, 1858, just in time to assure its full participation in the War of the Rebellion, which had been killing and maiming Union and Confederate soldiers for more than a year now. The sometimes-called "Civil War" commenced April 12, 1861 with bombardment of the Union Army at Fort Sumter, South Carolina by the Confederates. Will remembered dates and found this sometimes annoyed his friends, but it was helpful for birthdays and anniversaries. This day was July 20, 1862.

He expected to be a part of the war effort soon. He had arrived at Fort Snelling after a furlough visit to his parents' farm a week earlier. He was awaiting assignment when a skinny private had delivered a message yesterday directing him to appear at the commandant's office the next morning at ten o'clock. This was not ordinarily the way one received his orders, and he was baffled by his purpose here. He assumed it had something to do with the ongoing war effort and his duty assignment.

Most of his thirty-seven West Point classmates were engaged in combat on one side or the other. Several had served in both armies. Major Manning M. Kimmel had fought with the Union at the First Battle of Bull Run on July 1, 1861 and thereafter resigned to join the Confederate Army, where he was also serving as a major the last report Will had received. He was aware of a few who had died in the conflict, and there were likely more by now. One was Union and the other two, Confederate.

One of the dead Confederate soldiers had been his best friend at the Point, Jimmy Townsend. He had not sorted out all the moral aspects of the Civil War just yet. He saw it mostly as another failure of the politicians, but he admitted to cynicism where the operations of government were concerned. He had never spent any time in the South, but Jimmy had said he and his family were not slaveholders, and he had insisted that most Southerners were not. He had even expressed his personal opposition to the institution. Folks like Jimmy must have believed they were fighting for a greater cause.

The commandant's office door opened, and a short man with gray hair and a neatly-trimmed beard stepped out. Had he not been nattily attired in civilian clothing, Will thought the man might have passed for Robert E. Lee's double. Their eyes met for a moment, but before the stranger spoke, Will could sense he was being appraised like a horse scrutinized for prospective purchase. "Captain Wilhelm Erik Nilsson?"

Will stood, "Yes, sir." He stifled a reflexive salute, since the man was evidently civilian. "Mostly, I go by 'Will,' though."

"My name is Charles Hanscomb." He took a few paces toward Will and offered his hand, and Will accepted his firm grip, realizing only at that moment that he towered over Hanscomb. Will stood a few inches over six feet, and he estimated Hanscomb nearly a foot shorter. But there was something about his confident bearing that gave the man an authoritative and formidable presence. Will suspected ladies would have found him quite handsome. "I am President Lincoln's personal emissary. I was sent from Washington to confer with Governor Ramsey. While I am in the state, I had hoped I might speak with you. We have been tracking your whereabouts. Please come in."

Will did not know how to respond, so he was relieved when Hanscomb turned and led him into the commandant's office. He had expected to find the colonel there, but the room was empty, and Hanscomb claimed the colonel's chair behind the desk, gesturing for Will to take one of the chairs in front. He opened a folder lying on the scarred and coffee-stained oak desk and removed ten or twelve sheets of paper and began thumbing through them. His perusal was brief, telling Will he had previously read the documents.

He raised his head and looked at Will with piercing cobalt-blue eyes. "Captain. Impressive for a twenty-six-year old man without combat experience."

Will was a bit embarrassed about his rank, feeling he had done nothing special to deserve it. "The Judge Advocate General's Corps is generous with promotions. Otherwise, when a tour of duty expires, many lawyers resign their commissions after serving their commitment periods. Or those who joined the Army for traditional purposes may be tempted to seek commissions in the regular Army."

"You were commissioned out of West Point. How did you end up with JAG?"

"I never had a military career in mind. I sought admission to West Point for the free education. I always figured to serve my time and then go on to something in civilian life. JAG was looking for graduates to attend law school for two years and become lawyers—more free education. That's how I ended up at Yale." Will hesitated before deciding he could be frank with this man. "And I could fulfill my service obligation without getting shot at."

Hanscomb smiled and chuckled. "Then why did you resign your commission with JAG? You could have sat out the war in an office with occasional visits to a military tribunal. JAG officers are commissioned separately, and your rank is not transferable. You could face a demotion to first lieutenant."

"Guilt, I suppose. I happen to be a fair horseman, and classmates were fighting and dying in the war—on both sides. I just didn't feel right about not being there somehow. I had undergone some changes in my personal life that altered my perspective as well. And I wonder now if I was entirely lucid when I made the decision. Please, don't misunderstand me. Those who are serving in JAG are serving honorably, and the branch has a proud history. It was founded by General George Washington himself on July 29, 1775."

"You do know your history."

Will found himself embarrassed again. "It's a quirk of mine. I recall dates."

"A harmless enough quirk, I should think. Anyway, you should not make light of your military background. I have your history in front of me, and I have communicated with some of your former professors at the Point. Third ranked in the class of 1857. A marksman. First in horsemanship. I would rank that above fair. You were destined for a few stars if you had become a cavalry officer, according to your mentors. There was some disappointment when you opted for JAG."

"The stars are sheer speculation. I was never comfortable with the regimentation of Army life. I adapted to it, but it was contrary to my nature. I want to do my duty, but if I survive the war, my life thereafter will not be in the military."

"Well, your journey to the War of the Rebellion has been deferred by order of your Commander-in-Chief."

He had Will's full attention. "The President? I don't understand."

"All other orders have been suspended. You have been attached to the presidential staff indefinitely, and you will take your orders from me as the President's emissary."

"And I assume you have new orders for me? Of course, I cannot imagine where this is leading."

"You are going to stay in Minnesota, Captain, until your mission here is completed. And you will not incur the demotion I mentioned."

So far, he had told Will nothing, so he just nodded understanding.

"The President is forced to give his full attention to the rebellion, but he has these little gnats that keep distracting him—or, in this instance, given our locale, perhaps I should say mosquitoes. We are very concerned about the threat of an Indian uprising here, and the Union has no troops to spare to deal with this possibility. The President needs to know if this threat is real and if there is some way to abort it."

"And I am to look into this?"

"During our brief investigation, we learned that you hailed from Minnesota, and then we found out that you grew up just outside of what is now the Dakota reservation. The clinchers were your Indian blood and that you speak some of the Dakota Sioux dialect."

"I have probably had no more contact with the Dakota than others who were raised in the area. I am quarter-blood Dakota of the Sisseton band. My mother is half-blood. Her mother was a full-blood, who married a

Ron Schwab

French trader. My mother speaks fluent Dakota and insisted my sister and I learn it also. When I was a child, before the more recent influx of Scandinavians and Germans, I knew more Dakotas than whites. But you can see that despite my Swedish name, I am essentially an American mongrel. I would not pass for a Swede with my dark hair and brown eyes. And my complexion would not be considered Nordic by any means."

Hanscomb said, "Ambiguity in your heritage should be an asset here. Perhaps it will allow you to travel with less notice and suspicion among the Dakotas."

"I think any stranger passes with notice and suspicion among the Dakotas these days. I just returned from a visit to my parents' farm. It lies several miles north and east of Fort Ridgely. My father is very worried about the Dakota unrest, although most of his neighbors do not share his concerns. He was part of one of the early, small waves of Scandinavian immigrants and has lived here since he was sixteen years old. He has a sense of history, you might say. The newcomers, who have arrived since the Treaty of 1851, seem oblivious to the danger. It is somewhat understandable because there are so many mixed bloods, and a good number of Dakota have taken up farming and appear to pose no threat. It is a very com-

plicated society out there and not as stable as it might appear."

"I can see that your insight will be invaluable. All we want from you is reliable first-hand information that is untainted by any personal agenda."

Will could understand that. Indian matters were a toxic political topic in Minnesota, and many local politicians had strong military ties. Henry Hastings Sibley, a Democrat, had been elected the state's first governor in 1858 and had recently been appointed colonel of the state militia charged with protecting exposed settlements from the Dakota. With the Civil War in progress, his political party had fallen out of favor, but Sibley, who was barely fifty, was likely mindful that the winds of public opinion often turn quickly and would probably be preparing for that time. Will could see why Hanscomb might seek advice unfiltered by local politics.

"There is one thing I can do nothing about," Will said.

"And what is that?"

"The government is late on the annuity payments promised by the treaties. This is causing great stress to the Dakota people. And it provides fuel for those who want to take advantage of this unrest."

"We are working on this, and the President has already interceded with the Bureau of Indian Affairs and Treasury Department."

Chapter 2

CUT NOSE, ASTRIDE his gray, white-stockinged gelding, looked out over the Minnesota River valley from atop a scalped knoll. In the distance he could make out John Otherday's small farm. He knew every inch of the farm's building site intimately from nighttime scouting visits. One such night, he had cut the throat of a big dog that had barked ferociously and awakened the sleeping occupants of the house before attacking him. He glanced at the raised white scar on his wrist, a reminder of the beast's aborted effort. He hoped Otherday had guessed that the visitor who killed the cur was Cut Nose.

He hated no man more than Otherday. And the traitor would be among the first to die, after he watched the slaughter of his wife and children. Cut Nose intended to personally deliver a long and agonizing death to Otherday, only after he had first taken the coward's scalp.

John Otherday, like Cut Nose, was full-blood Dakota Sioux but was of the Wahpeton band, son of Red Bird, an influential chief. Cut Nose was Mdewakanton, who with the Wahpekute, occupied that portion of the reservation served by the Redwood Agency, commonly called the Lower Agency. The Sisseton and Wahpeton resided near the Yellow Medicine, or Upper Agency. The agencies were economic centers on the reservation with separate Indian agents responsible for distribution of government allotments and annuities to the bands.

Otherday had abandoned the Dakota ways and become a farmer Indian in the Hazelwood Community near the Upper Agency, casting his lot with white society and culture. Many other Dakotas had joined him, although they still constituted a minority. Those, who like Cut Nose, rejected the white man's path were often called "blanket Indians" by the whites.

Otherday, Cut Nose thought, had always been white beneath his brown skin. They were both the same age, forty-one summers now, but as boys they had never been friends. Otherday had often visited his uncle, Great Bear, who was Mdewakanton and lived in Cut Nose's village. But near his own village he had attended one of the mission schools, learning the white language and allowing his thinking to be twisted by the white teachers. He had even adopted a white name, "John." While Cut Nose had learned enough English to allow communication with the whites, he had not prostituted himself so much as to read and write the language.

He and Otherday had been strong competitors as boys, one or the other usually winning races, archery matches, and other contests of skill and strength with the other boys their age. Until one of such competitions, Cut Nose had been known as Mapeokinijin, in the Dakota language meaning "Who Stands on a Cloud."

The memory of that day was as clear now as if it had happened yesterday. It was during his fifteenth summer, only a few days after he had seduced his first woman, the young fourth wife of an old warrior absent from the village on a hunt. In truth, he conceded, he may have been the seduced. It mattered not. He still remembered her fondly.

A dozen loinclothed Dakota boys gathered in a clearing along a creek bank. Several started playful wrestling. Then, the winner challenged another. When Mapeokinijin was challenged, he sprang eagerly into the jagged ring formed by the onlookers and quickly dispatched the challenger. He was taller than most boys his age and proud of his muscular, athletic body. He considered himself the strongest of his contemporaries, and, as usual, was caught up in the competition.

He stood and cast his eyes about the clearing to identify his next victim and paused when he caught sight of Otherday standing in the trees at the edge of the clearing. He was a late-comer and apparently considered himself an observer of the competition. Mapeokinijin knew that Otherday was reluctant when it came to one-on-one wrestling contests for some reason. He seemed to lack a warrior's heart. He was stocky and short of leg, although still surprisingly fast in a foot race, but he would probably flinch at striking a death blow to an enemy. Mapeoki-nijin did not like him even then, and he called out a challenge:

"Come out from your hiding place, Otherday. You cannot hide from me like a mouse in the woods. I challenge you."

At first, Otherday hesitated, but he finally stepped into the clearing.

Mapeokinijin said, "I give you the advantage of first strike."

"No. I do not choose to fight you."

"You have no choice." Mapeokinijin charged him with arms outstretched to wrap about his opponent's waist, but just prior to contact, Otherday deftly stepped aside, and Mapeokinijin stumbled forward and landed on his chest in the dust.

His friends laughed, except for those few who knew his quickness to anger and obsession to avenge any perceived rid-

icule or slight. He looked up and saw Otherday displaying a smug smile on his face. The coward extended his hand in a gesture to assist him to his feet. Mapeokinijin decided then that Otherday must die. He slipped his skinning knife from its sheath and swiped it at the other boy's hand, narrowly missing. He leaped to his feet, crouching and moving toward the surprised Otherday, whose smile had disappeared, replaced now by tight-set lips. Unexpectedly, Mapeokinijin saw grim determination in his adversary's eyes, not fear.

He lunged with the knife, and Otherday stood his ground, latching onto Mapeokinijin's wrist and twisting sharply and wrenching it until the attacker released the knife and it dropped to the earth. Then, Otherday flung him away and he fell on his buttocks to the sound of still more laughter. Berserk with rage now, Mapeokinijin gathered his composure and approached more deliberately, while Otherday waited, apparently expecting to out-finesse him. This time, Mapeokinijin drove his head into the other boy's abdomen, leaving him gasping for breath. Mapeokinijin drove his fist into his opponent's jaw, sending him reeling before he straightened and struck back. Soon they were rolling on the ground, both bruised and bloodied. First, one had the advantage, and then the other. But Mapeokinijin sensed Otherday was tiring—too much time spent with the white man's school and books.

When he next had Otherday down, his hands went for his opponent's throat, his fingers closing in a death grip he vowed not to release. He lay on top of his adversary, driving a knee forcefully into Otherday's crotch. For the first time, the boy let forth an agonized scream. They were face to face now, and, nearly naked as they were, almost coupled like obscene lovers, thought Mapeokinijin as he squeezed the scream away from Otherday's mouth. It was at that instant that Otherday somehow found the strength to launch a final struggle, yanking frantically at Mapeokinijin's arms, forcing him to relax his grip. Otherday's head shot upward, and the agony was now Mapeokinijin's as pain consumed his face, and he realized the other boy's teeth were anchored in his nose. He jerked upward, but the teeth held like a vise, and he could feel the flesh of his nose tearing away and a river of blood flowing over his lips and down his chin. He tumbled off Otherday and rolled away, clutching at his mutilated nose.

He was embarrassed now to remember how he had howled in anguish like a papoose. He did not recall when or how Otherday disappeared that day, but he remembered he had feared that his entire nose had disappeared down his adversary's throat. Later he had been relieved to learn that only a sizable chunk of flesh from his left nostril to the lower fleshy part of the right side of his nose had been ripped away. The ghastly wound had left a disfigurement on his face but did not impair function, and he soon found it did not repel females. From that day forward Mapeokinijin became Cut Nose.

Cut Nose decided now that he would also take Otherday's wife before he scalped and killed her. It would be pleasing to watch his nemesis look on while Cut Nose impaled her with his rigid pole. When he was finished with her, perhaps he would even share her with other worthy warriors. She was a yellow-hair with a pleasant form, and he was now excited with thoughts of what he might do to her.

He had been visiting friends of the Soldiers Lodge at the Upper Agency rallying them to the upcoming war, but in the morning he must return to the Lower Agency for a meeting of the Lodge that evening. He wondered if Marta's man would be home tomorrow. The Soldiers Lodge did not meet until after sunset. There would be ample time for him to visit, and his musings once more triggered his endless hunger for her.

Chapter 3

ANJA LUND STOOD at the window of the Lower Agency's mission school and surveyed the rectangular grounds known as Council Square about which the agency's commercial operations were clustered. There were nearly thirty structures, including the agency office, a blacksmith's, at least four stores and trading posts, a large warehouse, stables, and Dickinson's Boardinghouse, where she expected to reside during the coming school term. School would not commence for another two weeks, but she had been too excited about her new assignment at the agency school to stay away. She had been unable to resist riding in from her parent's log house almost five miles north and east of the agency to prepare the single-room school for her pupils.

She was very aware she faced a challenge. Her class-room would include a good number of children of agency employees, traders, and other whites servicing the agency. Hopefully, some of the Dakotas would send their children, but the Dakota bands at the Upper Agency had a history of more participation in the educational offerings than those settled at the Lower Agency. She could expect a fair number of mixed-bloods, she had been told, and could look for as many as twenty-five pupils ranging in age from six to seventeen. Some would speak no English, and her fluency in the Dakota Sioux dialect had virtually guaranteed her employment.

She had just turned twenty years of age in March, but she had already experienced a year of teaching in a one-room school near St. Paul, where her parents had sent her to live with her grandmother, her father's elderly mother, to attend high school and another year of teacher training. Few in Minnesota had attained more than an eighth-grade education, most far less or none, and she was not unmindful of her good fortune. Her teaching opportunities here excited her, but she thought it improbable she would have returned to this rugged and desolate country if her fiancée, Lieutenant Matthew Hale, had not been killed in infantry warfare during some obscure battle in Virginia. His death, less than four months into the war, had devastated her and left her numb. After that first teaching year, she had decided to return home for a visit. She had been with her parents only a few days when she heard about the unfilled teaching position at the agency school.

"Miss Lund, I am arranging the books in alphabetical order by author. Is that all right?"

Anja started and turned away from the window. She had almost forgotten about Karina Johanns, the quiet sixteen-year-old who had volunteered to help ready the school for classes. Karina's father, Anders, was a friend of her own father, Larson, and he had inquired on behalf of his bookish daughter. In the three days they had worked together at the school, the two had become increasingly comfortable with each other, and Anja loved mentoring the girl, deciding she would occasionally use her as an assistant during the term. Karina's mother was full-blood Dakota, and like Anja the girl was bilingual.

"I think that's a good idea, Karina. I just wish we had more books."

"I talked to Reverend Goth at the Presbyterian Church. He's going to contact all the churches in the area about asking members to donate any extra books for the school. We'll get some, but there might not be many. Some folks just don't have books."

"That's wonderful. Thank you. Anything will help."

"Miss Lund?"

"You may call me 'Anja' when school's not in session."

"Your name is not pronounced like it's spelled."

"That depends. It's 'ahn-yah.' Norwegian. Not that different from your father's German. 'Yes' in German is '*ja*.'" She smiled. "Yah?"

"I guess. Papa does not speak German, but my grand-parents came from Germany, and they do sometimes. But I just hear. I don't see the spelling."

"I'm sorry. You wanted to ask me something?" She gestured to one of the student desks near the window. "Let's sit down." They took chairs side by side at a double desk.

"Yes. I would like to go to high school. Become a teacher. Like you."

"That would be wonderful. But, of course, you would have to go to St. Paul."

"That's where my grandparents live. I could stay with them."

"It sounds like you have this figured out. I stayed with my grandmother when I attended school."

"But I don't know if I qualify for high school. I would attend this school another year anyway. Maybe you would help me prepare."

"I would love to. And I can order a test that would enable us to determine if there are subjects you need to work on. It would also give us an idea what year you would qualify for. It would be nice if we could prepare you to enter at eleventh or twelfth grade level. I have no doubt your reading skills already take you beyond that."

"That's an exciting thought." She hesitated. "Was it hard for you—being an Indian and all?"

"I never thought about it. Of course, I am just quarter-blood."

"Really, I thought you were at least half. Like me."

"I can see why you would think that. I *am* a bit darker than you." She placed her hand on the desk and compared it to Karina's. Her almond-colored skin was tinted noticeably darker than the girl's. Not for the first time, she wondered about that. She also noted that Karina's dark hair, streaked with chestnut strands, was far lighter than her own long sable tresses.

"I didn't mean to offend you. Your skin is so perfect, and you are so beautiful."

"You didn't offend me in the slightest. Anyway, it was not a problem. There were many mixed-bloods in the school, probably half dozen full-bloods and even three free Negroes. I don't recall any troubles there, but I was never one to give such things much thought. I just focused on school." Until she met Matthew, anyhow. Fortunately, she was near graduation by that time.

"Well, you have made me less fearful. And I do want to take the test."

"I'm glad. Let's call it a day. I'll ride with you to your place."

They collected their mounts at the agency stable. Both young women wore practical denims, cotton shirts and moccasins for riding and working. Their attire did not draw notice on the reservation, where a wardrobe might consist of anything or next to nothing.

They rode along the winding trail among the trees that led to the Minnesota River bottom land Anders Johanns had only partly cleared for his small farm and where he spent most of his days working as a carpenter and furniture craftsman. Anja and Karina caught up on the latest gossip. At first their conversation was casual and light-hearted, but then, Karina asked, "Do you know about the Soldiers Lodge?"

"No. But remember I have been gone for some years. Is it a new building at the agency?"

"It is not a building. It is a society of Dakotas who are trying to stir up an uprising against the whites. They think they can drive all whites from the state of Minnesota."

"They can't be serious. They are a bit late. A few months back, I read an article in a St. Paul newspaper. The writer noted that prior to the 1851 treaty, there were only sixty-five hundred whites in Minnesota. Today, there are over two-hundred thousand."

"It is said the Soldiers Lodge is getting more members daily. The delay of the gold for the annuity payments promotes their cause."

"Are you worried about this?"

"More like terrified. I do not think people are taking this threat seriously enough."

"Who are the leaders of this lodge? Do You know?"

"Young Shakopee supports the lodge. He is known as Little Six."

"The chief Old Shakopee's son?"

"Yes. And Red Middle Voice is another. Cut Nose is said to be the most influential of the older warriors and may be the real leader of the Soldiers Lodge. You have heard of him?"

Anja sighed. "Yes, I have heard of him."

Chapter 4

AFTER BIDDING KARINA goodbye at the Johanns farm, Anja pondered angling southeast the short distance to the Redwood Ferry for a dry crossing of the Minnesota River. The river ran low and quiet today, however, and she knew of a nearby bend where the river widened and shallowed. She and her bay mare, Molly, had crossed at the spot many times over the years, and, while she might get the legs of her britches wet, she always enjoyed a bit of adventure. Even if the current caught them, they would be gently swept to a sandbar around the bend on the opposite side of the river. She removed her moccasins and stuffed them in her saddlebags and reined the mare toward the river.

The water turned out to be as friendly as Anja expected, and the mare soon gained her footing on the sandbar landing. Anja dismounted, slipped into her moccasins and led Molly up the gently sloping riverbank. Taking a long-established deer trail, she threaded through the oak and cottonwood trees that forested the river bottom there. In another half hour, she broke out onto a rutted dirt road that snaked its way with the river's course. Her parents' farm residence lay a mile northwest, a short distance off the road, where the woodlands gave way to open prairie, much of which was now cultivated for corn, oats, and wheat or harvested for hay, if not allocated for cattle and horse pastures.

The farm so diligently cultivated by Larson Lund had been established shortly before Anja's birth, while the Dakota still challenged the white man's occupancy. His marriage to a half-blood whose grandfather had been a respected chief had earned his presence reluctant tolerance. When the Dakota surrendered more territory to the Great White Father in Washington under the 1851 agreement, the Lund farm had ended up inside of the twenty-mile wide reservation carved out for the Dakotas, with portions of the Dakota land falling on both sides of the western branch of the Minnesota River. A subsequent treaty had reclaimed all land lying north and east of the river for the white man, and this had enabled Lund to acquire undisputed title to the quarter section of land—undisputed as far as Minnesota land title records indicated, anyway.

When she reached the farmstead road, Anja mounted the mare again and rode the horse at a slow trot down the road toward the house. She knew her father would not be home. He worked part-time for a freighter, making a long run to and from nearby Fort Ridgely to Fort Snelling. This caused him to be absent periodically long stretches at a time but provided income to supplement the farm, where income depended on ample rains and was inconsistent at best. He was not expected home for a few more days and would then have a two-week break before heading out again.

She reined in when she spotted the gray, white-stockinged gelding tied in front of the log house that had been so painstakingly crafted by Larson Lund. It even boasted an oak floor in country where many settled for packed dirt. Cut Nose was paying a call on her mother, Marta, as he had been doing for as long as she could remember. She dismounted and led Molly to the barn, where stalls were maintained for the mare and other horses. She would unsaddle and grain and brush her horse. If Cut Nose had not departed by the time she finished, she would remain in the barn until he left.

When she completed caring for Molly, she peered out the barn door and saw that Cut Nose's horse was still staked out in the yard. She sat down on a shaky milking stool in the stall with a stanchion, where the guernsey cow was milked twice daily, fuming as she waited, almost hating Marta Lund for what she was doing in the house with that man. She was sickened again by her mother's infidelity to her father.

Marta Lund was a dark beauty, with long straight hair like Anja's. She was just short of her thirty-eighth birthday, having been only seventeen when she gave birth to Anja. Larson was twenty years older, and the marriage had been sealed by payment of a dowry to Marta's father, a Canadian trader of Norwegian extraction, who did not care much for Swedes but foresaw a limited market for a half-breed daughter. Her mother's family roots were in the Mdewakanton band, and Marta had been raised mostly in her mother's village. Anja supposed that was how she had come to know Cut Nose.

Cut Nose had never visited often, usually no more than every month or two, and always when Larson was absent. Cut Nose had always been kind to Anja, often bringing crafted gifts like doeskin moccasins or intricately beaded bracelets or chokers. When he stopped by, Marta might join Cut Nose for a long walk in the woods across the road, always carrying a blanket. It did not bother Anja to be left alone. She usually preferred her own company to that of others and carried on many lives inside her head. She had not outgrown her daydreaming yet. As she grew older, she did not see so much of Cut Nose when school was in session, but, if she was home, her mother would often send her on a shopping mission to the trading post three miles down the road.

She could not remember when she first suspected that Cut Nose was stopping at the house for more than conversation and a cup of coffee. She could not wash away with hot water and lye soap, however, the image of her mother and Cut Nose when she had come home early from school. She had just passed her thirteenth birthday. The Dakota's horse had evidently been tied in the trees across the road, and she had walked blithely into the house unaware of his presence. Then, she had heard her mother moaning in her parents' bedroom and feared she might be ill. Anja had hurried to the bedroom and frozen at the open doorway when she saw the naked bodies of Cut Nose and Marta Lund entwined.

Anja had felt suddenly ill and whirled and quickly and quietly made her exit from the house. She retreated into the woods and remained hidden there until she saw Cut Nose ride away.

She had said nothing to her mother about what she witnessed that afternoon. But things were never the same between them. She had found it extremely difficult to talk to her mother after that, and she had found herself pressing even more urgently to be sent to St. Paul to further her education. Her mother resisted. She was happy without a formal education, she had insisted. Anja should be preparing to find a husband. Her father listened, though. He had spent some years in grade school and could read and write passably. He had often expressed regret that he had not found a way to advance his schooling. He heard her pleas and arranged for her to board with his relatives in St. Paul and found money to help support her there. And she would always love him for the priceless gift of her education.

She understood lust now. After learning Matthew was going away to war, she had given herself to him. And after that first time, she had required no coaxing. But she had betrayed no one, and she had been prepared to marry him if his company had not suddenly been ordered to action. She still missed him and ached for his touch.

As for her mother and Cut Nose, Anja knew whatever they did was beyond her control, probably none of her concern. She was sad for her father, who would always be her one and only father. But not long after she viewed her mother and Cut Nose engaged in heated intimacy, she had begun to wonder if she had been sired by the Dakota warrior. Did it matter now? She could not say. But the question gnawed at her, and she decided it was time to confront her mother.

Chapter 5

WILL'S FIRST STOP was Fort Ridgely, and he decided to travel by way of his parents' farm. Even though he had visited recently, he wanted to commandeer his claybank stallion, Warrior, to serve as his primary mount on his assignment, the purpose of which was still quite vague to him. Hanscomb had told him if he came across intelligence the President should be made aware of, Will would recognize it. By then, given the communication hurdles, Will figured it would be too late and had bluntly told him so. "We still need eyes and ears on the ground there," Hanscomb had insisted.

When Will trotted the blood-bay gelding he had selected from the Army's pathetic inventory into the yard, he saw that his father was loading the buckboard with household items, a few pieces of furniture, pots and pans, blankets, and canned fruits and vegetables. He dismounted and led the blood-bay over to the wagon. His father had seen him ride into the farmyard and stepped toward him and gave him a big bear hug, almost causing Will to drop the horse's reins. Will's father was strong as an ox and almost matched his height. And Erik Nilsson looked the Swede of stereotype. At a shade over fifty years, his straw-colored hair was turning white, and his fair skin was hidden by his perpetual summer sunburn. The wide-brimmed, Plainsman hat he always wore generally lost the battle to the sun's abuse.

Erik Nilsson released his son and stepped back. "Now this is a surprise, Will. A good one. What are you doing here?"

"Army business. Special assignment. I can't really talk about it."

"Sounds like you're a spy of some kind."

"Close enough, I guess." Will tossed a thumb toward the buckboard. "What's this all about?"

"I'm sending your mother to Fort Ridgely. The Army's encouraging folks to come in because of possible Indian trouble. I wanted to send her for a visit to Annette in St. Paul, but she refuses to go. She's tentatively agreed to go to the fort nights and come here days for now. I figure if I can get her to step into the fort on her own, it might be easier to push her in later if things go sour. It would help if you would back me up on this."

Will didn't bite on that proposition. His mother would recognize any conspiracy and cut loose with a tongue-lashing he preferred to avoid. His dad was a calm, stoic sort. Alexis Nilsson was anything but.

"I came by to recruit Warrior," Will said. "I'd like to use him as my main mount while I'm here and have this blood-bay tag along as a backup."

"He's your horse and he's done breeding for this season. Might do you both good to get out together. He's missed you something awful since you took off again."

His father was more rancher than farmer. He ran a fair-sized herd of mixed breed cattle, much of his production being sold to either nearby Fort Ridgely or Fort Abercrombie further northwest on the Dakota Territory side of the border with Minnesota. He also owned a dozen mares and raised horses that he sold either to the Army or other breeders. He didn't like selling to the Army at low prices and had increasingly sought out farmers in the market for good horse flesh. With the war, though, the Army's demand for horses had become insatiable, and he had resigned himself, as a patriotic American, to selling to the government.

Will still owned Warrior and two mares on the place, and his dad always insisted on paying breeding fees for Warrior's stud services and giving Will half the sale price for foals raised and sold from his mares. Will knew his dad still hoped to entice him back to the farm after the war. Who knew? Considering the war's casualty counts, Will was not inclined to speculate.

His parents owned a half section of land, a substantial holding for a western Minnesota farmer. Erik Nilsson's first one hundred sixty acres had been claimed under the Preemption Act of 1841, which essentially said that, regardless of Indian occupancy, if a person could claim and hold a property until treaties stole it from the red man and gave the claimant better title, it was the squatter's. He later acquired an adjacent quarter section from a neighbor whose wife had been driven to near insanity by the loneliness of the country, forcing him to sell out and abandon his farm. Now, with passage of the Homestead Act a few months earlier, his father had suggested Will might settle on another unclaimed quarter section nearby to add to the Nilsson empire. His father was an ambitious, hard-working man, and Will suspected he would always covet any land that joined his. He would unfailingly be a congenial and helpful neighbor. But he would be prepared to snatch an opportunity to buy a parcel of ground if one came up for sale.

Will hitched the blood-bay to the wagon, and they went in the house to announce his arrival to his mother. She was bent over the cast iron woodstove, tending to supper, when she turned and saw Will. She screamed with delight when she saw him and rushed into his arms. "Wilhelm, I cannot believe it," she exclaimed. She did not come near to knocking him over. Alexis Nilsson stood no more than five feet and might weigh a hundred pounds in water-drenched clothes. But as his dad always said, she was "tough as a boot." Erik Nilsson could claim credit for Will's size, and probably his calmer temperament and quiet ways, but there was no doubt he looked more like his mother's people. Fluent in French and Dakota, her first languages, Alexis spoke precise and proper English, but her speech was thickly accented. Having heard it all his life, Will barely noticed, but a stranger, he thought, might have difficulty understanding her.

"What a wonderful surprise," she said. "When you left, I feared I might not see you again for years. My heart was broken."

"The Army sent me back. I am to work near the reservation for now, but I don't know for how long. I can't tell you much about it. Frankly, my assignment is a bit of a mystery to me."

"It doesn't matter. We will have supper in an hour. I baked a ham—your father traded Fred Eastlicks beef for ham and bacon. And I'll fry some potatoes just dug from the garden. There will be leftover apple pie from yesterday. If I had known you were coming, I could have done more."

"Don't be silly, Mom. I either eat my own cooking or the Army's. Anything you serve up is a feast by comparison."

"Well, you go ahead and put up your horse and carry your things up to your room, and we'll talk at supper."

"Okay, but you should know, I'm just here for one night, and then I hit the trail. I'll probably be able to stop by a few more times while I'm in the area, though."

"Will, I'm just glad you're not fighting in that awful war down south. I'll never understand why you left the Judge Advocate General's Corps."

Will did not tell her that he did not understand it either. He was not commonly inclined to impulse and could not articulate his reasons without sounding more self-sacrificing than he considered himself.

His father had chores to finish up before supper, so Will led the blood-bay to the stable and grained and brushed the gelding. It was a pretty thing with the black mane and tail offset against the unusually dark red coat. The gelding was also a stronger horse than Will originally had judged. A man didn't really know till he had gone some distance in the saddle with a horse about the animal's stamina and endurance. This horse would do fine. He had taken to calling the gelding "Red," although some livestock folks thought it was bad luck to name a critter.

He had whistled Warrior up from the nearby grass. Once he had done his job with the mares, Erik kept him in a separate small pasture near the barn and didn't let him run with the mares and fillies after breeding season. Will knew that his stallion was a horny devil and could get ornery and try to mount a mare or filly that was not in heat when the mood struck him. On those occasions he could make a nuisance of himself, not to mention the risk of his hurting a mare with foal. Some of the breeding females were his daughters, and Erik traded services with other breeders' stallions for them. It was not always as simple as running all the horses together in one big pasture.

When Will finished with Red, he turned his focus to his stallion, which had been occupying the adjacent stall. He found the big yellow-hued horse pissed with the attention Will had been giving the new neighbor, snorting, whinnying, stomping, and banging against the stall partition. He was a gentle creature when he had his owner's undivided attention, but he was not good at sharing. He was a tad past ten years now but not all that mature when it came to his and Will's relationship.

Warrior's mother had died foaling him, and Will's father had promised Will the foal if he could save him. Will even slept in the barn with the newborn those first few months and milked the cow to provide a substitute, fashioning a cloth teat for little Warrior to suck until he trained him to a bucket. Warrior had decided Will was his mother, he guessed, and he even had to put up with the colt's weaning. As time went on, with his father's help, Will handled the training, and ended up with a rare beast that responded to voice commands and whistle signals. He came to know Warrior better than his younger sister, Annette. He would never tell her, but he missed the stallion more than Annette when he was away at school or serving his Army tour. He generally made it home for a spell most summers, but it made him sad sometimes he had lost so many precious days with Warrior.

After giving Warrior a graining and brushing he thought the horse had not really earned, he went back to the house, where his dad was just sitting down at the kitchen table. His mother was setting the bowls on the table, and he was glad to see she had harvested some ear corn and boiled it for supper. She knew he loved it, and he had just as well admit she spoiled him rotten. If his dad had not kept him on course with a prescription of hard work, Will wondered if he might not have turned out a lazy lout. But his dad always said a man never drowned in his own sweat, and he had not.

When they were all seated, his mother gave a quick blessing, which his father indulged but never rendered. He was raised Lutheran, but it didn't stick. Alexis had joined up with the Presbyterians because they maintained the nearest church, and she was devout as long the current preacher didn't disagree with her about some theological point.

They had not had a church anywhere near until Will was in his teens. His mother had wanted him to get baptized, and he dodged it until Annette agreed, and he finally joined the church with his sister. He had decided it was something he could do for his mother and thought he might have more interest someday. It worked for Annette, and she ended up roping a preacher who was on a year's assignment with the local congregation. They married and quickly produced three children. At least he had a religion he could claim when folks asked. It some-

times discouraged missionaries seeking heathen addi-
tions to their flocks.

As they ate, Will turned the conversation quickly to
serious business. "Dad, I have a few folks I need to track
down. Maybe you can help me find them. Levander Buck.
Ever hear of him?"

"I'm sure that's Billy. I think his middle name's William, and he took that on."

His mother interjected, "Hazel—that was his mother—called him Levander."

"Mothers tend to do that," his father observed.

Alexis said, "His mother died eight years ago, and his
father died before that. He was only eleven years old, as
I recall, when he became an orphan. Lots of folks offered
to take him in, including us, but he went to stay with old
Caleb Orth, the trapper, for a few years, and when Caleb
took sick and died, he was with a Dakota family at the
Lower Agency for a time. After that, he built his own tipi
along the river—maybe fourteen years old then. Can you
imagine?"

Erik said, "But he always made his own way. He hunt-
ed for his meat. Travelled around the whole area picking
up odd jobs—chopping wood, helping with harvest, and
the like. Everybody liked Billy, and if he came around at
mealtime, there was always room at the table for him.

And if he was doing a job on a place, he could count on a meal or two with a day's work. He worked for me at harvest several times and broke horses for me the past few years. When it comes to knowing horses, he'd give you a run for your money."

"Where might I find this Billy Buck?"

"Fort Ridgely, I'd guess. He's not Army, but he carries out scouting assignments and acts as a private courier for the Army. He's not more than nineteen, I'd guess, but he knows the woods and plains hereabouts better than most Indians."

"I was directed to talk to Captain John Marsh about other matters, so I guess Fort Ridgely should let me kill two birds."

"Yes, Marsh is acting commandant there for now. With the War of Rebellion going on, things seem unstable at the fort. Folks are worried all the troops will be pulled out. I don't know Marsh personally. I can't tell you much about him."

"Another man," Will said. "John Otherday."

"I know John. Full-blood Sisseton. He farms up near the Upper Agency. Blanket Indians don't like him much. Think he's too much white man. It's no secret he had a run-in with Cut Nose years ago. Story is he chewed off part of the renegade's nose in a fight and left him with a new name. Otherday has done well as a farmer and tries to get other Dakotas started in the business so they're not dependent on the government's money." He turned to his wife. "Alexis, isn't he some kind of relative of yours?"

She replied. "A distant cousin, but I hardly know him. He married a white woman. I never met her, but they say she's a pretty thing. He brought her back from Washington when he went with a Dakota delegation some years back."

Will said, "It seems to me half the families around here are either mixed-blood or related to the Dakotas in some fashion. If there is an uprising, how do the Indians decide who their enemies are?"

His father said, "It's not blood. It's how you live. Any man or woman who has adopted the white man's ways is an enemy. Some that are on the fence will have to choose. The farmer Indians are in as much danger as the white settlers. Some might be given a chance to join the blankets. John Otherday probably understands the situation better than anybody around these parts, red or white. He can give you more insight than anybody else can."

"I will be seeing him soon. Now, what about the two of you? You are obviously taking the uprising threat seriously."

Erik said, "I hope there is not a problem. I'm just taking no chances. I'll worry less if your mother is safe at Ridgely, but I'd feel better yet if she would visit Annette in St. Paul until this blows over."

Alexis snapped, "You are talking like I don't have a voice for myself, Erik. If I wasn't close by, you would hold out here till your scalp was hanging from some warrior's lance. I will not hide out in St. Paul. And I said I'd go to Ridgely and make us a nest either inside or outside the fort. But I am not staying there till you come with me. That's my last word."

"But I've got to be here to look after the stock. There's hay to cut. And soon there will be corn to harvest. That's why a lot of farmers aren't moving to the fort."

"You can't feed those horses and cows if you're dead, Erik."

Will was concerned about his folks, but he was not about to intervene. He took some solace in their proximity to the fort. They only had a few miles to go to reach safety—if there was such a haven along the west branch of the Minnesota River. There were still more Dakotas than soldiers and settlers by overwhelming numbers. The whites and their allies could potentially be swallowed by a swarm of hostiles. It might largely depend upon the loyalties of mixed bloods and friendly Dakotas.

Chapter 6

WILL HAD BEEN to Fort Ridgely many times. It had been constructed about ten years earlier to provide protection to the settlers after the 1851 agreement. His earlier visits had been essentially commercial, helping his father drive horses or cattle to the post for sale or to purchase supplies from a trader who had built a store outside the fort proper.

Today, before hitching Warrior and Red in front of the headquarters building, he surveyed the fort with a soldier's eyes and did not like what he saw. From a military standpoint the place was almost indefensible. There was no spired log barricade like most Easterners would have envisioned. For that matter, fortifications were virtually non-existent. Much of the military post was surrounded by rugged terrain with deep ravines, making excellent cover for attackers. The traditional Army structures, including barracks, officers' quarters, commissary, headquarters, and surgeon's quarters formed a square about the parade ground. The stable, warehouse, and a dozen structures were scattered some distance outside the perimeter. There was no water well.

Nearby Rock Creek and the Minnesota River apparently were relied upon for water sources. Ridgely extended southerly on a bluff overlooking the Minnesota River, but the bluff offered no great security because it overhung in a manner that obscured approaching attackers. Two stone buildings, the commissary and one barracks, might offer a last line of defense for a small number of occupants. Will seriously questioned if his mother would be any safer at this place than at home.

He walked into the post commandant's office. The desk corporal did not rise and salute, of course, since he was not in uniform and looked more like a frontiersman, or even a Dakota tribesman, attired in faded denims, buckskin shirt and moccasins. The only military signature on his person was the Army Colt holstered on his gun belt. His new Sharps rifle remained in the scabbard on his stallion.

The corporal looked up from his desk, staring at him quizzically with furrowed brow. "Yes? State your business."

He was no more than a kid so Will excused his abruptness. "I would like to see Captain Marsh, please. You may tell him that Will Nilsson is here to see him."

"What about?"

"You may tell him *Captain* Will Nilsson is here to see him."

The soldier's face turned scarlet, and he stumbled up, knocking over his chair, before coming to attention and saluting. "Yes, sir."

Will returned the salute, but not before the younger man had turned and headed for the captain's closed door. Momentarily, he returned with a stocky, balding man who appeared a few years short of forty. After giving his visitor a somewhat perfunctory greeting, the captain escorted Will into his office and invited him to take a chair in front of his desk. His brusqueness made it clear he was annoyed by Will's visit. Will supposed Marsh had already tagged him as a spy for folks higher in the chain of command. He would have been clueless as to just how high up the chain that reached.

Captain Marsh cleared his throat and waved a folded sheet of parchment in his hand. "I don't know what the hell is going on, Captain Nilsson, but I've got a message from Snelling that I am to give you full and prompt cooperation with any request for assistance and that Billy

Buck is to be employed to help with your mission, what-ever that is."

"I am only authorized to say I am to evaluate the Dakota situation here and report my observations. I was ordered to identify any problems and assess how they might be remedied or what military support might be required to put down an uprising. I would welcome your thoughts."

"My thoughts?"

"Of course, you are closer to this than anybody else in the Army. I would be remiss if I didn't include your views."

The scowl on Marsh's face faded. "Biggest problem. The government is late with the gold shipment to pay the guaranteed annuities to the Dakotas. Most are indebted to the traders, who will not advance more food supplies or goods until they are paid. Some of the Dakotas are on the edge of starvation. They're getting sick of the government's broken promises. This gives the Soldiers Lodge the perfect opening to stir up discontent and spur the bands to war. They are exploiting this unfortunate situation."

"Soldiers Lodge?"

"This is a loose organization of malcontents who are convinced they can drive all the whites out of the state.

The warrior, Cut Nose, is one of the most influential and apparently the leader. Mean bastard. Beware the Soldiers Lodge. But he receives support from Chief Shakopee—some call him Little Six. It appears Medicine Bottle and Red Middle Voice are cheering him on, too. Chief Little Crow is waiting at the fork in the road. He wants to be in charge, whether the road leads to peace or war."

"Is the lodge active on both agencies?" Will asked.

"Its roots are in the Lower Agency, and that's where the lodge has its strongest support. But they have supporters in the Upper Agency and are making inroads there as each day passes."

"Assume the worst. If there is an uprising, do you have sufficient troops to protect the people here?"

Marsh laughed uproariously. "Of course not. We're state militia brought under federal control by the Civil War. I have about seventy-five soldiers under my command here. We've started an effort to encourage outlying settlers to come to the post for protection, but all we can really offer is safety in numbers, as they say. I'm sure you have noticed what this sick excuse for a fort offers in the way of barriers to an attack. There are sixty-five hundred Sioux at the two agencies—not all warriors of course, but it would not take great military strategy to overrun us."

"I cannot argue that point with you. How many troops would it take to protect the settlers here?"

"Tell your friends at Snelling that one thousand combined infantry and cavalry would be a nice start. I am assuming that most of the civilians here would take up arms in their own defense."

"Troops are short because of the rebellion."

"How well I know. You asked, and I told you what I need, not what I expect to get. Any added numbers would be welcome."

"I will convey your concerns. That's the best I can do. I appreciate your frankness, Captain. Now, perhaps you can tell me where to find Billy Buck."

"He's yours for the duration. I would try the stables. He sleeps there and volunteers with the horses when he's not out on assignment. He's got some Indian blood, I think, or mostly lives like one anyhow. He'd rather be with horses than people."

Will subdued the temptation to inform the captain of his own Dakota ancestry and that he often preferred the company of horses to some people. He doubted, though, that the preference had anything to do with his Indian blood.

Chapter 7

ANJA REMAINED IN the barn for a half hour after Cut Nose departed the farm. Then she stepped out and walked toward the house, resolved to confront her mother, her body trembling with anticipation. When she entered the log structure, she found Marta Lund seated at the kitchen table, staring straight ahead as if unaware of Anja's presence, tears streaming down her cheeks.

"Mama, what is it?" Anja asked.

Marta seemed not to hear her.

"Mama, I saw Cut Nose leave. Did he hurt you?" Anja sat down in a chair next to her mother and placed a hand on her shoulder.

Her mother appeared to be aware of her presence for the first time and turned toward her daughter. "He would never hurt me," she said, speaking so softly Anja could barely hear her.

Looking at her mother now, it suddenly occurred to her that her mother was not an old woman by any standard but her child's. Her bronze-tinted skin was flawless, her dark eyes haunting, and her form slim and sleek despite bearing three children. Somehow it surprised her to realize most men would see Marta Lund as a beautiful woman notwithstanding she was approaching her thirty-eighth birthday, ancient from Anja's perspective.

Marta had not wanted for the necessities of life and had enjoyed a few luxuries during her marriage to the older Larson Lund. But she had suffered the devastation of losing her sons, John and Peter, within three days when the diphtheria epidemic struck in 1850. They would have been fifteen and seventeen now, Anja remembered. It had been a terrible sight to witness, as her brothers lay feverish and delirious, coughing and choking up white slime until they finally suffocated in their parents' arms. And Anja still bore the guilt of being untouched by the ravages of the disease.

Her mother had endured two miscarriages that Anja knew about, and Marta had worked hard not only to maintain a decent home but as a helpmate to her husband, milking the two cows twice daily, caring for the chickens and the garden, and working in the fields at harvest. Anja had seen her mother always treat her father with patience and affection and had thought they had a good marriage. Yet, there was Cut Nose. And now, Anja had to know.

She could not summon up a way to deal with the subject delicately. "Mama," she said, "I know about Cut Nose. I know you have lain with him. Many times."

Marta gave her daughter a startled look and then shrugged. Still speaking very softly and without emotion, she said, "I suppose you would know that. Yes, it was foolish of me to think otherwise."

"Is that all you can say?"

"What is there to say? I have lain with him for many years. He was my first. Before your father. Remember, for much of my life I was raised in a Dakota village. I am half-blood Mdewakanton, Cut Nose's people. The older girls and the women adored Cut Nose. He lay with almost any woman he wanted, and he wanted many. But I came to believe he liked me best. He said in time he would have taken me as his wife, but your grandfather traded me to Larson Lund for horses and money. My father did not think a true Dakota warrior would claim a half-blood, and he was a trader, who saw a squaw's daughter as merchandise."

Her mother was so matter-of-fact, Anja was stunned. "But after you married Papa, you continued to let Cut Nose visit and to have his way with you. I do not understand."

Marta surrendered a small smile as if calling up a special memory. "We had our way with each other."

"Do you love Papa?"

"Yes, of course."

"Then I do not see how you could have done this."

"I love Cut Nose, too. And I hungered for the moments we shared together."

"But you cannot love them both."

"Why not? Most Dakota men have at least two wives. Many have three or four and love them all. Why can a woman not love two?"

Her mother was being very difficult. Anja thought by now her mother would have broken down with remorse, but she was unapologetic. "Does Papa know?"

"I do not know. I have not told him, but he may suspect. If he asked, I would tell him. I do not think he would beat me or send me away."

No, Anja thought, her father loved Marta more than life, and brutality was not a part of his make-up. "Mama, think about this. Am I Cut Nose's daughter?"

"I can only say it would not be impossible."

Anja sensed her mother could tell her more but decided not to press. She had gained nothing from this uncomfortable conversation. She realized now the question might never be answered. On the other hand, she figured, determining that something was unknowable was an answer of sorts. She took her mother's hand. "I cannot grasp your reasoning, Mama, but I love you, and nothing can change what has happened all these years. But you were crying when I came in. You seem to believe you received much happiness from this relationship. Then how can it bring such sadness?"

"Because it is over. Cut Nose said I would not see him again. The coming war must bring an end to our meetings."

"War?"

"He says war against the whites is a certainty now. He said we should leave this place and go east. All whites that remain will be destroyed. Mixed bloods who do not abandon white ways will also be killed."

"They cannot chase the whites away. There are too many. And thousands more soldiers will come."

"I tried to tell Cut Nose that, but he would not listen. And he will die, but so will many others."

Chapter 8

C UT NOSE LEANED against an ancient cottonwood on a knoll above the creek bank where warriors of the Soldiers Lodge would be gathering.
The pow-wow would not convene until after sunset more
than an hour from now, but he was the self-appointed
guardian of admission. No man was better acquainted
with Dakota warriors than Cut Nose. He knew most by
name and reputation and could recite the lineage of each
several generations back. He decided whether a warrior
could be trusted with the lodge secrets and would expel
those he deemed untrustworthy.

No drunkards would be admitted. For several years
he had been a prisoner of the demon alcohol, groveling at
the feet of white men, begging for a drink. On one occasion, after a night of drinking, he had stumbled from the
woods and encountered the man the whites called Dr.

Mayo astride a fine horse. He had approached the man and asked if he might ride the animal. He had grabbed the bridle, and the doctor, apparently thinking Cut Nose was attempting to steal the horse, called him a drunken savage and struck at him with his quirt. Cut Nose released the bridle, and the doctor rode away, but word later reached Cut Nose that the doctor was accusing him of an attack with intent to take the horse.

One night in the German-settled town of New Ulm, he had watched as his drunken friend, Slow River, was pushed into a circle of white drunks and forced to dance naked for his drinks, while those surrounding him laughed and ridiculed him. A fat, drunken half-blood woman had joined him in the ring that night and tried to mount him, but to the delight of the crowd, his flaccid member had been unresponsive. He still burned at the humiliation pressed upon his friend by the whites that night. He had not touched the white man's poison since, convinced that alcohol was a brew invented to destroy the Indian tribes. And like many who conquer an addiction, he had become fanatically intolerant of the same weakness in others.

It was also Cut Nose's job to ferret out any spies who might be seeking to undermine the Soldiers Lodge's plans. He had eyes and ears in all the villages reporting to him, identifying which warriors could be trusted and those who could not. His network of personal loyalists made him the lodge's unofficial leader and a man whose private counsel was sought by wavering and uncertain chiefs.

Foremost among these was Chief Little Crow, a Mdewakanton of great influence, who had forged strong ties to the white community and even wore the white man's clothes and was building a new house on the Lower Agency. Little Crow did not seek war, but he did not want to lose power and influence among his people. Cut Nose thought Little Crow was raising his feather into the wind to see which way it blew. Cut Nose would see that it blew with the winds of war.

Warriors were starting to arrive at the clearing now and taking places at the fire circle carved out there. Young Flying Duck appeared with his drum and lit the fire that he had laid out earlier that day. Then he sat on the ground a short distance from the crackling flames, placed the drum between his thighs and began the steady beat. The gangly seventeen-year-old worshipped Cut Nose and was always nearby to do his bidding. The night was warm and humid, and the fire served no practical purpose, nor did the drum for that matter. But Cut Nose instinctively knew that men responded to staging and aura, and he, with Flying Duck's assistance, always tended to such details.

It was nearly sundown, and more than a hundred warriors had assembled when Cut Nose spotted an intruder from the Upper Agency: Silver Fox, son of Walks on Fire, a minor Sisseton chief, who was a vocal opponent of any uprising. Cut Nose slipped to the side of his ally, Fighting Elk, probably the largest of all the warriors in attendance and fierce as his namesake, who was standing nearby. He pointed to Silver Fox who sat in the third and last row of warriors encircling the fire. "He is not one of the lodge and cannot be trusted," Cut Nose said. "Take him away and send him back to the cowardly Sisseton without his right ear."

"Consider it done," Fighting Elk responded.

The big Dakota quietly slipped in behind Silver Fox, a small, gaunt-looking young man, bent over and locked his thick forearm about the intruder's neck and yanked him from the circle. The Sisseton choked and coughed, flailing his arms wildly as Fighting Elk drug him into the surrounding woods. Moments later, a terrified scream pierced the air, briefly drowning out the drumbeat. Soon, Fighting Elk returned, holding out a blood-soaked ear, which he handed to Cut Nose.

Cut Nose accepted the dripping ear and moved from the knoll, down the gentle slope to the fire circle. He signaled for the drumming to stop and then walked slowly around the fire, displaying the ear to the gathered warriors. Then, he spoke loudly, so all could hear, speaking Dakota, for no white man's words were permitted at this place. "This ear shall spy no more. Only those who are dedicated to war with the whites are welcome here. If you are not committed to driving the white man from our rightful lands, you must leave. If you do so now, you will not be harmed."

After several minutes of silence, one warrior stood and walked away. Then a second, and, finally, a third.

There was no agenda for the meeting of the Soldiers Lodge. The warriors rose spontaneously to vent their rage and hatred of the white men. Sometimes, the evening turned to chaos for a spell when three or four spoke at once. When the atmosphere began to calm, Cut Nose nodded to Fighting Elk, who stepped within the circle. Quiet descended on the clearing, as the big man wearing only a loincloth and moccasins stood before them. Warriors listened to Fighting Elk, who was an imposing and impressive figure with thickly muscled arms and shoulders. Moreover, his booming, mellifluous voice commanded attention and was almost hypnotic to his listeners.

Cut Nose recognized this and had contented himself with furnishing the ideas and, occasionally, the words for his friend to pour forth. He would intercede only for effect when appropriate.

Fighting Elk moved about the circle in front of the dancing flames, his form even more magnificent against the backdrop of the fire's glow. He paused strategically from time to time as he spoke, looking out at his comrades and casting his eyes from face to face.

"I was there," Fighting Elk said, his voice grave, "when the starving Dakota groveled before the trader, Andrew Myrick, at his store on Council Square of the Lower Agency and begged for credit to purchase food for their starving children. I heard him when he said scornfully, 'Let them eat grass.' I wept from the pain of seeing my brothers and sisters reduced to such a state. I cried from the contempt for our people shown by this man and all the other whites who have swarmed over our lands like so many locusts."

"And why?" he continued. "Because, once again, the white man extends his trail of broken promises. The gold that was rightfully due the Dakota people many suns ago has still not come. These are not gratuitous monies handed out by the father in Washington to villages of beggars. This is money owed in exchange for land ceded by our past chiefs, who thought the white man could be trusted. They foolishly believed that this paper the whites called treaties had meaning and that promises made would be promises kept. I have lived thirty-five summers now. When I was born, the lands that the whites now call Minnesota were all Dakota lands, and we only had to protect them from the thieving Chippewa from the north. But then the whites came, first, a few, and then, a horde."

Fighting Elk stopped speaking and walked a complete circle around the ring, shaking his head disdainfully, before speaking again. "Yes, they came, not as guests, but as trespassers. And the council in Washington told the settlers to come to our land, and they would help steal it. And they did, one treaty at a time, each reducing the amount of land owned by the Dakota and forcing us to move to a smaller place until now we have only this tiny strip of trees and rocks along the west branch of the Minnesota River. And the final insult is that the whites do not pay as promised. And our families go hungry. Does the council in Washington and its father plan for us to die and disappear so they may claim what little remains of our lands as well? Will we let them do this?"

Cut Nose started the chant. "No. No."

The other warriors joined in, and the chant echoed through the creek and river valleys.

Fighting Elk's voice rose among the din, and the chanters quieted. "We must drive these invaders from our lands. Their blood must soak our woods and prairies. We must kill them all—man, woman and child—so they will not sprout like weeds to suffocate our soil again."

Cut Nose yelled out another chant. "Blood. Blood."

The warriors took up the chant, working themselves into near frenzy. Then someone from the crowd, who had been previously cued by Cut Nose, called out. "But when?"

At this point, Cut Nose broke into the circle, and Fighting Elk slipped away. *"When, you ask? Soon. Within fifteen suns. Go out and tell those who are sympathetic to our cause to be prepared. We will inform the chiefs that there will be war with or without their leadership and that those who will not lead will become followers. Organize the bands for war. The signal will be the first death of a white man. The word will spread quickly." Cut Nose hoped to earn first kill.

Chapter 9

BILLY BUCK WAS a talker. He did not say, but Will doubted, as his parents had estimated, that the young man had reached his twentieth birthday yet. He rode his own sorrel gelding he called "Buster" and had helped himself to another sorrel gelding from the Ridgely stable as a second mount. Will took it Billy was partial to sorrels. Neither animal would attract a casual eye, but he judged the boy knew his horses. Both were rugged mounts and nicely put together. They just were not showy and would not interest a novice looking for a pretty thing.

Will guessed you could say the same for Billy. He was average height, a few inches under six feet, not quite skinny but not far from it. Tow-headed, his dirty hair crept from a coonskin hat and crawled down most of his neck. His eyes were his most striking feature—limpid, blue pools. Will could not imagine where Captain Marsh had picked up the notion Billy was mixed-blood. Any Indian running in his veins could not be more than a sprinkle. But the kid was a walking map of the lands along the west Minnesota.

They had ridden out of Fort Ridgley on the poor excuse for a road that led to the Upper Agency, or Yellow Medicine, as Billy preferred to call it, the same afternoon he had found Billy at the stable. They had stayed the night in a barn loft at the farm of Lars and Maria Halverson, friends of Billy's—everybody was Billy's friend, Will quickly learned—and he had wangled an invitation for supper and breakfast as bonuses. Well fed, he suggested they cut some wood before departing. Since the couple had adamantly turned down payment for their hospitality, Will agreed that was the least they could do. He had not engaged in such labor for a spell and was hurting now.

By noon the Upper Agency was in sight. Will suggested they rein off the road and eat the cheese and bacon sandwiches Mrs. Halverson had sent with them. Billy, of course, knew the perfect spot and led them to a spring-fed stream, where the horses could drink and the riders could fill canteens from the spring that tumbled from a stone outcropping like a virtual fountain. Billy had not asked any questions about the mission, but Will had taken his measure by now and felt he was entitled to know what the journey was all about. The young frontiersman would likely be more help if he knew what they were looking for. Of course, Will would be more help if he knew what they were looking for.

As they ate, Will explained to Billy that he had been assigned to evaluate the dangers of a Dakota uprising and to advise his superiors how such a possibility might be headed off or put down if it happened. He did not mention that his immediate superior was the President of the United States. "I've told you we are going to visit John Otherday. After we talk to him, I will likely write both a letter and a telegram for you to deliver to Fort Snelling. There is a telegraph connection there, and you will need to wait for a reply."

"Sure, I can do that. I've rode to Snelling lots."

"How long will it take?"

"With two horses and no more than a few hours' sleep, I can do it in twenty hours' time. I'd need a day's layover to rest me and the horses, so make it a three-day round trip."

"I would want you to wait for a telegram reply anyway."

"You didn't say before, but I figured you was Army. Officer, maybe captain. Too young for major. West Point, too. Not like our country officers. But you said you belong to Erik and Alexis. Ain't seen you there."

This kid's instincts were scary. "You've got it pretty much right. I've been away to school and serving my time. That's why you haven't seen me at the farm."

"Seen that stud horse you ride, though. No better-looking critter in these parts. Good as he looks, too. I get me a mare, what would it cost to have him poke her?"

"You can have a free service. I don't think Warrior would mind."

"That would be mighty generous. I'll take you up on that. So now that we're out in the open with each other, what do I call you? Captain or General or something?"

"Just Will. I'm not advertising I'm Army. And you're not a soldier."

"Will be after this job's done. I've decided to join up and fight the Rebs. Hoping they'll let me go horse soldier. Ain't much for walking."

"That's where you ought to be with your horseman-ship skills. Cavalry. I hate to tell you it's almost a guarantee you'll be in the infantry."

"That would be a hell of a thing."

"I'll see if I can help when the time comes."

His eyes brightened with enthusiasm. "You could do that?"

"No promises. If things go bad out here, I might be walking right beside you."

Billy lifted his head and his neck stiffened. He started sniffing the air like an old hound dog.

"Smoke. And it's not campfire smoke. Smell it?"

Will did his own hound dog imitation, but he smelled nothing except his own sweat. "No."

"You will. It can't be far off the main road. Want to check it out?"

"Might be a good idea."

They wolfed down the sandwiches and split the four ginger cookies their benefactor had sent along. They mounted their horses, and Will turned Billy Buck loose to find the smoke's source. He trailed behind on Warrior, as Billy veered off the main road and followed a road that was nothing more than faint wagon ruts. Will was starting to pick up the acrid scent now, and a few minutes later, he caught sight of the billowing gray plumes climbing skyward.

"No hurry," Billy called. "The place is beyond saving."

How he knew this without seeing the source puzzled Will, but he had already sold Will on his clairvoyance about such things. Sure enough, a few minutes later, as they rode over a rise, the smoldering rubble of a little farmstead lay before them. It didn't look like it had been much before the fire, perhaps a two-room shack and a stable that would have held three or four animals. Even the former outhouse looked like a one-holer, which was plenty, of course, if you didn't care for company when you took care of such business. Will suspected the two and three-hole privies folks put up were more status symbols than anything. He did not know what that said about Erik Nilsson who had built two sturdy two-hole structures, one for the men and one for the ladies. He guessed it protected the women folk from the unpleasant consequences of males with careless aim.

As they led the horses into the yard, Billy told Will the story of the place. "It's been burning since early morning," he said. "No bodies in there. We wouldn't miss the stink of human flesh being cooked."

"I suppose not." Although Will could not say if he would or would not. Either way, he was glad to hear Billy's verdict. "Where is the owner?"

"I'd guess he and his family are someplace on the Lower Agency waiting for war. This was Tommy Elk Killer's place. A farmer Indian. Full-blood Dakota, him and his wife both. Two kids. Some of the Indians have done real good farming and don't count on the government's money to come through—of course, they don't turn down their shares. Tommy was starving out here. Didn't have his heart in the farm. Didn't get much planted and got less harvested. He was a blanket Indian in his soul."

"So, you think he did this himself?"

"Well, he had some help." He pointed to the parched, dusty ground about us. "He didn't make all those unshod tracks on his own. Some of his blanket pals helped out. No dead critters about. He had some help driving off his few cows and calves. He wasn't forced out. It's just a message. Probably a message to the other Dakota farmers and mixed-bloods that it is a time for choosing. I think John Otherday will be interested in this."

"Then we had better tell him."

Chapter 10

THEY SAT IN the kitchen of John Otherday's frame, clapboard house, which had apparently been constructed within the past few years. It was a modest, single story structure, but Will could see the quality in it. The house had a planked floor and included a nice woodstove in the kitchen. Will could see a large stone fireplace in the parlor, so it seemed they were prepared for the hard Minnesota winters. It was not a pretentious abode, but it was not one that would be casually abandoned by the owners. Otherday had clearly adapted to white comforts and was carving out a permanent place in the foreign culture.

Otherday's buxom, blonde wife, Samantha, who appeared some years younger than her husband, served up three steaming cups of coffee while the visitors conversed with her husband at the table. Then Otherday suggested she might want to check on the children playing outside, a not so subtle hint that he did not particularly want her to hear the exchange.

"My wife is very frightened about the unrest on the reservation," he said. "I don't want her to get all worked up again. She is an Eastern girl and does not understand all of this. I wanted to send her and the children to St. Paul until we know it is safe again, but she will not go without me. And I cannot leave."

Billy said, "The settlers are all having that trouble. Most of the womenfolk won't budge if their men won't go."

Otherday sighed with resignation. He was a sturdy man with a dark, stern face. No doubt about his Dakota ancestry. There was nothing Indian about his garb. Today, he wore bib overalls and clodhoppers and had placed a straw hat on the table. Billy had said the man was a devout Christian, and Will would bet he would be just as comfortable in his Sunday go-to-meeting suit. He was very well-spoken, probably one reason he had joined Dakota chiefs at important councils in Washington.

Will sipped at his cup of coffee before he spoke. "John, I explained that I have been sent to evaluate the reservation situation. There is concern about an uprising, and the war with the Confederacy complicates the problem.

I have a lot of questions, but, first, I would like for Billy to tell you about something we came across earlier this afternoon."

Otherday turned to Billy, who obviously relished his moment on stage. Billy told him about the burning of the Elk Killer house and stable without undue embellishment and did not hesitate to give his own opinion about the implications. Otherday's expression shifted from solemn to grim as the boy spoke.

When Billy finished, Otherday nodded with understanding. "You are correct. The burning and abandonment of the farm will be taken as a sign by all the Dakota farmers. They can no longer keep one foot in the village of the traditionalists—or the blankets as the whites call them. They must choose. And if they do not return to the old ways, they will die with the whites."

Will said, "So you think an uprising is near?"

"I have no doubt of it. But I do not know how many will join. Most on the Lower Agency wish for a war, I believe. And those who do not wish it will have little choice but to go along or be ostracized, perhaps killed by their own tribesmen."

"And the Upper Agency?"

"There are three camps, I think. There are the war supporters, who are prepared to join any uprising. Then, you have those who will side with the whites, and finally the Dakotas, who are on the fence, as the white men say. They will wait and shift to whatever side appears to be winning the war. This last group may even make a majority."

"Do you think war is inevitable?"

"I think the arrival of the gold shipment to pay the agreed annuities could stop it. It would immediately take away the biggest argument Soldiers Lodge and their supporters have. And most Dakotas would be too caught up in the distribution of the payments to be excited about starting a war. This is not to say that the anger and resentment many feel for the white man's government will disappear overnight."

Will considered his remarks, which only confirmed his earlier conclusion. Arrival of the tardy payments would abort, or at least delay, the cries for war. But he had no control over that outcome. He could only report to Hanscomb the importance of expediting the money.

"How much time do we have?"

"A month. A week. A day. I cannot say. Something will happen, probably an event unplanned, and that will light the fuse. And the explosion will follow quickly after. When that takes place, men of goodwill cannot stop the war until it has run its course. We can only try to help as many as possible to survive. But many, many will die. We have come to take peace for granted here, and the rumors of war are not taken seriously."

"Do you have any thoughts about where I might go to learn more about Dakota preparations for war?"

"You must ride into the lion's den. Go to Redwood, the Lower Agency, and talk to the people there. Many will be blind and deaf to what is taking place about them, but you will find some who understand the gravity. I will be the watchman at the Upper Agency. I can make a list of people who live between the agencies and can be trusted. You can contact those persons for messages from me or give them messages to relay to me."

"Yes, you are making sense. We will head back that way this afternoon." Will turned to Billy. "It's time for you to make a run to Fort Snelling. While John writes up his list of contacts, I'll get my paper and writing case from my saddlebags and do a telegram and write a short letter for a gentleman in Washington. The post commander's office will see that these messages get proper priority. But you will need to wait for a reply to the telegram."

"I can do that. I'll get back as soon as I can."

"We need to choose a place to meet up."

"No need. I'll find you."

Will did not doubt it. He got up and retrieved the materials from his saddlebags. When he returned, he started the letter dated August 8, 1862.

Chapter 11

ANJA WAS THRILLED to have a classroom of nineteen students the first day of the school term. A dozen were children of white agency families. Three were mixed bloods, and the other four were full-blood Dakota. Given current tensions, she had been mildly surprised to have any Dakota representation.

Seating in the class was separated into three groups based upon educational achievement. She had five pupils who spoke little or no English, ranging from seven to thirteen years of age. Fortunately, Karina had tested well beyond eighth grade level, and Anja had decided to utilize Karina as a teaching assistant while helping the girl with a few deficiencies in preparation for high school. Karina's focus would be on the pupils who did not yet speak English. The language barrier would need to be crossed before these students ventured into any other subjects.

This first day had been devoted to distributing books and materials to the students and evaluation for placement at appropriate learning levels. She did not have adequate books to give one to each child for every subject, so she decided each child could take one book home after school was dismissed, and the next day they would exchange for one covering a different discipline. It complicated the teaching process, but Anja was determined to establish a rotation that would work.

After class was dismissed, Karina remained for a time to discuss teaching plans for the next day. The girl was very bright, and Anja was grateful for her assistance in the classroom and enjoyed her company. Despite their age differences, they were becoming good friends—as near to a contemporary friend as Anja would find in this isolated community.

After Karina started for home, Anja commenced collecting papers and class rosters she would work on in her boarding house room that evening. Thomas Galbraith, the Redwood agent, had sent out warnings to agency personnel and businessmen that, given reservation discontent, women and children should not venture out after dark. Otherwise, she would have returned to the school to work. She was nearly ready to depart when she heard a gentle rapping on the school door.

"Come in," she called.

The door opened slowly, and a tall man wearing a tan, wide-brimmed Plainsman hat, which he promptly removed, stepped in. She did not know quite what to make of him. His thick, black hair was military trim, but he wore moccasins and a buckskin shirt with faded blue denims. His dark eyes and the ocher tint to his skin suggested a bit of Indian ancestry, but the Dakotas would call him white.

"Ma'am," the man said, "I apologize for disturbing you. My name is Will Nilsson. I just rode in to the agency. I have been sent by the United States Army, and I need to talk to some of the folks at the agency. I saw the school and it occurred to me a school teacher might have an impartial view of the situation here. Tomorrow, I'll talk to the agent and traders and any other folks who might be helpful."

He seemed a gentleman. Besides, although his facial features were a little on the craggy side, they fit the man, and she found him rather attractive. He had a soft baritone voice that reminded her of Matthew. It struck her that it had been a long spell since she had found any man particularly interesting. This stranger piqued her curiosity.

"Ma'am?"

"I'm sorry. This was our first school day, and my mind has been wandering a bit." She stepped forward and offered her hand, "My name is Anja Lund. Yes, I can speak with you."

She gestured for him to follow her to her desk, where she sat down and nodded for him to take the seat in front. "Now," she said, "tell me how I might help you."

Will quickly explained his mission. "I've spoken to enough people to be convinced that the threat of an uprising is real. I am trying to get a sense of how much time we have and how we can do something to head it off."

"Yes, the threat is real. I could not even guess how much time there is to stop it, but, if it starts and the rage is turned loose, it will be terrible. I don't want to even think about the horror that will be unleashed. As to heading it off, of course, arrival of the gold would likely dampen the fervor of many. It would disappoint the Soldiers Lodge because the government's broken promises have provided the rallying cries."

"Yes, I have been told that several times."

"I do think time could be bought if the traders would open credit for food and supplies to the Dakota. I am told there is food in the warehouses to feed the bands for several weeks, but the traders have agreed among themselves they will extend no more credit until prior bills are paid. The annuities would allow the Dakota to do this. Of course, that will reduce the amount of funds available until the next annuity payments. They are always behind, and few have a real concept of the purchasing power of their monies. They rely upon the honesty of the traders' pricing and accounting to determine what they owe. I have made purchases in these stores and refuse to buy at the outrageous prices. I end up paying half of what the reservation people pay."

"I will speak with Agent Galbraith and some of the traders tomorrow and see if there is anything that might be done."

"I wish you good luck because they do not seem to grasp the seriousness of the situation."

"Aren't you concerned about your own safety here? And that of your students?"

"Sometimes. My mother is half-blood, although we reside on my father's farm off the reservation. It is unclear what immunity that offers."

"John Otherday says none at all."

"We do not control events. We can only react to them. I will not spend my life cowering in a cellar because of what might, or might not, happen."

Nilsson shrugged, but she sensed his disapproval. They talked for another hour, and she felt strangely comfortable sharing her opinions with this man. He listened, asked questions and challenged her thinking on some matters, but always respectfully. She had not generally had positive experiences expressing her thoughts to men on non-domestic issues in the past.

Nilsson slipped a pocket watch from his trouser pocket, gave it a quick glance, and said, "I'm sorry, Miss Lund, it is nearly five-thirty. I didn't intend to keep you this late. If we were in the city, I would offer to buy your supper, but I saw no evidence of a nice restaurant."

"Please, call me Anja." *Was she being too forward?* "And my supper is included in my boarding house rent at Dickinson's across the square. Mrs. Dickinson also serves meals to the public, if you are interested."

"I hope you will call me Will. And, yes, I am more than interested. I would much prefer anything she might serve to the jerky and stale biscuits in my saddle bags. I don't suppose they might have a room for the night? I wouldn't mind a room and a real bed. I had been planning to negotiate for a pile of straw in the livery."

"They have ample room. Visitors aren't much interested in staying over on the reservation these days."

"Then, if you will be so kind as to inform the hosts of another guest for room and supper, I'll put up my horses and join you later."

"I'll see you again soon then." She looked forward to seeing Will Nilsson again. Perhaps, he would ask her to chat in the guest parlor after supper. She supposed she would never see him again after tonight, but she thought it would be nice to learn more about him.

Chapter 12

WILL HAD HOPED to see Anja again this morning, but the soft bed had held him hostage longer than expected. Mrs. Emily Dickinson, who with her husband, Joseph, managed the boarding house, informed him that the young teacher had rushed through her breakfast and hurried to the school shortly after sunrise. His hostess placed a plate with a stack of hotcakes on the table, left the dining room, and returned with a butter dish and a glass cruet filled with hot maple syrup. She then filled his coffee cup again and took a chair across the table.

Mrs. Dickinson was a stout, matronly woman pushing forty, he guessed, and obviously hard-working. She had a cheerful, welcoming nature and had certainly made Will feel at home here. Anja had told him that Mrs. Dickinson handled operation of the boarding house, while her husband took on repair work and maintenance for other agency buildings. They had a son and daughter, who attended the agency school and helped with meals and laundry at the boarding house.

Will would have welcomed solitude and quiet to plan his day, but Emily Dickinson clearly had neither in mind.

"You and Anja talked a good spell last night, didn't you?" she asked.

How could he deny it? Mrs. Dickinson had found an excuse to enter the parlor with coffee or cookies every half hour or so, a cover, he assumed, for supervising the conduct of her guests. "Yes, we did. She is a very interesting lady."

"Well, you will be on your way today, won't you?"

"As a matter of fact, I would like to rent my room another night, if I may. I expect to spend the day here talking to folks. And, I thought I would ride on tomorrow."

"You ain't planning on trifling with Anja, are you? I won't have you doing that."

"Uh, no, I won't be trifling with her. But I hope to have a few words with her this evening."

The formerly friendly hostess glared at him with suspicion. He wondered what conduct was covered under the term "trifle." He did not have time, or he would have been willing to trifle with Anja Lund. She was a stunning, dark beauty and appeared to be totally unaware how she affected men. This man anyhow. Last evening had been the most enjoyable he had experienced for many months, and, after a bit more discussion about the Dakota crisis, they had shared stories and personal histories for several hours. It had been a long time since he loosened his tongue to any woman like he had to Anja, and he supposed he flattered himself to think she was very open with him. But, ever the realist, he knew the most he could hope for was one more evening to share conversation with an intriguing young woman. Will had the likelihood of two wars in front of him and no time to explore romance.

Mrs. Dickinson said, "Tell Anja to get out of this place. Now."

The woman's words were shockingly harsh and demanding, and Will about choked on a forkful of her delicious hotcakes. "Why should I do that?"

"Because this Lower Agency is a powder keg, and it's going to explode. Could happen today."

"Then why aren't you packing up?"

"I've got to convince my husband of the danger. We've been nothing but good to the Indians. Joseph and I pass on any surplus foodstuffs we come onto. I've gone out to the tipis and lodges with Doc Humphrey to help nurse some of the sick ones. Joseph says the Sioux shouldn't have no fuss with us."

"Under that theory, why should Anja be in danger? She hasn't harmed anyone."

"She's young and pretty. And some of the mix-breeds are hated more than whites. I've seen warriors eyeing her. Some don't mean nothing by it. Others would take war as an excuse to do what they're thinking."

"I'll have a word with her this evening. That's all I can do."

"I'm telling my husband tonight that I am leaving with the kids within three days. I'm going to start packing in the morning. Anja can stay here if she wants, but she will be on her own."

"You mean business, don't you?"

"I do. I can tell you're Army. What are you doing here anyway?"

Will did not know why these women read him as Army. Did he walk or talk funny? His wardrobe certainly wasn't fooling anybody. It didn't matter a lot, but if the local Sioux figured it out, he might earn a target on his back.

"Yes, I am Army. I am here to evaluate the situation."

"You're wasting your time. If you didn't bring a wagon full of gold, go back and tell your higher-ups it's too late to fix broken promises."

Chapter 13

WILL DID NOT see a friendly face on a single warrior loitering near the buildings lining Council Square. Some had tossed their blankets on the ground and seemed to be dozing. Others sat on benches in front of the several trading posts. Several just seemed to be pacing aimlessly from one end of the square to the other and then back again. The sun shone brightly, and a balmy breeze caressed the prairie this morning. But the tension in the air was suffocating.

Will decided to visit the agent's office first. It was some distance across the grassy commons from the boarding house. He figured the agent should be given the courtesy of a visit, although Anja had warned him that the man seemed clueless about the danger lurking at the agency. Like virtually all government employees, he was a patronage public servant, his main qualification being his Republican political party affiliation.

When Lincoln was inaugurated, loyal Democrats went job hunting. The pendulum would swing back some day, and the Republicans would be unemployed. It could be argued, Will thought, that the system assured a constant flow of inexperience, if not incompetence, throughout the government agencies. On the other hand, elected officials were less likely to have their policies subverted and ignored by unelected bureaucrats.

Be that as it may, Will found that Thomas Galbraith fit Anja's description of him. Whether it was bluster or not, he insisted no crisis existed at the agency and that he had firm control over any problems. He was a stocky, middle-aged man with fiery red hair and beard. As Will sat in his office, facing him at his desk, he picked up the unmistakable smell of alcohol and noticed some slurring of his speech. The man conceded he had no previous frontier or Indian experience, but he was very proud he had been involved in the recently admitted state of Minnesota's constitutional convention.

"Is there food in the traders' warehouses at the agency?" Will asked.

"Yes," he replied, "but they are united in their position it will not be released until the Dakota debts are paid."

"But they risk losing it all should there be an uprising."

"These people are children and must be so treated. We must be stern. And the Army should send troops to round up and punish the warriors of the Soldiers Lodge."

Will quickly determined he was learning nothing from the agent and bid him good day. Again, taking a suggestion from Anja, he decided to stop at the agency doctor's office. She had pointed out that Dr. Philander Humphrey, while a salaried agency employee, was not a political appointee. He was well-read and loved to debate politics and religion. A confirmed abolitionist, he could be reasoned with on most other topics, though, and working closely with those Dakota who would submit to a white man's care, he might be feeling the pulse of the Sioux at the agency. His twelve-year-old son, John, was a pupil at the agency school, and his wife, Susan, when stopping by to meet the new teacher, had expressed great anxiety about anger brewing at the agency. She had indicated she might flee with John and her two younger children if the atmosphere did not calm soon.

Unfortunately, the only insight Dr. Humphrey provided was further evidence of apathy and disbelief. The women were clearly taking the uprising threat more seriously than their male counterparts. "The Dakotas are

Ron Schwab

good people," Humphrey insisted. "They are rightfully frustrated, and I am embarrassed by the government's behavior. But we have lived in peace for some time now and intermingled freely. Just look at the mixed-bloods here. Unless I miss my guess, you are one of them. Our little community is the perfect example of racial and cultural harmony. I hope the Civil War will bring such acceptance between the white and Negro once the curse of slavery is exterminated."

Will concluded that Dr. Humphrey was a good man. He was also an idealist, more connected to life as he wanted it to be, than the harsh realities It often brought.

There were at least four stores or trading posts at the lower agency, most clustered about a half mile from Council Square. If he found time, he thought he might visit all of them, but he especially wanted to visit Andrew Myrick of the oft-quoted "let them eat grass" fame. There were four Dakota warriors in front of Myrick's store when he walked up, two sitting on a bench and the others perched on the edge of the porch. He was met with angry glares and clearly was not welcome here. His eyes locked with those of one of the bench warriors, who seemed to be especially unhappy with his appearance there. Clad only in his loincloth, he displayed a lean and muscular body, though he appeared to be the eldest of the gathering. Will would never forget him because of his disfigured nose, which appeared to have the part of flesh of one nostril torn away, leaving grotesque scar tissue that drew attention to his face. The warrior would have otherwise had what many might consider handsome facial features. He wondered if this could be the notorious Cut Nose.

He walked past the warriors and stepped through the open door of a single room with a crude, lopsided counter at the far end and walls lined with empty shelves. A thin, balding man with gray-stubbled cheeks and chin stood at the counter, eyeing him suspiciously. Dakotas were not alone in casting him suspicious glares at the Lower Agency this day.

"Who are you?" he asked, before Will could introduce himself.

"Will Nilsson," he replied. "I am an investigator for the United States Army." He thought his self-designated investigator title might get the man's attention. It did, but he was clearly not impressed.

"What the hell are you investigating?"

"The Dakota discontent. Army brass are concerned about trouble brewing on the reservation and want me to report on just how serious things are."

"Well, tell your generals things are damn serious, and it's going to get a hell of a lot worse if that gold don't show up. Those bucks outside are getting testy and making me nervous as hell. Me and other traders have got merchandise stored up in the warehouses, but if we put it out on the store shelves, these beggars will just walk in and help themselves. Cut my throat if I try to stop them. Some crazy devils out there. That Cut Nose is the worst."

"Have you considered opening up their credit? Buying some time? I've been assured the funds are being processed."

"The way the government works, it might be two years coming."

"I won't defend bureaucratic efficiency, but you know it won't be that long."

"Don't matter. I'm not giving in to these heathen thieves."

"If there's war, they'll break into your warehouses. I understand they had an incident at the Upper Agency, and your other store was involved in it."

"But they backed off. They're not going to go up against the Army's guns."

"What Army? What guns?"

Chapter 14

ANJA LEFT SCHOOL as soon as the pupils departed. She wanted to change before supper, admit-
ting that the prospects of another evening with
Will Nilsson motivated her some. Anja liked Will and had
found herself buoyed by thoughts of another visit with
him in the parlor this evening, knowing she would face
a bit of a letdown at his departure in the morning. The
chances of their paths crossing again were remote, but it
was nice to feel something again, although she could not
define what it was.

She was stopped by Mrs. Dickinson before she started
upstairs to her room. There was no welcoming smile on
the usually ebullient landlady's face.

"We're taking our children and leaving day after tomorrow, if not before. We're loading a wagon and will
cross on the ferry. You should leave, also, but you are wel-

come to stay here. You will be on your own for meals and laundry. We may return when this is over, but we are going to Fort Ridgely while we can."

Anja saw the fear in her landlady's eyes, and it ignited her own. "Has an uprising started?"

"No. But Joe has a Dakota friend, who warned him violence is no more than a week away. It's going to happen, unless the gold shipment arrives first. No one is safe. Whites, mixed-bloods, and even full-bloods, if they are suspected of siding with the whites."

The statement startled Anja. Deep down, she had thought her Dakota ancestry immunized her from danger. That's why she had been dubious about the uprising. Dakotas and French and English traders had been intermarrying for two centuries. Many in the Dakota villages carried white blood in their veins, and many of the settlers had Dakota spouses or themselves were mixed-blood. They had lived mostly in harmony for many years, the major difference being in whether they chose the blanket path or the farming trail in their daily lives. She could understand that the new arrivals from Germany and Scandinavia might be vulnerable. But the old families?

"Has Mr. Nilsson returned?" Anja asked.

"No. He said he would be here for supper, which should be ready in half an hour. I expect he will be along shortly. He seems like a punctual man."

Anja abandoned any thought of changing and went directly into the parlor to ponder Emily Dickinson's words while she waited for supper. She had just sat down in the rocker when Will arrived. He saw her when he entered the house and turned into the room. He smiled warmly, but she could sense he was very troubled. She supposed he had not been hearing encouraging words today, either.

As Will seated himself on the settee near her, Anja said, "We must talk after supper."

Will said, "You stole the words from my mouth. Yes, we must."

Two young store clerks joined them at the supper table. They both lodged at Dickinson's but were employed by different traders. Except for an occasional exchange of pleasantries and remarks about the weather, they all ate silently. Anja suspected their minds shared preoccupation with the Dakota threat.

When Anja and Will returned to the parlor, Anja wasted no time raising the subject that was foremost on their minds. "Did Mrs. Dickinson tell you what they are doing?"

"She mentioned plans to leave."

"She informed me that she and her family are vacating the boarding house as soon as possible. She thinks I should leave the agency, too."

"She's smart, and she's right. You should leave, as well."

"I can't just walk out on my students. But I was short some pupils today."

Will said nothing.

"The full-blood Dakotas were absent today. Do you think that's a sign of something?"

"It's a sign that it is time for a long recess."

"I will teach tomorrow and stay overnight and go home the next morning."

"Where is home?"

"My parents' farm—about half way between here and Fort Ridgley."

"Tell your parents that you all need to go to the fort."

"My mother is half-blood. She grew up in one of the villages now located on the Lower Agency. I don't think the Dakota would harm us."

"Others say that, I know. But John Otherday, and others whose opinions I respect, believe no one is safe. You should not rely on tribal relationships. During the heat of war, insanity rules and the rendering of death can even turn on whimsy. Please consider my suggestion."

"I will think about it."

"I wanted to speak with you before I left, Anja. I'm riding out tonight. I'm heading for Fort Ridgely. I don't think I should wait till morning. I am expecting Billy Buck to return with a message, and I want to make it easy for him to locate me."

"Billy Buck? I know Billy. He's helping you?"

"Yes. He seems to know his way around this country."

"He knows everybody and where to find them."

Will stood. "Well, I'd better get my saddlebags and gear from my room and be on my way. I'm sorry. I had looked forward to spending more time with you this evening."

Anja got up and faced him, finding herself at a loss for words. "Will, I'm sorry, too. Please be careful."

He reached out, put his arms about her and pulled her to him. And then he kissed her, his lips softly brushing hers before lingering until she responded, clutching him tightly and kissing him hungrily. When he released her, she could see in his eyes that he wanted her. She wondered if he saw the same need in hers.

"I will find you again, Anja. I promise," he said before turning and moving toward the stairway.

Chapter 15

WILL DECIDED TO take his horses across the river on the Redwood Ferry, which was less than a mile from Council Square. As he approached, he was not surprised to see the ferry was doing a lot of business, all traffic heading east across the river away from the reservation. Word must be getting around.

He did not mind waiting while some of the white family groups rolled wagons with belongings on the ferry for the trip across. He noted that the traffic was all one way. As he led Warrior and Red onto the ferry, he commented to the grizzled ferryman. "Busy place."

"It's going to get a hell of a lot busier. Traffic's all one way. Boss says he's going to keep it open. He's half-blood and related to Chief Little Crow, he claims. Thinks the Sioux will leave him alone. I wouldn't stay here if I was related to Jesus Christ. After my shift, I'm headed to the other side of the river and ain't coming back."

"I understand."

It was near nightfall now and cloud cover was shutting off the moonglow, but as they approached the other side, Will caught a glimpse of shadowy figures almost hidden against a backdrop of forest up the bank some distance. Reflexively, he caressed the butt of his holstered Colt. When the ferry was tied to the post moorings and the gangplanks lowered to meet the bank, the ferryman signaled Will to depart first, and he led his horses off the deck, keeping his eyes on the shapes near the trees. Finally, as he walked up the slope toward the road, he could make out the shadowy forms of a man and two horses.

The man walked toward him, leading the horses. "Will," he said. "It's me. Billy."

Will relaxed instantly, moving toward him and extending his hand as they met. "Well, you said you would find me, and you did."

"I heard you was at the agency, and I was going to cross and meet up with you there." He reached into his shirt pocket and pulled out a sealed envelope. "Telegram reply," he said.

Will took the envelope and opened it. He tugged out a sheet of paper and unfolded it, but it was too dark for him to read. He retrieved a candle and lucifer from his saddlebags, struck the lucifer on a stone, and lighted the candle. He held the burning candle above the telegram and read aloud: "CHASE APPROVED 71K GOLD STOP SHIPPED NY 8-11-62. STOP ARRIVES RIDGLEY 8-18-62 STOP C HANSCOMB

"The money is coming?" Billy asked.

"Seventy-one thousand dollars in gold, it appears. 'Chase' is Salmon P. Chase, Secretary of the Treasury, so this had some top-level attention. It's an ambitious transportation schedule but possible, I guess. Train goes to St. Paul. Wagon from there to Ridgley might be a challenge. That's a good one hundred twenty-five miles. Today's the sixteenth. If there aren't any problems, it could get to Ridgely day after tomorrow. But we don't even know if it is in St. Paul yet. I'm not optimistic about the arrival date, but we've got a promise on paper."

"Paper promises mean nothing to the Dakota. White man hasn't kept one yet."

"I suppose you've got a point. But it's more than we had a few minutes ago."

Now, what should he do with this information? It seemed to Will it was critical that authorities at the agencies be made aware of the imminent arrival of the gold. Perhaps they could convey the information to key chiefs

Ron Schwab

and ward somebody igniting the uprising. He needed to get to Fort Ridgley personally before the gold came in to oversee arrangements for distribution to the Dakota bands.

He handed Billy the telegram. "Billy, I would like you to take this to the Upper Agency and show it to John Otherday. Let him read it, but you should keep the telegram. We might need this yet." Will did not tell him that the sheet of paper might be needed to cover his butt, and not for hygienic purposes.

"Anything else I should tell him?"

"Yes. That I am returning to the Lower Agency to inform Agent Galbraith. John should notify the agent at the Upper Agency, and they should inform the chiefs and anyone of influence."

"After I talk to John, what do you want me to do?"

"We'll meet at Ridgley. I would like to be there when the gold shipment comes in."

Billy sprung onto Buster's back, settling into the saddle with a ballerina's grace, and disappeared into the darkness with the spare horse trailing on the lead rope behind. By the time the ferryman had finished supervising the removal of horses, wagons and people from his vessel, Will was ready for the return trip.

"Didn't you just come across?" the ferryman asked, when he led his horses back on the ferry.

Of course, he knew the answer. He was just curious or nosy, depending on how a man chose to take it. Will's disposition said nosy. "It was a nice ride. Thought I'd do it again."

He cocked his head and looked at Will in disbelief. "And back again?"

"Later."

After disembarking the ferry, he headed back to Council Square. He stopped at the livery to drop off the horses, glad to find Ezra Bently, one of the stable hands, was still on duty. He pondered reclaiming his room at the boarding house, but the skinny young man encouraged him to lay out his bedroll on a straw pile, and Will accepted his lodging offer. Ezra seemed to be welcoming company this night.

"Where can I locate Agent Galbraith at this hour?" he asked.

"Not at the agency. He left this afternoon. He said he was going to Fort Ridgely to collect recruits to escort to Fort Snelling. He recruits for the Army. I'll be going next month."

Will could not believe it. The agent pulling out at this critical time? Was he that oblivious to the seriousness of the storm building at the agency? Or was he getting out to save his own hide? His motivation did not matter; Will was left with a dilemma.

He asked Ezra, "Who is in charge when Galbraith's gone?"

"Don't rightly know. Place sort of runs itself most of the time. Nobody much notices if the agent is about or not."

"Ezra, I need to get a message to the Dakota chiefs. Immediately. How would I do this?"

Ezra was quiet a moment, rubbing his chin thoughtfully. "You could go to Little Crow."

"But I have heard he is friendly with the Soldiers Lodge."

"He's friendly with about everybody till he figures out where things are headed. He wants to be the big chief. I'm half-blood. My ma is a cousin of his. She thinks Little Crow just wants to be top dog. He really don't want to have a war, but if there is one, he wants to be running it. He gets along with the whites most times. They're building him a new house on the agency right now. He goes to either the Presbyterian or Episcopalian services most Sundays. Wears white man's clothes most of the time."

Will had heard all this before. It seemed like a long shot, but Little Crow sounded like his best bet to get word to the right people. "Where do I find him?"

"He keeps a tipi and a woman near the new house. That's where he would be easiest to get to. If he's at the village, it could be tricky business."

"Tell me where to find the new house. I can't wait till morning."

"He won't take a midnight visit all that good."

"It doesn't matter. This is important. The difference between war and peace."

Chapter 16

EZRA'S DIRECTIONS WERE simple to follow. Little Crow's house was being constructed within a mile of Council Square. From the foundation size, it appeared the structure would not be a modest one, more castle than house. Will had walked to the construction site and approached the tipi cautiously. He saw no signs of sentries, which he supposed would be unnecessary on the reservation considering the ratio of Dakota to whites. As he drew nearer, the sound of snoring from inside the tipi drifted to his ears. He decided to summon the chief in the Dakota Sioux dialect, thinking he would be less alarmed at being awakened with his own language.

"Taoyateduta," he called, and continuing in Dakota, "I must speak with you."

There was a stirring from within the tipi. "Who calls?" came the reply in Dakota.

"I am Captain Will Nilsson. The Great Father in Washington has sent me with an important message for you and all the Dakota."

There was a prolonged silence before the tipi flap was pushed aside, and a tall, gaunt man clad only in a narrow loincloth stepped out. He looked Will over with suspicion before speaking in more than passable English. "I do not know you. How do I believe your words?"

"I was told you are a wise man who will not be fooled by lies. And that you will have me killed if I do not speak the truth," Will lied.

Little Crow cast his eyes about, obviously searching the darkness to see if they were being spied upon. Will assumed he was more concerned about Dakota than whites. Then he waved for Will to follow him into the tipi. It was not all that much darker inside and he could make out a lump on the far side, which he guessed was a sleeping wife or companion. Will knew nothing about chiefly benefits, but the image of Anja Lund flashed in his mind, and he envied the guy.

"Sit down," Little Crow said, making clear the conversation would be in English. Perhaps he did not want the other occupant to understand their words.

Will found a place on a buffalo robe, and they sat facing each other not more than a few feet apart. Will decided to hit him with the message immediately. "The Great Father has told me the gold will come to Fort Ridgely after sunrise, probably late in the day. I have been instructed to tell your people, but I thought they should hear the words from their chief."

"They will say you bring another promise to be broken."

"I will go to Fort Ridgely to make arrangements for distribution. Send representatives to meet me there to confirm that the gold has arrived. Your people will be fed. We can stop a war and save many lives."

"You may speak truth, but warriors will say you try to trick them. I will give your words to other chiefs. I fear it is too late. Men do not stop a stampede by telling the buffalo to stop, even if they will run to the edge of a canyon and fall to their deaths."

Will felt he had a shaky commitment from Little Crow. He did not think the chief wanted war, but Little Crow seemed to be one of those leaders who led from behind. In short, he was more politician than chief. If his constituents wanted war, no matter how irrational the desire, he would join them in order to gain and maintain power. Suddenly, a flurry of excited voices broke through the night, the source apparently some distance away but moving closer.

"Go," snapped the chief.

He did not need to repeat his order, and Will quickly rose and slipped through the tipi opening. Off to the southwest, he saw a mass of at least a dozen shadowy, chattering forms coming toward the tipi. He sensed something important was unfolding, and, deciding he would likely be observed heading for Council Square, he raced for the doorway of the half-constructed house. He ducked inside, pressing his back against the exterior wall just inside.

As the voices approached Little Crow's tipi, Will heard the chief call for quiet and demand an explanation. Will spoke Dakota with reasonable fluency, but he had difficulty understanding when the dialogue moved too fast. Nonetheless, he could make out most of what was said, and none of the words were encouraging. Little Crow made no mention of the gold's pending arrival, but it was likely too late for that. The war had already started. Apparently, a small Dakota hunting party had triggered an incident some distance north and east of the Minnesota River and ended up killing three white men and two women. The warriors who had come to Little Crow were working themselves into a frenzy. He heard the chief declare, "It is time." The warriors began yelling and whooping and soon disappeared, presumably to prepare for battle.

As soon as they were gone, Will headed back to Council Square, realizing he must alert any vulnerable parties he could locate at the agency. But he also knew that there were too many homes on the agency side of the river for him to possibly notify everyone. And he had no way of knowing who might side with the uprising. If there was an attack, most would be surprised. His first stop was at Dickinson's boarding house. He reasoned that this might be the largest gathering of folks he could warn at this hour, but he had to admit Anja Lund was on his mind.

When he arrived, he was surprised to find that Joseph and Emily Dickinson were busy packing a wagon outside the boarding house. "We're leaving," Mrs. Dickinson said. "But nobody will listen to us."

"They had better," I replied. He told her about the killings north of the river.

"My God, it's started. There will be no stopping it."

"How many boarders do you have?"

"Ten. Seven rooms."

"I'll tell them."

"Your lady friend is in room five, second floor."

Will turned and rushed for the entrance and moved down the main floor hallway, pounding on each door until someone opened it, warning that the uprising had started and urging an exodus to Fort Ridgely. One man cussed him out for waking him. Another shrugged and returned to bed. Most got up and dressed and started collecting their belongings.

He raced upstairs and knocked first at Anja's door, which was first at the top of the stairs. He was surprised when she promptly opened the door, and he saw she was already dressed in a green cotton shirt, faded denims, and moccasins. "Will, I thought I heard your voice from downstairs. I picked up enough to tell me to get ready to move out of here. I'm leaving most of my things here. I'll either return for them when it's safe or live without them."

"Stay with me," he said. "I'll warn the others on this floor and then get my horses at the livery and alert as many people as I can. I have an extra mount, if you need one."

"My mare is at the livery, too. I'll be right with you." She turned back into her room, and he stepped to the next door. By this time, everyone had heard the commotion, and one middle-aged man had even stepped out into the hallway. After Will conveyed the bad news to the others, he turned back to Anja's room and saw she was waiting in the hallway, holding a small carpetbag in one hand and a shiny Henry rifle in the other. He had not pictured her as a gun-toting woman but had only seen her wearing a dress in a schoolroom and the boarding house. In his conversations with her, though, he had garnered hints that there was a complex woman hidden behind her prim and proper façade, and her lingering kiss had suggested as much. He realized now that he was starting a journey with Anja Lund that might lead to places unexpected and not necessarily happy.

When they reached the livery, Will informed Ezra about the new developments. The young man stood there in stunned silence for several moments before he spoke. "They'll come for the horses by daybreak, but it's my job to stay with the critters. Maybe they won't bother me none since I'm half-blood. What do you think?"

Anja replied, "I don't think that guarantees anything. I am guessing there is no plan and no rules. It will depend on what warriors you are up against. Dakota blood might help you with some. Others might see you as a traitor if you are getting along with whites. My advice is to get the hell out, if you aren't joining with the uprising."

"I don't know nothing about being Dakota. I'm a farm boy from north of the river. I can't even talk their language."

"You had better saddle up and go," Anja said.

"I got a job here, but I'll think on it."

"Don't think too long."

Chapter 17

ANJA AND WILL agreed to split up to warn homes within sight of Council Square. She identified the families that would likely side with the Dakotas so Will would incur less risk of encountering hostility. They agreed to rendezvous in the trees on the bluffs above the Minnesota River at the first trace of sunrise. From that vantage point they could view most of the agency grounds and several of the nearby Dakota villages. They would also be able to monitor activity at the Redwood Ferry to determine if crossing was still safe.

Anja first rode to Reverend Samuel Hinman's Episcopal mission, where the church maintained both a school and chapel for services. She had always found Hinman an agreeable, though somewhat naïve, young man but sensed that he looked down upon the agency school a bit for its lack of religious instruction. She woke him from slumber in the adjacent manse, and he did not attempt to hide his skepticism about the prospects of an uprising. "That cannot be possible," he insisted, "Chief Little Crow attended Sunday services here yesterday morning and was most congenial."

She did not have time to debate, and, satisfied that the young preacher would not be returning to bed, she mounted Molly and reined the mare westward toward the cluster of stores and trading posts northwest of Council Square. She warned the traders or their employees who had cabins in the area, disappointed at the unwelcoming reception she received from most. They seemed deaf to her words.

She saved Andrew Myrick's store for last. She did not care for the weaselly man and knew he would be hostile to her message. He slept above his store most nights, so that's where she hitched her mare. She hammered loudly on the door for several minutes, not caring whether she annoyed him. She started when she heard a voice above her.

"What the hell do you want?" growled Myrick, his head and the barrel of a shotgun sticking out of the store's second-floor window.

"The Sioux are on the warpath," she said. "You had better be getting to Fort Ridgely."

"Who are you?"

"Anja Lund."

"The Indian woman up at the school? Why should I believe you? You're one the heathen varmints. Get the hell out of here."

She shrugged and returned to her horse. She had tried. As for his insults, she just shrugged them off. Every race and culture had their share of those kind of people.

She heard gunfire to the south at the same instant blurred rays of sunlight appeared on the eastern horizon, and she wheeled Molly toward the bluffs where she was to meet Will. He, Warrior, and Red were hidden in the forested high ground when she approached, but Will stepped from the trees and waved for her to join them. Halfway up the rocky escarpment, she dismounted and led the mare into the cover.

Will seemed pensive and thoughtful as he surveyed the land below. "Gunfire's in the direction of the ferry. There are lines of wagons and people waiting to board, but I think the attacks are directed at folks in the cabins. I'm surprised they didn't cut off the ferry first thing, but I don't think there is any plan. There seem to be small bands of Dakotas just roaming at random, looking for somebody to kill. And still they haven't decided who to kill, it seems."

Anja looked in the direction of Council Square, and she could see small clusters of painted Dakotas moving from building to building. Most were carrying steel-headed war axes and either a shotgun or rifle, although some had bows and a quiver of arrows. Gunfire was steady now, and she saw a man race from the livery with a warrior in pursuit. *Oh, my God, it was Ezra.* She gasped with disbelief when the axe blade came down on his skull and split it like a melon but could not turn her head away when the Dakota began chopping at the young man's neck and finally kicked the bloody, decapitated head into the dusty roadway.

The agency area quickly turned to a large slaughtering ground, white clerks being drug from burning buildings and scalped alive before mutilation of their bodies started. She knew the incessant screaming would haunt her the remainder of her life. The more fortunate victims were taken down by shotgun blasts before the butchery commenced. Her eyes moved to the cluster of traders' stores in the distance. Same scene. She saw a man escaping from the rear of Myrick's store, running, but with a noticeable limp, before arrows drove into his back like needles into a pin cushion. She was certain the runner was Andrew Myrick, and she suspected the warrior now taking his scalp would claim special honors for his trophy.

So entranced by the unfolding scene was Anja, she only now became aware that she had been squeezing Will's hand so tightly she had dug her fingernails into his flesh She reluctantly slipped her hand from his. "It's horrible. Worse than I could have ever imagined. And there is nothing we can do."

"No. Some have escaped, but their chances of making Ridgely aren't good. I saw Dr. Humphrey and his family headed for the ferry, but there is more gunfire down that way. I'm afraid they'll be too late. Maybe they can hide till help comes. But I don't know how much help anybody will get from the fort. They are terribly undermanned. I don't know if they can withstand an attack if the Dakotas ever get organized."

"I must warn my parents. I know you need to get to Ridgely. And I must warn my assistant, Karina's, family. They live on this side of the river not far from here. I can show you a shallow crossing and then we will have to separate."

"No. We stay together. I can't take a direct route to Ridgely, and you know this country better than I do. Is your parents' farm between here and the fort?"

"Yes. We won't want to take the main road to Ridgley anyway. The Dakotas will be swarming to the road. And we can get to Karina's house in twenty minutes."

"Then let's ride."

"We walk. Follow me."

They led their horses along a narrow trail that snaked through the woods until Anja saw the four Dakotas blocking the trail. They were fierce-looking with their angry eyes glaring from menacing painted faces. Will was behind her ten paces and did not see them until he drew closer. She feared he would draw his Colt.

"Don't make a move for your pistol. Not yet."

She recognized the Dakota with the black warpaint coating his face and a red stripe running from his forehead, over his nose, and to his chin. Cut Nose. He stared at her, and she wondered if she really saw his eyes soften a bit. Then his eyes shifted, obviously looking at the man leading two horses behind her. She saw hatred again and then detected some uncertainty. Something strange was happening here, but their best chance was to wait them out. Two carried shotguns. Cut Nose carried a rifle and a war-axe. The fourth apparently preferred his bow. Her Henry was secure in its scabbard, and she would be dead before she could retrieve it. Will might take one or two down, but not all four, before they overtook him. The Dakotas were no more than twenty feet in front of her.

Cut Nose was obviously their leader and stood to the front of the group. He turned to the others and, speaking Dakota, told them to let the man and woman pass. The others protested.

"The woman is Dakota," Cut Nose told his comrades. "We will not harm her."

A young warrior said, "I need a second wife. She can live, but I will take her."

Cut Nose said, "No. If you try, you must fight me first. To the death."

The young warrior, his face painted half yellow and half black, looked sullen but said nothing else.

A stocky warrior with streaks of gray in his braided hair said, "The man is not Dakota, or his blood has been bred out. He has the look of a warrior, but a white warrior. We should kill him now."

"Later," Cut Nose declared, "not now. Let us go." He moved off the trail and into the woods, heading northerly toward the river, and the others followed, looking over their shoulders with disdain and disappointment.

"I don't believe this," Will said, coming up beside her. "We should be dead by now. Or I should be."

"That was Cut Nose," Anja said.

"I figured that much. I saw him outside of Myrick's store. He took an instant dislike to me, and I don't think my status has improved. Why did he pass on the opportunity?"

"You did understand what they were saying?"

"Pretty much, but that didn't explain why. Cut Nose knew you."

It was a statement, not a question, so she did not reply. Then it suddenly occurred to her, and her heart pounded like a drum in her chest: The Dakotas were on the trail that led to Karina Johanns's cabin. Only they were walking away from the home. They had already visited.

Chapter 18

CUT NOSE SENSED Swims Like Otter and young Beaver Tooth were still angry with him for allowing the tall white warrior and Anja to pass unharmed. Otter simply liked to kill. He was a large, powerful warrior, but Cut Nose would be a frail ancient before Otter would have the courage to challenge him. He was a violent and cruel coward, whose favorite prey were women and small children. Beaver Tooth had just wanted to drag Anja to his buffalo robe and enter her with his unmanageable youthful spear. And he had just taken a woman not more than an hour before the encounter. Cut Nose did not mind being past the days when reason came from beneath his loincloth.

His friend and blood brother of many years, Round Bear, had simply shrugged off the incident on the trail. He killed easily enough but lacked the bloodthirst of some. He did not torture or mutilate his foe, other than to take a prized scalp only after the unfortunate one's death. He had never seen Bear kill a child, although he might take down a woman who attacked him, especially Chippewa women, who could be very dangerous.

Cut Nose respected his friend's approach to war and shared it. He wanted to kill the whites and drive them from Dakota lands, but he preferred the infliction of instant death. He killed women and children, though, because it was necessary to keep the invaders from reproducing like rats and overwhelming his people with their seemingly endless numbers. His weapon of choice was his stone-headed warclub, and he scoffed at torture and mutilation, although he saw the manner of administering death as each warrior's choice.

Round Bear no doubt understood why Anja had been allowed to pass unharmed. He had waited in the woods sometimes while Cut Nose and Calling Dove, known by whites as Marta Lund, coupled. When the girl was very small, the stocky, gentle Round Bear had even entertained Anja with tricks and games on occasion to distract the girl from seeking out her mother.

They did not talk about such things, but he supposed Round Bear wondered if Anja was a child sprouted from Cut Nose's seed. Anja's dead brothers, lighter-skinned than their mother and blue-eyed, had clearly been sired by Larson Lund. Fittingly, they had succumbed to a disease brought by the white man to infest the Dakotas. But Anja was darker than most mixed bloods and more beautiful than any white woman could hope to be.

The four Dakotas had retrieved their horses from the ravine where they had been hidden while the riders made their stealthy attacks on settlers on the south and west sides of the Minnesota River. They had crossed the river, calm and slow-moving today, with no difficulty. It was not mid-morning yet, but the sun shone brightly and warmed their backs. It would have been a good day for fishing or a hunt were it not for the gunfire and screams that echoed from all directions.

As they moved out of the woods, and onto the road that led to Fort Ridgely, Cut Nose surveyed the twisting wagon trail in both directions. Many Dakotas had preceded them. Overturned wagons blocked easy passage, and white bodies of every age and sex littered the roadway. He decided other Dakotas would be clearing out the white farms near the main road. Best hunting would be further north and east into lands claimed by the whites, so he led his small war party up a less-traveled access trail. He had an ulterior motive. He planned to split up the war party after a few attacks, so he could veer off to

the Lund farm and assure himself Calling Dove had escaped. He cared not about the man she called husband
but hoped he would not have to kill the Norwegian invader himself.

They rode nearly a mile along the trail before they
came to a farmstead that included two small log houses.
These probably lodged several generations of a white
family. The body yield could be substantial here.

They dismounted and staked their horses and approached the houses on foot. As they neared the building site, a young woman clearly with child, carrying a
pail, emerged from the barn and caught sight of them.
She screamed and dropped the pail, dumping milk on
the ground, and ran back into the barn. Momentarily, a
somewhat older man with a pitchfork in his hands, appeared in the barn doorway. Cut Nose could hear the
woman crying and sobbing. He wished she would not be
so afraid. She should face her death with courage.

He was distracted for a moment when a naked, tod-
dling child came out the nearer house and started to walk
on uncertain feet in the direction of the man, who was
apparently his father. Swims Like Otter broke toward
the child and grabbed his legs, swung him into the air
and began slamming his head against the side of the log
house. The white man yelled, "No. Stop. No." He raced

toward Otter with pitchfork poised to strike, but the roar of Round Bear's double-barreled shotgun drowned out even the woman's screaming, and the man crumpled to the ground, his upper body and neck a massive lake of blood. Otter turned around, the child hanging like a dead rabbit from his hands and the head a mass of mush. He dropped the little boy next to his father and knelt and removed his knife from its sheath.

It was no surprise that Beaver Tooth headed to the barn to deal with the woman. Cut Nose signaled Round Bear to investigate the house the boy had come from. He cast a look of disdain at Otter, who had pulled down the man's britches and was carving away his genitals, so he would not plant seeds for more whites in another life. Otter had no pride and would doubtless claim a scalp he had not earned.

Cut Nose tried to shut out the hysterical screaming of the woman as he approached the other house, shotgun in one hand and his favorite war club in the other. There were shoe and boot prints in the dust near the house, so he was certain it was not an abandoned house. He had been uneasy about the quiet there. Perhaps the occupants had escaped to Fort Ridgely. When he was no more than ten feet from the door, however, it opened slowly, and he was faced by a scrawny, white-haired woman with a butcher knife clutched tightly in both hands.

"Go away," she said, her voice little more than a whisper. "We have helped your people when they were sick, given food to those who came here hungry. I don't understand why you are doing this."

"Nellie," came a croaking voice from behind her. "Who you talking to? I heard a shotgun fire."

The woman said, "My husband is sick. It's his heart. He is helpless and needs me."

Cut Nose spoke in English. "Put knife down. Go to your man and get on knees. Pray to your God, and you both die fast."

She looked at him, her eyes incredulous. "You expect me to just give up to you heathen animals?"

Cut Face shrugged.

She released the knife, and it dropped at her feet and clattered on the doorstep. She turned and walked back into the house. Cut Nose followed her but paused in the kitchen to scan the tidy cupboards and the woodstove and all the knickknacks that he thought cluttered the place. He had been in many such homes but never got over their strangeness. This room made him think of Calling Dove. The woman disappeared for a moment, but he found her in what he knew to be a bedroom, which was like a true Dakota's buffalo robe—where a man slept and lay with one of his women.

The old woman knelt next to the bed, one hand holding that of a skeletal, pale bearded man whose eyes were closed. He could hear her mumbling words too rapidly for him to comprehend. He moved up behind her and raised his warclub. The stone head arced downward and drove deeply into her skull, and she toppled over without so much as a gasp. He repeated the strike and caved in the husband's forehead. Cut Nose did not need to confirm their deaths. He knew when he had struck a death blow. He turned away and walked out of the house.

Outside, he noticed the young woman's screaming had subsided to moans and sobbing. Beaver Tooth would have emptied his seed into her by now, perhaps more than once. Cut Nose hoped he would kill her soon and stop the suffering.

Round Bear came up to Cut Nose as he walked toward the barn. "Should we torch the place?"

"I think not. There may be much to scavenge here once the whites are driven away. It would be a waste to burn it now. Some of the fools are destroying things we might use, even cattle and hogs that might feed our people. I will not do this. We should take any good horses with us and set free any other animals that are in the barn. Where is Swims Like Otter?"

"He is in the barn with Beaver Tooth."

"Is he mounting the woman?"

"I think not."

Round Bear fell in beside Cut Nose as he moved again toward the barn. Before they entered, Otter came out, with a squirming, bloody baby clutched by an ankle with his hand. Beaver Tooth followed with a hammer and spikes he had found in the barn. Cut Nose entered the building, where he found the naked young woman stretched out on the dirt floor, her fair-skinned face framed by long, flaxen hair. Her glassy, azure eyes seemed to be staring up at him. Her throat made a choking sound with each breath, but she lived notwithstanding that her abdomen had been sliced open from between her breasts to above to the curly, blonde hair that covered her secret place. Her nipples had been cut off to assure she would not suckle a child in another life, although he doubted if whites would be granted such existence by a just Great Spirit. He knelt by the woman, lifted his warclub, and ended her misery.

They released two of the five horses that were in the stalls. "You may each take one of the others," Cut Nose said. "I have something I must do alone. Tell all you see that the Soldiers Lodge will meet tonight. You should find Little Crow and tell him his presence is desired if he wishes to lead this war. Like the white eyes, we must plan, and there must be a general."

"I can do this," said Round Bear.

When they led the three horses out of the barn, Cut Nose saw that the baby's hands and feet had been nailed to the side of the barn and that the tiny body with its head drooping forward was suspended there. The blood was drying and forming a brown crust on the pale form now. He looked closer to confirm that the creature had died and saw that it was a girl child. He felt a moment of remorse that it had all come to this but reminded himself that this was one less white to perpetuate their race. One less to steal the Dakota land.

Chapter 19

CUT NOSE, ASTRIDE his gray gelding, approached the Lund farmstead through the small pasture north of the buildings, choosing to avoid the trail that passed for a road in front of the house. He did not know if his Dakota brothers had struck this far north of the river yet, but he did not wish to confront any passing settlers just yet. His main concern was Calling Dove. He hoped she had heeded his advice and departed the vicinity. Fort Ridgely would fall soon, and there was no true haven nearby.

His body tensed when he came upon the dead milk cow and two young heifers stretched out in the tall grass. The cow had wounds in her neck and shoulders indicating shotgun blasts. The others had been taken down by arrows. All had been disemboweled in the search for the liver, which would have been eaten fresh and bloody immediately upon removal. A Sioux delicacy, to which some medicine men attributed strength and invulnerability. Cut Nose had seen more than one foolish warrior die in reliance upon that notion.

He rode ahead slowly, but he saw no sign of movement in the farmyard. He dismounted and approached the buildings cautiously and quickly confirmed that the war party had moved on. Dead chickens were scattered about the yard, some with twisted necks but others had died from gunshots, a senseless waste of ammunition that might soon be desperately needed for killing the white hordes.

In front of the barn lay what remained of a naked Larson Lund in a pool of blood. His hands and feet had been chopped off and dropped near the body, and the usual amputation of the genitals had been performed. Often his evidence of manhood would have been stuffed in the victim's mouth, but his head was missing. He cast his eyes about the yard but did not see it anyplace and thought that strange. If not tossed near the body, the head would ordinarily have been anchored to a post or other object to further terrorize any of the enemy who might approach this place.

He looked in the barn, aware he was delaying his visit to the house. The two or three riding horses had been taken, but a mule team in a shared stall had collapsed and died after having their throats efficiently cut. When he stepped out of the barn and walked slowly toward the house, he recognized the corpse of a large short-haired dog, its head battered by a tomahawk or war club. He remembered the animal. Affectionate and gentle, non-threatening. She probably had not attacked but made the mistake of being in some warrior's way.

The door to the house was closed but not locked, and he opened it and stepped into a small enclosed entryway occupied by a few chairs, a big wash tub and a basketful of clothes. Shelves full of things the white man used lined one wall. He went into the kitchen and found Calling Dove sitting at the small table, the front of her dress blood-soaked but apparently not with her own. She seemed oblivious to Cut Nose's presence as she gazed at the pale, blood-smeared face of Larson Lund, whose pale, blue eyes stared up at her from the head resting on the tabletop.

Cut Nose felt a tremor of fear dance down his spine. Calling Dove was behaving very strangely. If her mind had flown away without her, she could be bad medicine. Such people should be avoided. "Calling Dove," he said, speaking Dakota, for she had always insisted they use the people's words when they were together. "I have come to help you."

She did not look up at him but replied in English. "I am no longer Dakota and will not speak your tongue. If you wish to help me, take your club and kill me now."

"No. I cannot do that."

"I do not understand you. Speak English."

The strangeness had overtaken her. He would not argue with her. "I say, I cannot help you."

"Of course not. How many have you killed today? How many more will you kill tomorrow? How many Dakotas will die? But when this is done, and it will be, the white man will win, and the Dakotas will move again and suffer more. You will die and it will have been for nothing. Nothing." She still refused to look at him, but she gently caressed the face on the tabletop.

Words would not come to Cut Nose, but Calling Dove's words unsettled him. They were like a curse or at least an omen that portended ill.

Marta said, "You cannot answer, can you? But you will learn the truth of what I say." She shook her head from side to side. "My poor, kind Larson. You were so good to me. I never knew you to raise a fist to any man. Always patient and reasonable. I loved you, my dear, and long to be with you. Please forgive the savage lust within me.

You knew, didn't you? About Cut Nose. And you guessed about Anja. You never said a word, but I am sure you did. I am sorry I betrayed you. But I am not sorry about Anja. You are her father. She loves you and knows no other. She will always be Larson Lund's daughter and carry your soul with her. Blood is nothing."

Cut Nose moved toward Marta and reached out to place his hand upon her shoulder.

"Do not touch me," she snapped. "It is done between us. I will probably burn in hell because of what we did. Maybe my sins brought Larson to this end. I cannot believe any just God would punish him for what I did. Nothing makes sense. But I do not want to go on. Kill me. I beg you. Kill me."

"Calling Dove, do not speak like this. Come with me and be my woman. It will be as we wanted those many summers back."

"My name is Marta Lund. If you refuse to kill me, go away. Now."

He hesitated, and then he turned and walked out of the house. It saddened him that he had not looked into those doe-like eyes one more time, and he felt an emptiness no woman had ever made him feel before. But he had lied to her. He would never have taken her as his woman. Her head was not right, and he could not bring such bad medicine into his lodge or robe. It worried him some that he might already have been tainted by her proximity in the small room.

Chapter 20

THE FARMSTEAD WAS nestled in a clearing a good mile from any road. Access was essentially by way of a trail network made up of paths much like the one that brought them to this place. Will noticed a trail heading west that would have been wide enough to squeeze a wagon through, but it had not been used frequently enough to carve out ruts. It was certainly not a farm in any traditional sense, and he wondered how a man might eke out a living in the middle of the woods.

As they dismounted at the edge of the clearing, his question was answered. He caught sight of large, elegantly-carved letters attached to the barn: "Johanns Furniture." Anders Johanns was evidently a wood craftsman. With his workplace located on acres teeming with oak, walnut and other hardwoods, Johanns's raw materials could be harvested on site.

When they led the horses out of the woods, he saw nothing amiss. He noticed the wide barn door was open, but that would not have been unusual on a summer day. "I'll check the building," Will told Anja, "if you want to see if anyone is in the cabin."

He walked slowly toward the barn, his eyes searching the yard for any sign of a disturbance and finding none. Perhaps the family had not been home when Cut Nose and his little war party stopped by. It occurred to him also that Anja had said that Karina's mother was full-blood Dakota. That might have been a ticket to the family's immunity from attack. But, then, why would the warriors have even bothered to come here?

When Will reached the open barn doorway, the notion of immunity dissolved. Slung over a sturdy sawhorse and surrounded by an assortment of beautifully crafted chairs and tables was the partially-clothed body of a middle-aged man he assumed was Anders Johanns. The thick salt and pepper hair on top of his head was split by an angry, scarlet divide where an Indian's scalping knife had done its work. He moved closer and realized that the man's hands had been removed and lay on the ground near the corpse. And they had been neatly sawed away from the arms, not hacked off with an axe as the Dakotas would have been expected to perform the task.

A white craftsman. What better way to extract revenge than to take his hands with his own tools? Will flinched at the thought, and he would bet his yellow stallion that Anders Johanns was alive to watch and feel his wrists giving way to the blade of his own saw.

He lifted the body off the sawhorse and stretched it out on the dirt barn floor, taking note of the mutilation of the craftsman's crotch. Seeing a dusty horse blanket tossed over a stall partition, he retrieved it and covered the body and armless hands. He searched the barn-workshop to confirm the Dakotas had left no other artwork behind but found nothing. There were no horses or other animals in the stalls. He figured the Dakotas had been anxious to make other visits and did not have time to travel with extra horses and had probably turned them loose and scared them off.

"Will?"

He turned and saw Anja standing in the door opening, framed by the sun's morning glow. "Yes. Bad news here."

"You've covered him. What did they do to him?"

"Are you sure you want to know?"

"Yes."

"Scalped, of course. Genitals removed. Hands were sawed off with his own saw."

"Oh, my God. Do you think he was alive when they did these things?"

"Yes. No other wounds. He just bled out. Hopefully, he passed out early on." Will was being more clinical about the poor devil than he felt. "What did you find?"

"His wife, Rachael, is dead. I found her naked in her bed. I am certain she had been raped. Her throat was cut. Her scalp wasn't taken. No other mutilation. I suppose it might have something to do with her being full-blood. But her life wasn't spared because of that."

"The girl?"

"No sign of her. That's why I came down here. I thought you might have found something. But I was afraid of what it might be."

"Horses are gone. Do you think she might have escaped or been away from the house?"

"Possible. But not likely as early as it would have been when the war party hit the place."

"There is nothing else here. I'll go up to the house with you. I think we should bury these folks. Maybe Karina will turn up yet, alive and well."

"Pardon me, if I am turning pessimistic. She is such a pretty and bright girl. The thought of what those animals might have done to her sickens me."

There was nothing he could say to console her, and he feared they had not seen the worst of it yet. Gunfire still echoed through the river valley, and plumes of smoke were rising across the river now, an indication that the war was moving north and easterly. Perhaps toward Ridgley. Will could not help but think of his parents. Had the uprising spread to the Nilsson farm? Had his mother and father received any warning? Had they escaped to Fort Ridgely? This was not a single war, he thought, where armies planned and strategized. There might be a hundred wars going on out there with small war parties, like the one that attacked the Johanns farmstead, striking out on their own and hitting farms and villages at random or exacting revenge for perceived wrongs against them.

The house, which like many in this part of Minnesota was constructed from native stone and logs and, not surprisingly, reflected a master craftsman's skills. They stepped onto flawlessly laid oak flooring no doubt installed by Anders. The interior had not been ransacked. The tidy, small parlor just off the kitchen was in condition to receive guests. Rachael Johanns had obviously been a good housekeeper. A woven rug covered the area under the settee and a polished oak rocker.

It was a compact single-story house, but Karina enjoyed a separate bedroom that had space for a single
feather-bed and a chest, as well as a little bedside table
with an oil lamp and several books on it. One corner had
a nice clothes rack for a few dresses and other garments.
Her parents' bedroom was much wider but similarly furnished. As they stepped into the room, he was relieved to
find that Anja had covered the dead woman's body with
a blanket and had even wrapped a pillow case about her
neck to hide the angry slash in the throat. Somehow it
made him feel less invasive. He could not help but notice
the Sioux woman had a pretty face, and he guessed she
was in her mid-thirties, probably some ten years younger than the man he found in the barn-shop.

"I should look for a shovel in the barn so we can bury
them," Will said. "We've got to move on if we are going
to check your parents' place." He had already decided he
would report in at Ridgely after that. Then, if his own
parents had not come in, after sending a courier to Snelling with a report to Hanscomb in Washington, he would
look into their status.

"But we need to find Karina."

"We will try to track her down, but we cannot search
now. If you wish to wrap Rachael for burial, I'll see what
I can do for her husband. I'll come back and carry the

body out after I dig a common grave. It will save time, and maybe they would have liked that thought."

Will could tell she thought he was being cold about it all, but she nodded her approval. Little did he know that this was nothing compared to the carnage he would witness in the days and months ahead.

He stepped back into the parlor when something caught his eye. The deep notches in the rug. The settee had been moved very recently.

"Anja," he called. "Could you step out and help me a minute?"

Anja came into the parlor and looked at him questioningly. "What is it?"

"I'm going to lift the settee. Would you grab the rug and pull it out? I want to look at something." He lifted and manipulated the settee's legs, and she tugged and worked the rug free.

He slid the settee away from the area. The lines were barely discernible, but it was clear that a trapdoor was snuggly imbedded in the floor, the oak planks in perfect alignment with those surrounding it. He knelt and ran his fingers along the edges until he found a tiny depression just large enough for his index finger to slip in. It was apparently designed to allow a person to raise the edge just enough to secure a grasp with the other hand

and lift it. But he could not budge the door, which answered his question.

"Anja, I think Karina is under the trapdoor, but it seems to be locked. If you would knock and call to her, she might reply. Her father probably lined the floor and trapdoor with a sound barrier, so an invader wouldn't hear movement or noise below. But it works both ways. She probably can't hear much of what's going on up here."

Anja stretched out on the floor and pounded on the trapdoor. She yelled, "Karina, it's Anja Lund. It's safe. You can come out now. Open the door."

Silence.

"Maybe she's not there." Anja said.

"Maybe. But try again."

This time there was a response by a tapping on the underside of the door. "Anja, I am unlocking the door," came a muffled voice.

Will watched, waiting for one side of the door to rise, but soon all four came up. Locks on each side, to reduce clearance problems should the trapdoor be spanned by the settee. Anders had given this a lot of thought. He took the trapdoor and lifted it from the opening and a wide-eyed young woman emerged and stumbled out and fell sobbing into Anja's arms.

"Something terrible happened, didn't it? Mama or Papa would have come for me."

Anja took Karina's hand and eased her down on the settee and began to explain gently in a soft voice Will could barely hear and did not wish to hear. Instead, his curiosity led him to explore the hiding place.

He was surprised to find that a steep stairway with a handrail dropped into the darkness. At the bottom, he bumped his knee on a small table that had an oil lamp with a few scattered lucifers on it. He lighted the lamp and promptly realized it was a day-to-day necessity in the hideaway. Shelves along two of the walls were teeming with jars of canned fruit and vegetables and other foodstuffs. The light would have been necessary to both store and retrieve the items hidden here. Jugs that he suspected were filled with water would allow for long-term survival in this place. The walls were all made of perfectly mortared stone, which did not surprise him in the least. The cellar was much larger than he had expected and doubled as a safe retreat and functional part of the house.

He found a double-barreled shotgun leaning against one wall adjacent to a straight-back chair, where presumably Karina had waited out her ordeal. It was loaded. This was an interesting place, and he would have liked to study it in more detail, but he had grim work to attend to. Will grabbed up the gun, snuffed out the light, and started his climb back up the stairway.

Chapter 21

THANKFULLY, ANJA KNEW of a crossing that gave them access to the northeast side of the Minnesota River. The gunfire and screams coming from downstream told Will the Redwood Ferry was out of business. The rapid rate of the gunfire seemed odd to him. The Dakotas appeared to be receiving serious resistance from some of the defenders.

They had taken a saddle from the Johanns's barn, and Karina was now mounted on Red. She was subdued but composed now, holding up well considering they had just buried her parents less than an hour earlier.

Anja had taken Karina under her wing, and Will admired her ability to calm the girl and help her to collect her senses after the brutal deaths of her parents. Anja had permitted the girl a brief glimpse of her mother's face, but a view of her father's mutilated body had been forbidden despite a near tantrum. Anja had said simply, "You do not want this to be the last memory of your father. Trust me on this."

They led the horses cautiously through trees and brush toward the river road. Yells and screams, and more gunfire, told Will the war had overflowed to this side of the river. The crying of children shot shivers down his spine. The Sioux far outnumbered the whites in southwest Minnesota, and most whites were not well-armed. Many homes owned no more than a single rifle or shotgun used for hunting. Few farmers owned a pistol. The Dakotas and settlers had been at peace for many years here, evidenced by the large number of mixed-blood families. The thought of needing guns to defend against attacks from Dakota neighbors had likely not occurred to most whites. Weapons of all kinds were a part of Dakota culture, however. The majority owned either shotguns or long-rifles. A fair number carried muskets, and Will had seen a few revolvers proudly brandished by warriors on the reservation. And, of course, the inventory of traditional weapons was plentiful—knives, war clubs, hatchets, lances, bows and arrows.

Will had promised Anja they would check on her parents, and he was increasingly concerned about what they might find at the Lund farm. He knew Anja had believed her mother's Dakota heritage would protect Marta and Larson Lund. That illusion had been obliterated at the Johanns place. He was certain Anja's confidence had been shaken by the atrocities committed there, but comforting Karina seemed to be her focus now.

Will led the way on a deer trail that snaked through the woods. Karina followed him, and Anja had fallen in after her. They had arms enough for all, but he was uncertain about Karina's skills with the shotgun. She insisted she could load and squeeze a trigger, so he had fashioned a rope-sling for the gun to slip over the saddle horn and stuffed all the shells he could find in her saddlebags. He hoped her prowess with the weapon would not be tested.

They were less than a half mile from the road when the agonizing cries reached his ears, and he signaled a halt. There was no gunfire, but something terrible was happening in the direction of the road. He tied Warrior to a low-hanging oak branch and pulled his Sharps out of its scabbard. "Stay here," he said. "I want to check this out."

He moved toward the shrieks and screams but drew his Colt and wheeled when he heard steps behind him. He was at once relieved and miffed when he saw Anja and Karina only a dozen paces back. He guessed military rank did not carry weight with Anja.

When she caught up with him, she said in a near whisper, "We stick together."

He glared at her long enough to let her know he was not pleased with this development and then turned and hurried ahead. Soon they were near enough to the commotion to have a line of sight through the trees. They saw a lone buckboard wagon on the dusty roadway. Two men and two women lay scattered in the road, their heads bloodied. The wagon's team had been cut free. Three mounted Sioux watched two others as they climbed into the wagon, which was packed with personal belongings and at least five children. One of the mounted warriors leaned from his horse and yanked a baby Will had not previously observed from the wagon box, swung his war axe down on its head and tossed it in the road as if it were garbage.

The warrior nudged his horse along the side of the wagon searching out another small victim, but by this time Will had a cartridge in his Sharps and the rifle cradled to his shoulder. When the Indian reached again to grab up another child, he squeezed the trigger. The gun roared, and blood exploded from under the Dakota's jaw, and he tumbled off the horse and dropped like a sack of flour on the road.

He quickly reloaded, but Anja had already moved ahead of him and off to the right. Her Henry cracked twice, and one of the Indians on the wagon crumpled over and fell forward, collapsing among the hysterical children. The other stood up, war axe in hand, and looked in the direction of the gunfire. Will aimed, squeezed, and dropped him backward over the edge of the wagon box. The remaining two Sioux disappeared down the road. He reloaded and started to walk cautiously toward the wagonload of children, who seemed to be slipping from uncontrolled panic to stunned shock now. When the unmistakable roar of a shotgun blast came from behind him, he swung his Sharps around, ready to fire, but saw that Karina had answered his question about her shotgun prowess. A painted Dakota was stretched out on the ground no more than twenty feet from her, his bare midsection a bloody mass from shredding by the buckshot. Karina's face was grim and cold as she reached into her trouser pocket and plucked out another shell from the handful she had taken from her saddlebags. She looked at Will, and he nodded his approval. "Thanks," he said.

When they reached the wagon, Will pulled the dead Dakota out and drug him to the roadside. He was sickened to find they had arrived too late to save a small boy, no more than four years of age, who had been hacked beyond recognition. They helped the other four children, three girls and a boy, from the wagon, and Anja and Karina ushered them back into the woods.

The other two Dakotas Will deposited with their tribesman. He clustered the settlers' bodies further down the road and a few feet into the trees. He placed the remains of the slaughtered boy and the baby girl with them. They were apparently two couples and the parents of the children, but he had no way of matching spouses or children and was not inclined to ask one of the children to identify them. Perhaps later Anja might elicit descriptions that would help. The adults were all on the young side, the men probably in their mid-thirties and the women in their late twenties. The men had been shot down and scalped, and the women had suffered axe and clubbing wounds. There was no other mutilation, which he speculated had been interrupted by their arrival. There would be no time to bury these poor people, so Will tried to identify landmarks that would help with recovery of the bodies should that be possible before predators moved in and did their work.

When he joined Anja, he found that she and Karina had the children calmed down, though they were naturally distraught and frightened. He learned that the children shared a last name, because the men had been brothers. The boy, John Castor, was a good-sized ten-year-old and was the eldest and spokesman for the rescued. He explained that his parents were Peter and Katherine and that the murdered boy and baby girl had been his siblings. The girls were children of Jacob and Mary. Rose and Lily were eight-year-old twins. Lorena had turned six that day. The Castor boy was holding up with admirable courage, taking on responsibility, Will supposed, because he was the eldest of the lot. Often the reality of the horror struck later.

Will signaled Anja to step away from the group to speak with him. "We have to get these children to Ridgely. I don't know if any place is safe right now, but that's the best we can do for them. Did you ask if they have any other family?"

"Yes. They do. Or I hope so. Their grandparents, Jonah and Maria Castor, left for Fort Ridgely several hours before the other families. They all operated a good-sized farm together apparently. A very close and seemingly compatible family."

"We can't take the roadway to Ridgely. It's like running down a chute to the slaughter house. Do you know how to get to the fort through the back door, so to speak?"

"I do." It was a familiar voice but not Anja's. He turned and was greeted by Billy Buck. And he had to admit he

Ron Schwab

was damned glad to see this kid. "Billy. How in God's name did you find us here?"

"I was headed back from the Upper Agency. I knew all hell was breaking loose and figured you might use some help if you hadn't got your ass out of the Lower Agency by now." He looked at Anja. "Beg pardon, ma'am."

Will noted that it was the first time Anja had smiled in a long spell. "We're glad your ass showed up. From what Will's said about you, we can use your help." She stepped forward and extended her hand. "Anja Lund."

He accepted her hand and doffed his coonskin hat. "My pleasure, ma'am. Remember you from back a ways. I'd be just a mite younger than you—not much. But I ain't had much schooling, so I never saw you at the school house. Caught me a glimpse of you at your pa's farm sometimes. You're not one I'd forget. Know your folks. Larson and I talk a lot. Salt of the earth."

Will interrupted. "So how did you find us?"

"I was going to cross the river to the Lower Agency but figured the ferry was long gone by now, and I knew about a crossing down this way. Appears you did, too. That big stud horse of yours has got a notch in his shoe. Picked it up in the mud along the river's edge so knew you'd come this way. Heard the commotion, so it wasn't hard to find you." He nodded at Karina, who was looking at him with obvious curiosity and interest. "That pretty gal can handle the scatter gun mighty good. I took out one Indian back there with my knife, but one got away before I could catch up with him."

"She did just fine, and it sounds like we were lucky you came along."

"You could introduce me to the little lady."

"Let me do it," Anja said.

After Billy and Karina were properly introduced, Will informed the others he would go back down the trail and retrieve the horses. Billy joined him because he had tied Buster and his big bay with the others when he came across them. "What's happening at the Upper Agency?" Will asked.

"Dakota were raising hell up there, too, when I rode out. Not all the chiefs are buying in to it, though. Otherday's talked some of the families into gathering at the warehouse, but if things get bad enough, that won't work long. Bastards will burn the place down. He's a good man, though, has lots of connections among the friendly Wahpetons and Sissetons. And he ain't afraid of nobody. A warrior named Spirit Walker is organizing friendlies to help settlers escape. Otherday mentioned Little Crow's half-brother, White Spider, as somebody at the Lower Agency who would help whites and mixed-bloods."

"Well, right now, my first concern is to get these poor kids to Ridgely. Then I can talk to the commanding officer and make a better appraisal of the situation. I'll need to get another message off to Washington."

"If I'm going, I'll need some other horses. These are about tuckered out. The bay wouldn't live through another run that soon."

"I might want you here, anyway. We'll talk about it at Ridgely."

Chapter 22

WITH THE CHILDREN joining them, they were forced to double up on some of the horses. Johnny Castor volunteered that he could ride bareback just fine, so he rode Billy's spare bay. The twins split up and rode double with Anja and Karina. Lorena, the birthday girl, who had not spoken a word since her escape, sat behind Will with her hand clutched tightly to his shirt. Billy ranged ahead and periodically circled the perimeter of the party on the lookout for hostiles.

Billy had assured Anja that he had a route in mind that would take them within a half mile of the Lund farm. There was a ravine there where he and Karina could hole-up with the children while Anja and Will scouted the farmstead. She did not want to leave the Castor children unprotected, so she welcomed his suggestion. At the same time, she wondered if part of his motive was to spend some time with Karina. She was not unaware of the eye contact the two had been making since their introduction. She hoped Billy understood Karina was just a child yet. At age sixteen a girl was still a child, was she not? Of course, her own mother and many others she knew had been married and with child at that age. She guessed it didn't matter. The girl was too grief-stricken to think of romance, and a friend wherever she found one should be a positive thing.

Anja and Will rode between rows of corn not more than a month from harvest, attempting to gain some cover during their approach to the Lund farmstead. Anja looked up into the blue sky of what should have been a perfect day and was struck by a surge of cold fear when her eyes shifted to the black harbingers of death swooping and dipping over the farmyard ahead. Vultures, so many of them, they formed a rolling cloud over the area.

When they reached the barnyard, she saw the still corpses lying next to each other not far from the barn. A half dozen vultures, beaks tearing at exposed flesh, danced and fluttered about the bodies. They reined in their horses and surveyed the building site to confirm there was no Dakota threat.

"Anja, let me go in first."

"No," she snapped, and gave her mare a soft dig with her heels and rode slowly into the yard.

The vultures scattered, and broad wings lifted them from the earth until they joined the ghostly army above, soaring and waiting for the next opportunity. They had time, for there were countless banquets set for scavengers along the Minnesota River this day and would be for many days to follow.

She dismounted, and Will followed her lead. She stepped toward her father's naked body and that of her mother's, fully clothed and face down, with a bloody arm tossed over husband's chest. She felt the bile rising in her throat and screamed when she saw it: the ghastly face of her father, its eyes ripped out and nose torn away by vultures, on a head lying several feet away from his body. She screamed again and again, sobbing uncontrollably before she vomited. Will raced into the barn and returned with a saddle blanket and covered Larson Lund's remains. Then he put his arms about Anja and held her close till she was cried out.

Anja knew she would carry the image of the scene to her grave, and she only now fully understood the horror that would trail Karina, the four children, and countless others long after the drums of war were silenced. She slipped away from Will and knelt by her mother, gently turning her over and examining her body for the fatal wounds. It was then she saw the butcher knife lying under her still limp form. Her eyes turned to the bloody arms and wrists, and she suddenly realized her mother had died some hours after her father, not long before their arrival, in fact. And she had killed herself.

She did not object when Will suggested she return to the others while he took care of burial. She showed him where she wanted her parents buried: in the family plot at the edge of the farmstead adjacent to her brothers' graves. She said a common grave would be fine, and then she rode off, unsure when she would return, if ever.

Chapter 23

BILLY BUCK THREADED the needle's eye leading the bereaved and struggling band through twisting ravines and over unbroken trails to the fort. He picked up plenty of war party signs and caught sight of several bands of warriors roaming the prairie, trying to search out settlers heading for the fort. This always triggered a change in course, but, finally, by late afternoon the battered flock rode onto the grounds of Fort Ridgely.

For a man with a penchant for order, Will had ridden into a chaotic hell. Civilians of all ages and sexes milled around aimlessly on the parade ground. Those with apparent missions had to bust through the crowds to get to their destinations. They had encountered a dozen soldiers building barricades when they came in from the ravines and gorges northeast of the fort. Men were turning over wagons, stacking bags of dirt and sand, and occasionally rolling a boulder into place to obstruct the Sioux in the increasingly likely event they attacked and tried to overrun the place. Again, Will thought of the bureaucratic foolishness that ordered the construction of a fort without barriers in the middle of seven thousand unpredictable Dakotas.

They dismounted at the edge of the parade ground, as far from the mindless mob as Will could place them. Anja and Karina sat the children down in the shade outside the big, stone commissary while Billy and Will staked out the horses nearby. They had been watered at a spring not more than an hour earlier, and they agreed the mounts would be fine until they found a place to put them up for the night. They reunited with their companions to discuss their plans, but Will faced something of a quandary. His military obligations took priority, but he could not abandon his new friends. It struck him how fast and tight bonds formed when folks faced death and shared tragedy together.

He told his companions, "I must see the commanding officer immediately and then I'll return here. Billy, I would like you to come with me. We should discuss how to get a message to my superiors."

He also wanted to fill Billy in on the terrible scene at Anja's home. When Anja had saddled up to leave the

Lund farmstead, she had said, "I don't want the Castor children to know about this." The remainder of the ride had been in silence. Will had thought then that he was riding with a convoy of new orphans. He could not help wondering if he had also become one this day. When Will and Anja had rejoined the others, Billy had looked at him expectantly, and he had given him a negative shake of his head. But Will was sure Billy had guessed the news was not good.

Anja said, "Karina and I will take the children and see if we can find their grandparents. If not, we will make other arrangements for them or bring them back here."

"Thanks. I appreciate that." He turned and waved for Billy to join him and started to walk toward the headquarters offices at the opposite end of the post.

"And Will?" Anja called from behind him.

He stopped and looked back. "Yes?"

"I will inquire about your parents. Erik and Alexis, right?"

"Right. Thanks."

Outside the headquarters offices Will encountered Lieutenant Thomas Gere. He had a worried and haggard look that told him Will did not need to inquire about his day. He liked the young officer and considered him quite bright, if inexperienced. He had been told Gere was only nineteen years old, which would be possible in the state militia. The rank might not hold on transfer to regular Army.

"Lieutenant, who is in command of Fort Ridgely?" Will asked.

"If you mean at this moment, sir, I am. Tomorrow, Lieutenant Timothy J. Sheehan will be. Early this morning, Captain John Marsh was in command. As a captain, you are the highest-ranking officer on the post, and I suppose you could claim the right to command. I can almost guarantee Lieutenant Sheehan would gladly step aside."

"You are leaving me totally confused, lieutenant."

"Understandably, sir. When we heard of the uprising, Captain Marsh rode out this morning with fifty soldiers to put it down. I assumed command in his absence as the next ranking officer. I was left with only twenty-six soldiers, and we commenced working on fortifications for defense. Meanwhile, settlers were already starting to roll in with their families—the smart ones."

"And where did Marsh go?"

"The Redwood Ferry. That's where he intended to cross. But they were ambushed there and overwhelmed. Five wounded soldiers have limped in so far. They reported that Captain Marsh is dead along with most of his troops. By all accounts, it was a slaughter with the savages scalping and mutilating every soldier who went down."

"I heard gunfire when we crossed the Minnesota this morning. That must have been the source."

"I would say that is likely."

"Well, you may assure Lieutenant Sheehan I will not be challenging his command. That's not my assignment. But I do have a question. Have you heard anything about the gold shipment?"

"Yes, sir. It arrived today at noon with five armed guards who had to fight off attacks by two small war parties. The Indians, of course, had no idea what was in the wagon." August 18, 1862. A date Will would remember. The day the delinquent annuity funds arrived at Fort Ridgely. The date the Dakota war commenced.

"One day earlier and hundreds of lives might have been saved." All because of bureaucratic snafus, Will thought. His cynicism made another huge leap that day. "Where is the gold?"

"Buried beneath the floor in a corner of the commissary, sir. It's in a sealed keg. Weighs two hundred twenty pounds, one of the guards said. Nobody's going to pick it up and walk away with it. The guards that escorted the wagon here will guard it in shifts till further orders are received from Washington. Of course, if the Indians overrun us, they'll still get their gold, with our scalps as a bonus."

"How many soldiers do you have now?"

"Less than thirty fit to fight. Lieutenant Sheehan should add fifty tomorrow morning when he returns from an unrelated mission, if my courier makes it through and he gets my message. He's about twenty miles from here and should bring his infantry soldiers to reinforce. I also sent a courier to Agent Galbraith with his recruits at St. Peter. They should be here late tomorrow if we're lucky. They're untrained, but they will be armed. And that's another fifty men."

"Well, count me as another gun, but my immediate concern is to get a message to Snelling. It's important because it will include the text of a telegram to be sent to Washington. I would like your permission to allow Billy to select a man, civilian or military, to do this."

"Go ahead. I will take responsibility. Right now I am trying to set up a defense. I would welcome your advice, sir, if you would stroll about the fort grounds and share your thoughts with me."

"I must tell you I have no combat experience."

"I am aware of that, sir. But I know you are a West Pointer with some formal training."

"I'll take a stroll."

Chapter 24

BILLY VOLUNTEERED TO seek out a suitable courier. Will entered the headquarters and borrowed paper and pencil from the corporal at the front desk and wrote out the telegram and letter for Hanscomb. It occurred to him that since the war had arrived, he might have no further purpose here, and in his letter he told Hanscomb as much.

He begged two envelopes from the corporal and went back outside. It was starting to get a bit dusky, so he took his walk around the fort's perimeter before he ended up in the northwest corner, where they were to meet Anja and Kirsten, knowing Billy would find him with his seeming bird dog senses. He was impressed with the work Lieutenant Gere had done and would tell him so. There was considerable work ahead, but he appeared to have identified the civilians who could assume responsibility and be relied upon, because there were a fair number of ununiformed men directing the fortification efforts.

His only serious concern was that all six of the fort's Howitzer cannons were lined up in a row facing the river bluffs. But Ridgely was vulnerable from all sides, especially the opposite end from where the powerful weapons were now positioned, the side that faced the ravines. Will thought he would suggest placing a cannon at each corner of the fort proper, holding two to be moved wherever the greatest stress came during any battle. He was still hopeful an attack would not happen and that the preparations would prove unnecessary.

When he returned to the commissary building, he found Anja sitting on the ground on the east side near the horses, her back pressed against the building wall. She appeared sad and pensive but calm. He let himself down beside her without speaking. She reached into a cloth bag, plucked out a big sandwich and handed it to him. "Thanks," he said.

"I've got one for Billy, too."

"He will be here soon, I think. He's on an errand for me." He took a healthy bite of the sandwich and was surprised to be greeted by fresh bread and beef that was almost hot. "Good. A nice surprise."

"They've got enough food for now. The Army's warehouse was recently replenished and some of the early arrivals were able to drive a few head of cattle with them. With this many people, a long siege will make food a problem, though."

"Let's hope it doesn't come to that. The kids aren't with you."

"We found the grandparents. It was so emotional. The terrible sorrow. The joy of reunion. It will take a long time to sort those feelings out. But the grandparents are not old folks. They will raise those kids. Do what they've got to do and find happy moments again in time. I have got to believe that, of course. I tell myself that if I repeat it enough, I will believe and then it will happen."

He did not know how to respond, so he returned what he considered a lame reply. "I understand."

"I met your mother."

She said this right out of the blue and caught him by surprise, but he was elated by this news. "So my parents made it in?"

"Your mother. Not your father. She's quite angry with him. Claims he tricked her and said he would be an hour behind her. She's been here since mid-morning. She seems to have taken charge of cooking and food distribution. She's working out of the bakehouse and wants to speak with you. Karina stayed to help her, and I said I would be back to help, too. I should say that your mother told me I could help out there, and it wasn't quite an order."

"Yeah, that's Mom. She takes charge of everything but Dad. He rarely argues with her head-on, but he knows how to dodge and slip around her. After dark, I'll ride out to the place and see what's holding him up. It's only a half hour from the fort. Maybe you can let Mom know." He just hoped the delay was caused by stubbornness and not Dakotas.

Faint traces of a smile crossed her lips. "You don't want to deal with your mother either, do you?"

He confessed, "Not unless I've got Dad with me."

He suddenly felt guilty talking about his parents to a woman who had learned of her own parents' horrible ends just hours earlier. He was relieved when Billy came around the corner of the commissary and joined them.

"Sit a spell," Will said. "Anja's got a sandwich for you."

He sat down on the other side of Anja. He seemed taken by both the young women in their party, and it was apparent to Will that Billy Buck was not an innocent when it came to the ladies. This young man knew everything about the river country and everybody who lived in it and likely had a good handle on where his visits might be welcomed.

They carried on their conversation, with Anja sitting between them. "I got your courier," Billy said. "Curley Coburn. About your age, I'd guess. Maybe you know him."

"No. I know Dad does business with some Coburn families."

"I'll bet your pa got some stud fees from Arnold Coburn, Curley's old man. Curley's gelding is a spitting image of Warrior. They shouldn't have gelded the critter. He'd give old Warrior some competition. Anyway, Curley will grab an extra mount and will be saddled up in an hour, if you want to meet him at the stable and see what you think of him. I told him what he needs to do, but you'll want to be sure he understands."

"If you vouch for him, that's good enough for me. I'll be there. We need to put our horses up someplace. Any ideas?"

"I wangled three stalls in the stable. Used your rank. Warrior gets his own. Others will double up. Fair number of stalls vacant if not for settlers coming in. Lot of horses got stolen or taken down at the Redwood Ferry attack." Will decided he was getting a little too dependent on this kid. Soon he would be escorting him to the privy.

"And," Billy added, "I've claimed a hay pile in the stable where we can all bunk tonight."

Will assumed by "all" he was including the ladies in their strange band. He thought that would be crossing the line of propriety but chose not to address the issue, figuring Anja and Karina would be lodging with the other ladies. "I've got to take a little ride later. Do you think you can find me another horse? I don't think we can work ours any more today."

"I can do that. This ride—would you like some company?"

He hesitated but decided his trip home was personal business. "No. Just an errand I have to run."

Billy looked at him suspiciously, and he would swear Anja's eyes shot darts his way. He got up stiffly. He had not been in the saddle this much for a long while, and his butt and lower back hurt—and about everything else. "I have to speak with Lieutenant Gere. Billy, why don't you and I put up the horses, and then I'll talk to the lieutenant after I send Curley Coburn on his way."

Anja jumped up with an agility that made him feel like a doddering old man. "Billy and I will put up the horses. You go ahead and see Lieutenant Gere."

"Don't you remember that you have an assignment from General Alexis Nilsson?"

"Not all of us are afraid of Alexis Nilsson."

Ouch.

"Sure," Billy said. "Anja and I will take care of the horses."

Will suspected his enthusiasm was more for the company than the task.

Later, when he arrived at the big stable, which stretched almost the width of the parade grounds and lay south of the road entering the fort compound, Billy and his friend, Curley Coburn, were waiting near the stabled horses. Curley's fingers clutched the reins of a powerfully-built claybank gelding, a younger version of Warrior. Will instantly coveted the horse.

The horse's owner was a short, stocky man, who did not have the look of a rider. He doffed his hat when he approached, revealing a skull that was bald as a marble. He appeared fit and muscular though, and Will thought the ladies probably found him a handsome man with his penetrating steel-gray eyes and a neatly-trimmed, short-cropped, blond beard.

"You must be Curley Coburn," he said, extending his hand. "I'm Will Nilsson."

He took Will's hand in a firm grip. "Yes, sir. Feel I already know you, Billy's told me so much about you." Will figured Billy probably knew more about his life's history than he did.

"Are you up for a ride to Fort Snelling?"

"Yes, sir. Billy and me has talked about a route. Cross-country. No roads where the red devils will be waiting. Cut off miles that way, too. I can do this for you, sir."

"Are you Army?"

"No, sir. Used to be. Will be again, I guess. I plan to join up to fight Rebs in a month or two."

"You can drop the 'sir' then."

"Sorry, sir. Got the habit."

Will was not going to argue the point. He slipped the envelopes from inside his shirt and gave Curley delivery instructions. "I want you to wait at Snelling until you receive a reply to my telegram. That may be a day or two."

"I can do that, sir."

Chapter 25

WILL HEARD GUNFIRE before he rode over a grassy knoll that overlooked the Nilsson ranch and saw the flames dancing on the barn roof and illuminating the farmstead like a giant lantern. The house, much of which was constructed of native stone, still stood and that seemed to be the focus of the seven or eight Indians sweeping back and forth in front, riding low and firing their shotguns or rifles at the house. A few with bows were loosing flaming arrows at the roof, but so far the arrows had burned out without igniting anything.

He dismounted, yanked his Sharps from its scabbard, grabbed some cartridges from his saddlebags, and got down on one knee. He was a confident marksman, and the yard was less than a hundred yards distant, easily within his five-hundred-yard range. He inserted a cartridge into the breech and searched for a likely target. One Dakota dismounted and raced for the house with war axe upraised. Will worried that there was no response from inside. He aimed, squeezed the trigger, and the rifle boomed. The Dakota stumbled and fell in front of the doorway.

That got the other Dakotas' attention, and they wheeled their horses away from the house, gathering near the burning barn. He could hear them yelling excitedly and pointing in his direction, although he could not make out the words. He reloaded, thinking he should ride away and find a hideout. He knew the terrain here and thought of several hiding places where they would never find him. But that would likely just send them back to his dad, which would mean his mutilation and death, if he was, in fact, still alive. Will was efficient with his Sharps and could get off eight to ten shots per minute, but if they all charged the hill, he did not have much chance of taking them all down. At close range, his Colt might get one or two if they didn't take him down first.

By the time he had thought out his dilemma, the mounted Dakotas were charging the slope, spread out with some distance between them to afford more elusive targets. He fired and dropped another one from his horse as an arrow plunked into the earth a few inches from his knee. He loaded again and fired, missing the Indian, who had swerved just before he squeezed the trigger. Before he could get another cartridge in the breech, a Dakota appeared off to his side, hanging low from his horse's back. He was so near that even in the darkness Will could see the fierce eyes peering from his painted face. And the disfigured nose. Cut Nose.

He struggled to his feet, pulling his Colt from its holster, but Cut Nose, seemingly fearless, tried to ride him over with his horse and knocked Will down, jarring his gun from his hand and launching it into the tall grass. The warrior leaped upon him with upraised war club, and he saw the weapon arcing downward and grabbed his attacker's wrist. But his arm was powerful, and, although he deflected the full force, Cut Nose struck a glancing blow on the right side of his forehead above the eye. The blow stunned him and he nearly blacked out, but somehow his instinct for survival kicked in and he rolled and rammed a knee in the warrior's groin and dodged a second strike. He grunted and toppled off Will and rolled away. Will was a larger man but doubted he was as strong as Cut Nose. When he spotted his Colt in the grass, he easily abandoned fighting ethics with his life at stake. He readied to dive for it, when he heard rifle fire nearby, and it did not seem to be aimed at him. He went for his pistol, expecting Cut Nose to pounce on his back. He grasped the pistol and swung around to fire, but the warrior had disappeared like a ghost in the darkness.

"Will," a voice called. "You okay?" It was Billy's voice.

He struggled to stand up, but, yes, he was okay. Dizzy. His head hurt like blazes. But he was alive. "Yeah, I'll be all right."

Billy rode up the slope, leading his horse, no doubt spooked by all the gunfire. "Three of them got away. The one you was dancing with and two others down on the flat."

"You saved my life, Billy. I was good as dead. I owe you. But what in the hell are you doing here?"

"Orders."

"Orders?"

"Yep. From Miss Anja Lund. She told me to follow you, and said if didn't, she would. Sent her new Henry with me. Mighty fine weapon. She said I'd better bring it back. Guess I'll get me one of them things when the government pays me for this job. Of course, them folks is damned slow to pay as our Dakota friends have learned."

Will suddenly realized that he wasn't thinking straight. His father was down the slope in the house. He could be bleeding to death. "My dad. He's in the house. It looked like he was still putting up a fight when I got here. But then things went quiet."

"We'd best take a look."

When they had dismounted and headed up to the house, Will called to his father, "Dad, it's Will. Don't shoot."

"You're safe. I've used up all my shotgun shells."

Will fought back tears when he heard his voice. He wasn't ready to lose his father. He never would be. And then he thought of the people who had lost their fathers today. And mothers. He felt he was owed something terrible by the devil for his good fortune.

They went in the house and found Erik Nilsson sitting at the kitchen table, his shotgun leaning against the wall. He seemed unperturbed by the Dakota attack.

"Well, hi there, Billy. I didn't know you were out there. Sit down. I still had some hot coals in the stove, and I'm warming up some coffee."

"Howdy, Erik. Glad to see you're doing good."

Billy took a chair and sat down, and Will joined him.

Will's dad said, "The barn's gone, but at least they ran the horses out first. Might find those that the Dakotas didn't steal. They didn't kill any of the cow herd, but that doesn't mean they won't. Depends on how long this war goes on."

"Main thing is you're okay," Will said.

His father got up and retrieved some tin coffee cups from the cupboard and spread them on the table. Then he removed the coffee pot from the stove and began to fill their cups. "I'm okay, huh? Wait till your mother gets done with me."

Chapter 26

C UT NOSE WAS late for the gathering of the Soldiers Lodge. The attack on the big Swede's farm had been whimsical and not well thought-out. They had not been prepared for the ferocity of the man's defense and had lost two warriors before the arrival of Stalking Wolf, the name he had assigned to the tall man he had first seen outside the trader's store. The feeling had struck him instantly that his fate and that of Stalking Wolf were intertwined. He had taken this as an omen, but he was uncertain about what it meant. He only knew that the man, and the thought of him, made him uneasy and agitated.

Only hours later, they had met on the trail, and he should have killed the man then. But Anja had protected him. He could not kill her, and he had flinched at destroying this demon in her presence. She was unaware of it, but the blood of a great warrior coursed through her veins, and he had sensed she would have fought to her own death to save this man.

And then tonight Stalking Wolf had appeared like an evil spirit on the hilltop and intervened to save the Swede. And they had fought, hand-to-hand, and the man's strength had matched his own. Cut Nose's man-parts still ached from Stalking Wolf's assault, but he was confident he would have won the struggle had not another rider appeared just as mysteriously as Stalking Wolf had. The ghost rider had turned a magic rapid-shooting thunder-stick upon the Dakota warriors. He had taken that opportunity to make his own escape, but he lamented now that of the nine warriors in their war party, only three had escaped the wrath of the white men. He wondered if the Great Spirit had thrown a veil of protection over his foe. He could not doubt now that Stalking Wolf carried powerful medicine, and it would be best to avoid him. But that might not be possible if the merging of their life journeys was inevitable.

He shook off his thoughts as he approached the council fire, disappointed as his eyes searched the circle and found no more than twenty warriors present.

His friend, Round Bear, greeted him, "You are late, friend."

"I came across another war party and was asked to join them on a raid. I did, and it did not go well. Six warriors died. I have told you of the man I call Stalking Wolf."

"Yes, the man who was with Calling Dove's daughter."

"He appeared and killed warriors with a deadly thunder-stick, and then another man came with a rifle that rained many bullets. When only three of us remained, we rode away. Stalking Wolf is bad medicine. It is better that we stay away from him." Cut Nose was not going to tell Round Bear or anyone else about his unsuccessful personal combat with Stalking Wolf.

"There are few warriors here tonight," Cut Nose commented.

"Many still raid the whites. Others are preparing for the attack on New Ulm tomorrow."

"The Germans? We must attack Fort Ridgely. The fort has few soldiers now. The massacre at the ferry has left their defenses weak. Other soldiers are elsewhere."

Round Bear pointed in the direction of the ravine that funneled into the council area. "Little Crow comes. He told me he desires to speak with you."

Cut Nose waited for the chief to approach, but he could barely tolerate the fool. He was the first signer of the 1851 Treaty that ceded Dakota lands to the whites. He had been the whites' friend and constant apologist. If a white man wanted to ravage the Dakotas, Little Crow would drop his loincloth and bend over. And now he dared to call himself a war chief.

Little Crow was accompanied by Chief Mankato and Chief Big Eagle and a dozen older warriors. Cut Nose grunted an acknowledgement, waiting for Little Crow to speak first.

Little Crow said, "I want to attack Fort Ridgely when the sun rises. What do you think about this?"

Cut Nose was surprised to find himself agreeing with the chief. "Yes. The fort has few soldiers to defend, and it will take much time to prepare the settlers there for battle. They have probably sent for more soldiers. We should do this now."

"But the young warriors want to attack New Ulm. They say there will be much plunder there. The Germans have much food and many guns in their houses and stores. And there are no soldiers."

All of this was true, thought Cut Nose, but New Ulm was a town of nearly a thousand people, with probably several hundred males owning guns to defend the town. For some reason, many of the Swedish and Norwegian settlers did not even own a gun. The Germans tended to have several in their homes. Also, the populace would be swelling with refugees, who would provide more defenders. An attack on New Ulm should be carefully planned. Fort Ridgely could be overrun with numbers. The existing vulnerability could change with the addition of troops. He thought about this, and there was a prolonged silence before he spoke. "I agree that the attack should be against Fort Ridgely, but you are the chief. You must control your warriors."

"There is no punishment for not listening to a chief. One is a chief only if others follow."

"Then why do you come to me?"

"Because other warriors listen to you. You make no claim of leadership, but all know that you are the leader of the Soldiers Lodge. That makes you more powerful than any chief. This war is more yours than mine to lose."

It struck him then that Little Crow's words held some truth. The Soldiers Lodge had taken advantage of the white man's lies to build the little fires of anger and rebellion throughout the bands. And its members had nurtured those fires until the flames burst out of control and roared through the Minnesota River valley this morning. But he had no ability to direct the journey of such a fire. "Look at the lodge members seated around our council fire tonight. There are no more than twenty. Usually, we would have ten times that. I cannot stop the wind. It has its own life and blows where it wishes. Tonight, it blows us to New Ulm."

Chapter 27

I T WAS THE second day of the war, and Cut Nose led a war party of ten warriors from the Soldiers Lodge north and east of New Ulm. They had burned houses and barns on the outskirts of New Ulm, but the occupants had already escaped to the town. He calculated that by ranging some miles beyond the town, they would find settlers who had not yet received word of the uprising or thought themselves too far removed from the conflict to be in danger. He was still skeptical about the New Ulm attack and had pulled away from direct participation.

Instead, he would find other means of inflicting damage this day and prepare for the attack on Fort Ridgely tomorrow. He had promised Little Crow he would use his influence in the Soldiers Lodge to rally warriors to the fort assault, and he had been invited to a council with the chiefs following the New Ulm battle for purposes of planning the attack on Fort Ridgely.

As they rode across the plains, Cut Nose caught sight of a wagon pulled by a team of oxen moving slowly on the road that would eventually take the driver to New Ulm. He signaled his warriors to follow him toward the wagon, and they moved their horses at a lope across the prairie. As they neared, he saw that a young woman was driving the wagon, and another woman sat beside her with a shotgun or rifle across her lap. Seven children were seated in the wagon bed. He led the war party into the road to block the wagon's passage until the woman stopped the wagon, perhaps twenty steps away.

Cut Nose dismounted and walked toward the wagon with only his war club in his hand. Beaver Tooth, astride his pony, rode to his left, and Swims Like Otter moved to his right. When he was directly in front of the oxen, they paused. Speaking English, he said, "You move from wagon. Get on knees and pray."

The yellow-haired woman holding the gun raised it to fire. "Go to hell," she shrieked.

Before she could get the shotgun to her shoulder, Beaver Tooth, struck her on the forehead with the butt of his own shotgun, and she plummeted off the wagon, her weapon dropping between the oxen. The woman was dazed but conscious, and Beaver Tooth leaped off his horse, grabbed the woman's long hair and drug her to a ditch along the roadside and began to tear off her clothes as she flailed and screamed. A boy, not more than nine summers, Cut Nose thought, jumped and began to run back up the road, but Swims Like Otter quickly rode him down and felled him with the blade of his war axe.

The woman who had been driving the oxen placed her head in her hands and began sobbing uncontrollably, "Please, no. Spare the children. Take them captive. I know some have been taken by your people to be adopted or held as hostages. Kill me. But don't harm the children."

"No time for children. Do what I tell you and nobody suffer. Now. Move from wagon. Get on knees or warriors kill you and all suffer more."

The woman stopped crying and turned back to the children in the wagon box. "Climb out of the wagon, children, and do what this man tells you." The children—the eldest, a girl about the same age as the boy Otter had killed, and the youngest, four or five summers—obeyed. A few began to cry as they climbed down from the wagon. Others just looked perplexed.

Cut Nose noticed that Beaver Tooth had finished with the woman. Her protests had been reduced to whimpering now, while another warrior took his turn. Beaver Tooth watched, waiting to torture and mutilate the woman after any who wanted her had their opportunities. It would upset Beaver Tooth, but Cut Nose intended to kill the woman as soon as he completed his current duty. He ordered the woman and children to form a circle around him in the road, facing outward. Some of the warriors stood outside the circle to slay any who might run. If any should be so foolish, the apprehending warrior could dispose of the runner in any manner he chose.

Cut Nose instructed the captives to kneel in position for prayer and was pleased to find they obeyed. He did not want this to be difficult for them. The woman began to recite a prayer he had heard others speak, "Our Father," and some of the older children joined in as they sobbed. His war club took the oldest child first, and, guessing their ages, reserved the youngest for last, and then, finally, the woman.

He went to the whimpering woman just as Beaver Tooth had knelt with his knife to commence his work. He shoved the warrior aside, and, like the others, he killed her with a single blow. Beaver Tooth was not happy.

By Cut Nose's count his war party killed nearly twenty whites before ominous, black clouds filled the sky with little warning and soon exploded with torrential rains that drenched the warriors and dampened their enthusiasm for the war. It was late afternoon, so they returned to the southwest side of the river. Other warriors were trickling in as Cut Nose arrived at his village, and he learned that his little party of warriors had killed more whites than all the Dakotas amassed at New Ulm.

The attack by as many as five hundred warriors had failed miserably. The attackers had burned down a few houses on the town's outskirts and killed or wounded more than thirty whites according to Tells Stories, Cut Nose's friend, whose name was born of the warrior's propensity for exaggeration. Besides, he knew that his own small party had done the damage to the homes to which Tells Stories alluded.

The chiefs had planned to launch flaming arrows on the town and reduce it to cinders when the rains came and doused the flames before a single arrow struck a target with success. The discouraged warriors thereafter began to peel away from the battle.

Later, at the council meeting in Little Crow's village, Cut Nose found the chiefs and senior warriors disinterested in discussing the New Ulm failures but enthused about prospects of an attack on Fort Ridgely the next day. Little Crow assured the others they would gather a force of no fewer than six hundred warriors. Little Crow would lead warriors in an attack from the northwest, Little Six would bring warriors from the southwest, and Medicine Bottle would move a force through the ravines east of the fort. Cut Nose volunteered to pull warriors from the Soldiers Lodge to join Medicine Bottle. He felt the fort was most vulnerable near the eastern ravines and he hungered to be the first to break through the crude fortifications.

After the war council, Cut Nose found he hungered for a woman. He suffered no shortage of accommodating women, but tonight there was no time to hunt and seduce, so he decided to visit the moon lodge, as he often did. The moon lodges were located outside the village proper and women who were in their moon took up residence there while menstruating. Many thought women had great spiritual power during this time, and many warriors believed that even nearness to a woman during her moon might weaken or taint their medicine. Cut Nose thought such concerns foolish and looked upon this time as opportunity.

His medicine was good tonight, because he found Happy Squirrel at the lodge, and she was always a willing partner. As a fourth wife of old Chief Many Horses, she lacked for attention in her robe. The elderly first wife had demanded another wife to take on more of her work. The chief had insisted his additional wife must be young and pretty to enhance his reputation for great virility, which was, in fact, a dying ember, probably the reason the first wife did not object.

Cut Nose had shared Happy Squirrel's robes many times and suspected her son, Fast Weasel, carried his blood, but they, of course, never spoke of it. There was no other occupant in her moon lodge, and Happy Squirrel was glad to see him and made him feel so welcome he spent the entire night in her robe.

Chapter 28

ANJA AWAKENED AN hour before sunrise to find herself in the straw pile snuggled against a sleeping Will. They were fully clothed but sharing a wool Army blanket she had begged from a young clerk during a trip to the warehouse on an errand for Alexis Nilsson. August nights sometimes got chilly along the river, and the blanket had proved useful. If other ladies had seen her covered in a blanket with Will, they would have been scandalized. But did anyone really care right now? She did not.

She had planned to stay in the stone Army barracks last night where most of the civilians had been moved, but the accommodations offered a hard floor and sweating, smelling bodies packed like cigars in a box. Not that she smelled like a bouquet of roses herself right now.

She had been with Alexis when Erik Nilsson strolled in as casually as could be and taken the tiny woman in his arms and kissed her on the lips in front of the entire cooking crew. Alexis had blushed and pushed him away, but Anja could tell that the wily husband had softened his wife's tough bluster.

"Sorry I'm late." Erik had said.

"What took you so long?" Alexis had asked, glaring at him suspiciously.

"I decided I needed to turn out the horses and do some chores in case we didn't get back for a spell."

Anja could tell he was lying, so she figured Alexis knew it, too, but was happy enough he was alive she was not going to press the issue. Not then. She had read between their words and envied what she saw between them after their many years together, the comfortable friendship spiced by a spark of passion. She wondered if she might find that someday. It was different than what her folks had shared. Larson Lund had her mother's friendship. Another man had the passion.

Will had not come in with his father, although she was certain he had retrieved him from the farm. By the time Anja had been able to retire for the night and decided to claim quarters in the stable, Will was sleeping. She had just tossed the blanket over him and crawled in beside him. He had mumbled something that sounded like, "I'm glad you're here," and went back to sleep. If she had heard him correctly, she shared the sentiment.

She rolled out from under the blanket and tucked her side of the cover up against Will. She sat up. She needed to pee and tried to remember where the latrines and privies were located. With all the refugees, the accommodations usually had lines at them, but, at this hour, she might not be forced to fight for relief. She envied men at times like this, when they could just go water the grass behind the stable.

When she sat up, she realized for the first time that Karina lay several feet away on the other side of her with a saddle blanket covering her torso and shoulders. And next to her, but not indecently close, lay Billy Buck. Funny that she was judging decency, she thought. She was the one who had spent the night indecently near to a male companion. To hell with it all. In another day their scalps might all be hanging from Dakota lances.

When she returned from the privy, her friends were still sleeping, so she went to the horses' stalls and brushed down Warrior, Red, Molly, and Buster. The Army had apparently reclaimed the gelding Billy was using for backup, because the horse was not with the others. As the first shards of sunlight slipped through the windows and open doorways and cast a dusty light upon the stalls, she studied the horses that had served them so well. They seemed in good shape considering the work pace they had endured. She loved horses, and, along with the loss of her parents, she lamented the disappearance of the riding horses from the farm and was saddened by the senseless murders of her father's draft team, Sampson and Delilah.

She looked with admiration upon the magnificent stallion, Warrior, thinking he would be the perfect sire for Molly's first colt. Molly should go through two or three more heat cycles before winter cut them short till spring. She wondered if she might talk Will into a breeding. She smiled at her thought. Between Warrior and Molly, of course.

"It's nice to see a bit of a smile on your face."

She started at the sound of Will's voice. He had slipped up on her like a damned cat. She turned and realized he had been gazing at her, studying her as she evaluated the horses, and wondered how long he had been standing there, not more than five feet away.

She said, "I was just thinking. Molly should come in heat again in about two weeks. If you're still around—and we're both alive—I thought it would be nice to breed the two. I would pay a stud fee."

"No fee. I think Warrior has earned a little pleasure. Molly, too. I think they would produce an outstanding foal. An excellent idea. And maybe the foal will make you think of me on occasion over the years. I like that thought."

"You sound like you are going away. You won't live nearby?"

"Not soon, if ever. I'm a soldier. I am here until I receive contrary orders, and then I will be assigned to a cavalry unit in the South for the war's duration. I refuse to plan life beyond that. Bad luck."

In that instant she determined she would draw firm lines when it came to their relationship. She vowed she would not repeat the heartache she had endured with Matthew's death. Her partnership with Will Nilsson would stop at friendship.

She quickly changed the subject. "What's on your agenda today?"

"I am going to see if I can round up a cup of coffee and a biscuit, and then I will speak with Lieutenant Gere and see what his reports are on Dakota movement. If an attack here is anticipated, I will stay and help defend. If not, Billy and I are going out on a scout to see what has happened out there and if there are any civilians who need our help. The lieutenant can't spare any troops to attempt rescue missions, but a lot of the folks who have shown up here report kids and spouses who have disappeared and may just be wandering around or hiding out there someplace."

"I would like to go with you. If you find children or injured victims, you will need more than just the two of you." He seemed to be thinking about it. She hoped he said "yes," because "no" was not an acceptable answer.

"I would appreciate your help with this. And another gun could come in handy. Shall we see if we can talk my mother out of coffee and a biscuit?"

"Yes. And I will show you that the fine woman cannot intimidate me into working in one of her makeshift kitchens today. She has dozens of women and girls available for that anyway."

Chapter 29

THE FOUR RODE away from the east side of Ridge-ly into one of the ravines. Anja had handled Will's mother perfectly. She had cleverly avoided his mom's all-seeing eye and sneaked out of the fort. Will was impressed with Anja's refusal to be intimidated.

It was unclear to him how Karina came to be with them. She was just there when they readied to move out, saddling Red and squeezing her shotgun into the noose Will had fashioned earlier. She was too young for this, but he did not have the heart to send her back. Her family had lived on the south side of the river near the Lower Agency, and it appeared almost all at the fort were strangers to her. And a sixteen-year-old on the frontier was much older than those he had encountered in the Eastern cities.

As usual, Billy rode out front, ranging wide to keep a lookout for hostile Dakotas. As they emerged from the ravine and climbed onto the flatter grasslands, Billy came riding toward them and reined in and waited for the others to reach him. "Ran into old Broken Horn up ahead. He's heading east with his wife and two kids as far as they can get. They're full-bloods, but friendlies, and don't want no part of this. Says the Dakotas are going to attack New Ulm today. He thought it would be a good time for him to get the hell out."

"It sounds like we won't do any good moving toward New Ulm. We can't help the Germans, and they're not going to hit Ridgely today, so let's head upriver and circle to the east when we head back in."

"Makes sense, but we need to keep an eye out. Broken Horn says there will still be roving bands out that don't want no part of the New Ulm battle. For what it's worth he says more than five-hundred warriors from the Upper Agency are headed north to Fort Abercrombie. That's a long way out there, and those folks ain't anywhere near help."

Bad news. But Will knew all he could do was report it. They took to the road between Ridgley and the Upper Agency, stopping to collect scattered corpses and drag them into vacant houses or other outbuildings to shelter them from scavengers when they could. There was no pattern to the killing he could detect. Some places they found bodies of entire families. Others, the women's remains were absent. In some instances, several of the children were unaccounted for. Billy speculated that some of the women and children were being taken captive to be absorbed into the tribe or held for ransom. Such decisions were likely not thought out but depended upon the whims of members of the war party, whether someone had a use for the captives or if there was time to deal with the nuisance of taking women or children back to the village.

Billy said he would like to veer off the road a mile to check Henry and Mathilda Richter's farm. They were a childless couple in their sixties, he informed us, and had always been kind to the Indians who dropped by to visit, usually offering food and sending them away with flour, coffee or some other commodity in demand. Billy had broken horses for Hank Richter and enjoyed a good number of meals in Mathilda's kitchen.

As they approached the house the stone chimney and rooftop came into sight, and they were encouraged that the farmstead had not been burned out. As they entered the yard, they received a familiar grim story, however. What remained of a frail-looking man, naked, scalped and disemboweled, lay staked and spread-eagled in the barnyard. Beside him sat a big, short-haired dog with sad eyes, bloodied, but standing watch over the mutilated body of his master.

Billy said, "That's 'Sniffer,' Hank's redbone coonhound. Hank raised him from a pup. Probably two, maybe three, years old. Dog never left Hank's side. Still won't, I guess."

They dismounted and Billy went to the dog, while Will cut the leather thongs that anchored the dead man's wrists and ankles to the stakes. The rust-colored coonhound sat fast while Billy's fingers gently tested his wounds.

Billy said, "Sniffer's got a knot and cut on the side of his head. The bloody mess on his hip is where he took the edge of a shotgun blast. Ought to try to pick out some of the buckshot when there's time, but he'll live. My bet is the Dakotas left him for dead, and he woke up later."

Will had not been aware of their slipping away, but he turned and saw Anja and Karina had disappeared. They had no doubt headed for the house. He got up to join them.

Billy said, "I'd like to bury these folks. I'll see if I can find a shovel in the barn. I'll dig a grave in the garden where the soil's soft. Assuming Mathilda's dead, I'll dig it wide and shallow."

Will could tell these folks were special to Billy and could not deny him his wish. Besides, their day was half gone, and the only living thing they had come up with to rescue so far was the redbone, and he was not certain about his fate yet. Anja and Karina met him at the door of the house.

Anja said, "Mrs. Richter's dead, too. Usual female mutilations. Scalped. Raped, I'm sure."

Her voice was cold, matter-of-fact, almost like she wasn't speaking of a real person. He thought they were all starting to deal with the carnage that way. Maybe that was how people held on to a bit of sanity.

After the Richters were buried, Anja asked, "What about Sniffer?"

Will said, "He could be a danger to us if he barks at the wrong time. For our own safety we ought to put him down."

And the redbone picked that moment to walk over to Will, stand at his feet and look up at him with those pitiful eyes. Everybody else, including Billy, who would know Will was speaking the truth, glared at him with anger and disbelief that he would suggest such a thing.

Will patted Sniffer on the head and said, "I guess he can follow us if he wants." And he did.

They rode back toward the main road, Sniffer trailing with a bit of a limp. They were passing by a wooded area when Will looked over his shoulder and saw that the red-bone had stopped and was staring into the woods. Billy was well ahead, but he signaled Anja and Karina to stop. He reined Warrior around, and he loped back to Sniffer. The dog kept staring into the trees and started whimpering. There was something in there. Will wished Sniffer could tell him what.

By this time Anja and Karina had joined him. "I think he wants me to take a look in the trees."

Anja said, "Let's all look. If it's Dakotas, there can't be that many, or they'd be all over us by now." Good point.

They staked their mounts and approached the woods. Will carried his Colt in one hand, and his partners had their weapons ready. Sniffer raced ahead now and disappeared into the trees. Then he heard voices. Children. A few laughing. Several sobbing. He dodged through the thick brush and weaved through the trees until he broke into a clearing and found the source of Sniffer's worry. At least a dozen weary, bedraggled and frightened children were scattered about the clearing. One little boy clung to Sniffer's neck, giggling while the dog licked his face.

Anja and Karina stepped into the clearing with astounded looks on their faces but quickly put down their guns and moved to the children who seemed most in distress. A girl and a boy, both early teens, Will guessed, stood off to one side and appeared to be in charge. The boy carried a shotgun, which he assumed was loaded, and it appeared he had stuffed extra shells in his trouser pocket. He looked tired but determined. Will approached the pair and introduced himself. "I am Will Nilsson. Our group is from Fort Ridgely. We've been out searching for folks who need help getting to the fort.

The boy said, "I'm Jed Ireland. This is my twin sister, Louisa. We've been hiding out here for a day. We saw a bunch of Indians coming our way when we were headed for Ridgely, and my pa told me and Louisa to grab the little ones and head for the trees. He sent his only gun with me. Ma wouldn't leave him, and he just kept driving the team down the road. I could see the Indians swarming over the wagon, and I heard my ma screaming. I know they're dead." Tears squeezed out of the corners of his eyes and rolled down his cheeks, but he did not break down.

Louisa jumped in. "There's five of us Irelands. Mary, Emily and Joe go with us. Mary's the baby. That's Emily holding her, and Joe's next to her. There are eight others that we stumbled onto or found us. Three Pettijohns. Others were alone. We've been here since yesterday afternoon. Figured out how to get to the main road, but we didn't know if it was safe. Thought we'd move on tonight and try to find the fort."

"We'll get you to Fort Ridgely. But stay here for a bit. Try to assure the others everything's going to be okay. I need to leave for a bit to talk to our scout, Billy Buck."

"We know Billy," the twins said simultaneously.

Will told Anja and Karina he was returning to the horses to see if Billy had come back. When he broke out of the woods and got to the horses, he looked to the northwest where Billy had headed and saw a cloud of dust moving his way. He hoped Billy was hidden in that cloud, because it was too late for him to make it back to the cover of the woods. The horses would have given them away anyhow.

Billy rode up and practically leaped off his horse. "We got company," he said. "Grab the horses and get them to the trees. War party. Six Dakotas, and they spotted me."

Will did not have time to tell Billy about Sniffer's discovery. They gathered up the horses and led them well back into the woods.

Will yelled to Anja and Karina, "Bring your guns but have the kids stay where they are. Hurry."

He had pulled his Sharps from its scabbard and grabbed ammunition from his saddlebags. When Anja and Karina arrived, he said, "Spread out. If they've got shotguns, we need space between us."

They all hunkered down in the brush and waited. In moments the warriors appeared on the horizon and headed in their direction. He had faint hope they would pass them by, and, of course, they did not. One of the warriors spotted the disturbance in the earth and hoofprints where the horses had been staked. Several slid from their mounts and walked around the area like bird dogs picking up a scent. Their eyes turned toward the trees where the group was hidden. Will could not hear much of what they were saying, but there was no doubt, as the others dismounted, they were going to take up a search.

He whispered to his comrades. "We need to take them down fast. All of them. Karina, you aim the shotgun at the middle of the pack and give them both barrels. I'll take the one that ends up furthest left, and, Anja, you start on the right. Billy, you go for any stragglers. Wait for me to say 'fire.'"

The Dakotas were nearly one hundred feet out, as he spoke, and as they moved toward the woods, they wisely began to spread out. The apparent leader of the party and another warrior moved somewhat in front of the others and in the center of the cluster. Perfect for a shotgun's range.

Will let them approach as near as he dared without the risk of disclosing their presence and then softly said, "Fire."

Their guns exploded. The Sharps drove lead into the center of a Dakota's chest, and the warrior stumbled backwards and fell. One warrior was left standing and began to run, but Will heard the two cracks of Anja's Henry before the warrior staggered a few steps and pitched forward, landing on his belly. Impressive work, Will thought, as he stood up and stepped out from behind their cover. Trained soldiers would not have been more efficient. He walked among the scattered bodies to determine whether any Dakotas survived the ambush.

One warrior tossed back and forth on the ground, obviously in pain and waiting for someone to end his suffering. Another raised himself up on his elbow grasping his other wrist with his hand. Billy knelt beside him. "I think Karina's scattergun turned his hand to ground meat. What do I with him, Will? I ain't much for killing a man that can't defend hisself."

"Can you tie off the bleeding with something?"

Karina came up and removed a leather strip she had strung through the beltloops of her britches, which stayed up fine without it, and handed it to Billy. He began cinching it about the surprised Indian's arm.

Confirming that the other four were dead, Will examined the other wounded warrior. He had a bullet lodged between the base of his neck and shoulder, but it was not bleeding profusely, and Will's uneducated guess was that he would survive to kill another day given the opportunity. After his experience with Sniffer, it was easy to conclude they lacked executioners for the defenseless in their party, so speaking Dakota, he gave the prisoners two options. The Indians could take their horses and get out, or they would be taken to Fort Ridgely for medical treatment, after which they would likely be held as prisoners. He got a split verdict. The warrior with the shoulder wound got to his feet and pointed in the direction of the Lower Agency. The other, who identified himself as Skunk Eyes, opted to surrender. Will considered this a wise decision. A military surgeon might have to amputate his hand, but he would likely live. The odds shifted to death if he returned to his village.

The wounded Dakota departed on his horse, but they held on to the other horses. Skunk Eyes would ride his, but that left four extras. The transportation problems were resolved now, although some might be forced to walk part of the trek to the fort.

Chapter 30

ANJA SUNK INTO her bed of straw, exhausted after bringing the children into the fort and then placing them with temporary caretakers. Fortunately, the Ireland and Pettijohn children were greeted by aunts and uncles who had been watching for the families to come in. Two children were placed with grandparents, and the others were placed in the care of neighbors. Anja found it was becoming harder to take pity on herself. She was old enough to make her own way in life. These poor kids had been tossed abruptly into incomprehensible loss and chaos that left them dependent upon others to step up and take over their care.

Skunk Eyes had seemed almost relieved to be a captive and had insisted he was a reluctant warrior and that many others were as well. Anja thought that his statements were plausible, though self-serving. Many of the

Ron Schwab

Dakotas faced retribution if they did not support the war, and she thought it human nature to support one's people regardless of moral niceties. She suspected the same could be said of many dying for the Union and Confederate causes. For many, loyalties probably had more to do with geography and the community in which one lived than personal commitments to anti-slavery or states' rights, or any other banners under which the war was being waged.

The post surgeon had advised that the Dakota's hand would be amputated above the wrist but that he would likely survive, barring putrefaction of the wound. Skunk Eyes had been suffering enough pain by the time of their late afternoon arrival at the post that he offered no resistance to whatever the surgeon chose to do.

To make matters worse, the group had been struck by a sudden rainstorm several hours before reaching the fort, leaving everyone soaked and even more discouraged. She had been too stunned by the scene at her parents' farm to grab extra clothing from the house, but a woman had given her a pair of bib overalls and a cotton shirt she would no longer need because of the death of her thirteen-year-old son. Anja had spread her wet clothes out to dry, but it was a hopeless effort until the sun showed up again.

Nightfall had dropped its black curtain over the fort now, and she worried about Karina's absence. She was soon relieved, however, when the girl appeared with Billy. She came up to Karina and plopped down at her side. "Billy found me some dry clothes. The britches and shirt fit perfect."

Of course, Billy would have scavenged something. Anja did not want to know how he figured out the size. She asked Billy, "Have you seen Will?"

"Yup. He'll be along soon. He's talking to Lieutenant Gere. Guess he ain't in charge now, though. Lieutenant Sheehan got back with fifty men from Company C, Fifth Minnesota, this morning. More good news is that Agent Galbraith and Lieutenant Gorman marched in with another fifty from Renville's Rangers, Company B, just a few hours ago. Gives us a fighting chance if the Dakota attack tomorrow."

"Do you think that's going to happen?"

"More than likely. Joe Big Horse rode in not a half hour ago. He says it's coming for sure. Big pow-wow tonight making plans. Joe's full-blood, but he's not blanket. He's a friend of John Otherday's. There's a fair number like Joe who favor the whites and can go back and forth unnoticed. The war's start was a surprise, but from here on it shouldn't be hard to find out what's planned. Of course, there's always the roving bands like Skunk Eyes's bunch raising hell. Nobody tells them what to do. They carry on their own little wars."

"What if they strike tonight?"

"Don't think so. The devils hit New Ulm today, and it didn't go so good. The town held. They got to work up to attacking the fort. Some say Indians don't attack at night, because, if they get killed, their spirits will get lost and wander forever. You'd think when daylight came, it would just find its way again. Anyhow, unless they can surprise somebody, the dark works against them as much as our side. Don't make sense to me that they'd come tonight. But the guard's been doubled or tripled. We'll know if they show up."

Anja pulled her blanket over her but was certain she would not sleep this night. A few minutes later she dropped into deep slumber. She was awakened briefly when she felt something snuggled beside her. Will must have come back. She lifted the side of her blanket for him to slip under, when she felt something wet on her face. She pushed her hand gently against a hairy chest. *Oh, my God.* It was Sniffer licking her face. She surrendered part of the blanket to the big coonhound and found she didn't mind the warmth generated by the dog's body. His closeness was a comfort. She should not have been surprised, she supposed; Sniffer had been hanging close to her ever since they found the dog, and she had worked for the better part of two hours plucking buckshot from his hide while the hound lay stoically on his side. She had also rubbed a soothing salve provided by the surgeon over his wounds. She had a feeling now she was the chosen one.

It was not yet daylight when Will shook her awake. Sniffer still slept beside her but raised up when he saw Will and waited for some scratching behind his ears.

"Some watch dog," Will remarked.

"He trusts you," Anja said. "I don't think a stranger would get this close."

"I suppose not. You do know you've been adopted, don't you?"

"Yes. I think we've adopted each other." She stood up. "Did you get any sleep last night?"

"No time. Lieutenant Gere asked me if I would take charge of some of the able-bodied settlers on the east side of the fort and shift the group to wherever weakness in the defense lines develop. There will be an attack on the fort today. According to intelligence that came in from our Dakota friends this morning, Medicine Bottle will lead a force down the ravines from the east and northeast. Little Crow and Little Six will bring warriors from the other sides, especially from the northwest and southwest. Gere's a kid, but he's got it figured out if Sheehan has the sense to cut him enough slack. And I think he does."

"Where do you want us?" She knew he wanted to send Karina and her to stay with the women and children, but he had the good sense not to suggest it. Besides, they were desperate for guns, and she was not giving up her Henry.

"Northeast corner, not far from the howitzer. That's where I'm going to start out. There is an abandoned stable I don't like in that direction that gives some cover to the Dakotas, and the mouths of the ravines are wider there to allow the attackers to spread out faster. There is also a row of log huts behind the stone barracks that could be a nuisance. Sergeant McGrew is in command of a dozen soldiers at that corner and seems to be experienced with the twelve-pound howitzer. He'll do damage if they don't run him over first. We must make sure that doesn't happen."

Chapter 31

C UT NOSE LOOKED around as he prepared to enter one of the ravines east of Fort Ridgely. He estimated that at least one hundred fifty warriors would be attacking the fort from the east. Three other bodies of warriors would be striking from the other sides. The fort was surrounded, and there was no place for the whites to retreat. They must crush the invaders.

He and Round Bear would lead nearly fifty warriors against the big gun at the northeast corner of the fort. Beaver Tooth and Swims Like Otter had also just joined them. They were formidable warriors, whose habits he did not always approve, but they would be welcome fighting assets.

He did not like the big guns, and without their thunder the fort would fall quickly. There would be no quarter, and every white would die. Not a single woman or child would be spared this time. The fools who had taken prisoners guaranteed that soldiers would follow to recover the bounty. The Soldiers Lodge would see to their destruction once the white soldiers and trespassing settlers had been driven out.

The sun was at its highest when the warriors swarmed into the ravines. Cut Nose was not pleased with the lateness of the hour. He had argued for attack at dawn, or earlier, catching the whites by surprise and before they had more time to shore up defenses. But, again, Little Crow and the other chiefs had wasted time debating. *Talk. Talk. Talk.* Their tongues were impotent weapons that had never killed a white man.

As they moved silently through the twisted ravines and approached the fort, Cut Nose crept ahead of his followers before stopping to hide behind a bank of dirt and peer out at the point of attack. He decided he would send a third of his warriors to seek cover behind the old stable and a like number behind the northernmost log huts. He would lead the others in a direct charge against the defenders surrounding the cannon. The two-story, stone barracks that lined the eastern side of the fort west of the huts concerned him. He had been told that women and children were secured there but he feared soldiers might have claimed the second floor, where they could rain fire upon the attacking Dakotas. He saw no sign of movement behind the closed windows, however.

He instructed Round Bear to inform the other warriors of his plan and to split their attackers. "Otter and Beaver Tooth will attack with us," he said.

Cut Nose waited impatiently for the sound of gunfire west and south of the fort. That would be the signal to attack. Then he heard it, the cracking of rifles and roars of shotguns. He signaled his warriors, and they poured out of the ravine. Out of the corner of his eye he saw Medicine Bottle's other screaming, whooping hordes south of his position racing toward the fort.

He led his warriors on the direct charge as the other two groups branched off to find protection behind the buildings. He was surprised that the enemy's guns were silent as the Dakotas neared. His own band began firing their own guns and arrows, and he saw one of the whites behind a wagon bed clutch his chest and fall. Then the defenders' guns cut loose, and two warriors fell. The gaps near the cannon had been filled with civilians, and he recognized one of them. Stalking Wolf. And he froze for an instant when the man raised his rifle and fired in Cut Nose's direction. Round Bear, who had been leading the charge at his side, stumbled backwards and dropped, a bloody borehole between his eyes. He dodged and veered away, realizing his other warriors had already retreated.

Before he turned away, he saw her, and it further unnerved him. Anja, dressed like a farm boy, firing a rifle that spat out bullets faster than any he had ever seen. What kind of people were these who made warriors of their women? Had they no shame?

The warriors regrouped beyond the range of the white men's guns, and Cut Nose surveyed the scene. They must disable the cannon, which had not fired yet, and he personally must kill Stalking Wolf. He saw that all but a few of the other warriors had reached the cover of the huts and old stable and were assaulting the whites from their positions. He hand-signaled that they should join him on the next charge.

Then the cannon belched and roared and launched its smoking ball toward a cluster of Medicine Bottle's warriors. It hit the earth and exploded, sending shrapnel in all directions while warriors screamed and fell or limped away. It had been a devastating and demoralizing strike. And what were they doing now? The cannon was being rolled forward and past the line formed by the huts for a better angle and sight on the Dakotas. And Stalking Wolf and Anja were moving with a dozen fighters surrounding the big gun. This must be stopped.

He readied his own shotgun and signaled the attack. The remnants of his band charged again, and the warriors moved from behind the buildings, all heading toward the cannon to destroy its defenders and take control of the powerful weapon. But his focus was on Stalking Wolf. Warriors dropped around him, but he ducked and weaved to within easy range of his nemesis, who was reloading his thunder-stick and concentrating on warriors charging from behind the old stable. He aimed and squeezed the trigger. The gun did not fire. It was dead—jammed. He lowered the weapon just as he saw Anja turn toward him and aim. He stood straight and faced her, prepared to meet his death at the hands of one of his own blood. Their eyes met. Her eyes shifted, and she turned her rifle on a different warrior.

The earth was scattered with his tribesmen now, and the huge gun had been rolled into firing position. Again, he retreated with his band. More than half dead or wounded badly. He was deeply saddened by his friend, Round Bear's death, enraged because it had been inflicted by the loathsome Stalking Wolf. And it troubled him that Anja stood at this man's side and fought those of her own blood. There was a mysterious bond between those two that he despised.

The man's medicine was powerful. He should have been a simple kill. But his spirit had been stronger than Cut Nose's gun. It was another bad omen that Stalking Wolf continued to appear wherever Cut Nose might be. It was beyond mere coincidence. But what did it mean?

The fighting continued through the afternoon and well into the night. The Army finally manned the windows of the barracks' second floor, and the cannon exploded with regularity. Medicine Bottle's forces were making no further incursions. Cut Nose's heart was no longer in the battle. He fought on mechanically and dutifully but without enthusiasm. Word from the other chiefs gave no reason for hope this day. At best, it was a standoff, which was effectively a victory for the besieged and vastly outnumbered whites.

But the war was not ended. One battle did not make a war, thought Cut Nose. Many settlers had been exterminated, and this was only the beginning. New Ulm would fall and all the smaller towns. Most of the settlers had already been driven from their farms and many of them killed. And Fort Ridgely would be visited again. It was almost a relief when rain came again that night, and the chiefs agreed upon a strategic retreat from Fort Ridgely.

Chapter 32

I T APPEARED THE Dakotas had abandoned their attack for now, and it seemed unlikely they would initiate another tomorrow. They would need to lick their wounds and consider their battle plans. Will had no illusions the war was ended. The Indians had not been defeated. Their casualties were not overwhelming, nor were the Army's. It had been hammered into his head at West Point that wars were never predictable. The statement had never been truer than here, mostly because there was no real commander-in-chief for the Dakotas. Indian chiefs had authority only while others would follow, and the conduct of this war was dispersed among many chiefs and warriors with their own supporters and agendas. Over the long haul, Will suspected this would be the Dakotas' downfall.

Several buildings outside the fort's perimeter had been burned, but Ridgely proper had not incurred irreparable damage. Guards, of course, had to be posted, but Lieutenant Sheehan had sent out a detachment of soldiers to confirm no hostiles remained near the fort. Near midnight Will and his comrades had found supper at one of the many food stations scattered about several buildings and the parade grounds. A slow rain had dwindled to a drizzle by the time they collapsed on their common bed of straw in the stable. Sniffer, evidently not holding a grudge about being tied in the stable with the horses during the battle, crawled between Anja and Will. He noticed Anja had spoken scarcely a word after the fighting and had maintained near silence during supper, as well. Something was troubling her, but he did not pry. She had lost her parents in a horrible fashion and seen more death the past few days than anyone could imagine witnessing in a hundred lifetimes. And she had killed or wounded more than a few with that Henry today. Why would she not be troubled?

The official start day for what would become known as the Dakota War of 1862 was Monday, August 18. Will would never forget the date, but he figured this time, for a generation in these parts, anyway, he would not be alone. When they got up on Thursday, August 21, day four of the uprising, the sun had decided to visit again. The blue skies and bright rays improved Will's outlook. Anja's funk lingered.

Nobody at the fort was enjoying a day of rest following the battle. Preparations were underway for the next assault by the Dakotas, which friendlies assured would be coming. It seemed that Ridgely was a symbol of white power over the Dakotas, but the fort was too undermanned to put down any uprising. Officers were preoccupied with trying to organize civilians into a potent fighting force. There were insufficient rifles with which to arm all of them, however.

Lieutenant Gere told Will the Army had been informed by the friendlies that the chiefs were awaiting reinforcements from allied Sissetons and Wahpetons of the Upper Agency and that another attack could be expected Friday or Saturday. The tanks at the springs near the Minnesota River had been destroyed and the water poisoned by the Indians, and Lieutenant Sheehan recruited volunteers to dig a water well within the fort proper, a task that was several years tardy.

Will's official responsibilities were in limbo until Curley Coburn returned with a message from Washington. Will suggested to Billy that the two leave the fort and search for more survivors. He thought Anja and Karina might stay behind this time, but Billy let the plans slip to Karina, and she mentioned the new quest to Anja. When Billy and Will started saddling their horses, the ladies appeared and began saddling their own mounts. As the searchers rode out, Sniffer fell in behind.

They counted something over forty dead that day, but the search party made several forays that collected some fifteen survivors, many in the woods along the river, others in hiding near their burned-out farmsteads. Two were women, one severely wounded by an arrow lodged in her abdomen. She had escaped with her baby boy into nearby brush, but her husband and two older children lay dead in the yard, their naked bodies suffering the usual degradations. Sniffer had ferreted out the woman and her baby, as well as several of the concealed children. Will judged most of the escapees near miracles. Children had often been rushed into hiding by their parents, scattered like fleeing mice into nearby woods or creek beds, wandering for several days until rescue came.

Some of the survivors mentioned the capture of a mother or siblings, giving some hope for reunions when the terror ended. There were no stories of captive adult males, of course. The death toll was quickly climbing into the hundreds, and he wondered how many others were lost or hiding and might yet die if not found. Will decided the living would be his mission.

Anja and Karina took over the care and comforting of the children as they collected them, and Will realized it would have been foolish for him and Billy to have taken on the search without their help. Anja still did not say much to her partners, but she turned a different face to the rescued women and children and gently coaxed them to summon the strength to complete the trek to Fort Ridgely.

That night, after supper, Will took a shift with the well diggers. It was a wide pit with six men digging as those above pulled up buckets they filled with dirt and sand. The sand was wet now, and that suggested they would hit water soon. Workers would continue throughout the night to make that happen.

Later, Will collapsed on the straw bed next to Sniffer. Anja appeared to be sleeping, but he would have bet his last dollar she was awake.

Chapter 33

WILL FELT SHEEHAN and Gere were doing admirable jobs preparing for the inevitable second attack. The well was completed before sunrise the morning of Friday, August 22, which was a significant achievement. A long siege could be withstood by the occupants with scant food supplies but not without water. Scouting reports confirmed Dakotas were moving in the direction of Fort Ridgely in numbers that could double the force that launched the earlier attack. Perhaps as many as a thousand warriors would be converging on the fort. Counting civilians, the fort could rally a force of no more than one hundred seventy-five fighting men of whom no more than half had any training or experience at warfare. The Sioux were expected to attack mid-morning.

Over three hundred women and children depended upon the successful defense of the fort, but few were passive. Women were busy melting spent bullets and molding them for reuse. Ammunition that was too large in caliber for the rifles was located, and the ladies shaved the balls down to fit. Others focused on keeping the defenders supplied with food and water. Some volunteered to reload rifles or pass ammunition to the riflemen, and a half dozen women, following the examples of Karina and Anja, were prepared to take up battle stations with their own rifles.

This time the fort was better fortified. Additional barricades had been constructed, several made of wood, four feet high and running as far as 100 feet. The cannoneers had a better sense of their range and where to strike with most effectiveness. Sergeant McGrew had somehow successfully negotiated a twenty-four pound howitzer for the corner Will and his partners would help defend again. Still, the enemy numbers seemed overwhelming. The cannons would be key. The big guns could fire almost any ammunition. In addition to the Army solid shells and explosive shells, they could fire cannister shells filled with large buckshot that turned the weapons into giant sawed-off shotguns. Anything that could be stuffed down the bore could also be fired, and the fort occupants had gathered nails, horse shoes, door hinges, and anything made of metal for ammunition.

Will was surprised, as he was nursing a cup of steaming coffee outside the stable entry, when Curley Coburn rode in on Warrior's look-alike progeny. He dismounted and walked up to Will and thrust an envelope in his hand.

"Looks like just in time for the party, sir. Gave Lieutenant Sheehan a message from Fort Snelling first. He ain't going to like what he reads. Sibley ain't going to be here anytime soon. He's put together a thousand men or more, but he's in no hurry moving this way. Doubt if they've reached Mankato yet."

Sibley was Colonel Henry H. Sibley, trader, former delegate to congress, governor, and citizen soldier. Will knew that the man had the reputation among professional soldiers as being more politician than military commander, but he would be bringing a serious force for the Dakotas to reckon with. Will opened the envelope, plucked out the telegram, and unfolded it and read the message. LETTER SNELLING ONE WEEK STOP STAY IN FIELD UNTIL CONTRARY ORDERS STOP HANSCOMB.

"Thanks, Curley. Good job. I may need you again. Would you keep me posted on where I can find you?"

"Yes, sir. I can do that. Don't look like I'm going any-place but here soon. If you'll excuse me, sir, I'm going to see if I can scare up some coffee and grub someplace."

"Go to the commissary and look for a scrawny half-blood woman who's bossing everybody. That's my mom. Tell her I sent you. She may grump at you some, but she'll see you're well fed."

"Thanks, sir. I'll do just that."

Curley led his mount into the stable and found a boy to care for his horse and then headed across the parade ground. Will looked at the telegram again. Obviously more detailed instructions were being sent by letter, which would be held for pickup by courier at Snelling. Otherwise his mission remained as nebulous as ever. The sound of gunfire kept him from pondering the message further.

Will ducked in the stable, retrieved his Sharps, and raced for the fort's east boundary. He found Anja, Billy, and Karina already in position near McGrew's big how-itzer. The defenders along the east side had nearly dou-bled since the first battle, and Will was glad for the real-location of guns here, especially since the stone barracks crammed with women and children was directly behind their position. If they were overrun, the attackers would take the barracks, potentially throwing defending husbands and fathers into panic that would pull them away from their positions.

It appeared to Will that the Dakotas had not changed their strategy at all since the first battle. According to Billy, one of the friendly Dakota scouts had informed him that Chief Medicine Bottle would still be leading the attack from the east. Little Crow was the general battle leader, and Chiefs Mankato and Big Eagle would be overseeing the attacks from the northwest and southwest. But the sole plan was apparently to overwhelm the fort by superior numbers, which made a certain sense but had its flaws.

Warriors were already surging from the ravines by the time Will joined the others. There were many more Dakotas than swarmed the defenders at the first battle, but their own firepower was greater now and better positioned. Indians generally tended to engage as individual combatants and did not fight in structured units. Their warfare was largely undisciplined and spontaneous. They quickly overtook the old stable but just as rapidly abandoned it or died when Sergeant McGrew turned his twenty-four pounder on the structure and collapsed it into flames and rubble.

The cannons broke up the mass of Dakotas. Will took down two with his Sharps, and, standing beside him,

Anja was dropping more than her share because of the Henry's rapid firing. Then, from behind him, Will heard the screaming of women and children from the barracks. He wheeled around and saw that somehow Dakotas had broken through the barricade and were streaming toward the stone building. He saw three or four before they disappeared behind the building, but he feared others had already entered the building. He nudged Anja and pointed and then headed for the barracks. He pressed a cartridge into the Sharps as he ran, and he had his Colt revolver holstered at his waist, an effective weapon at close range.

Will swung around the corner of the building and saw that the attackers had not broken through yet, but two stout warriors were swinging war axes with vicious strokes against the heavy oak door, splintering away the barrier and on the verge of gaining entry. Others, strung out along the outer wall, were shattering windows and struggling to climb in but were being deterred from inside by a pommeling of heads and hands by boards, sticks, and other objects pressed into service as improvised weapons.

The door. Once they broke through the door, there would be no stopping them. He leveled his rifle and squeezed the trigger, and one of the Dakotas dropped his axe and slumped to the ground. The other turned away from the door and looked around. Unfortunately, the crack of the Sharps had got the attention of all the attackers, nine or ten of them, and they turned their attention to the intruder. He did not have time to reload the rifle, so he shifted it to his left hand and drew the Colt from its holster.

Several of the Dakotas fired their own guns, and he felt the burning in his side as a hostile bullet tore into his flesh. They were charging him now, and he knew he could not take them all down. He emptied the Colt's chambers and stopped a few. Then the crack of gunfire rang in his ears and several more went to their knees. He saw Anja out of the corners of his eyes, and Karina stepping up beside her.

One of the wounded Dakotas, with black and yellow paint covering his face and his eyes wild with rage, stumbled and then charged Will with war axe upraised to strike. Will lifted his hand and dodged to ward off the blow. He blocked the handle and diverted the weapon's course, but the axe's butt still struck his forehead and sent him reeling. He heard another gunshot before blackness consumed him.

Chapter 34

AFTER ANJA'S RIFLE delivered a bullet to the chest of the Dakota who had struck Will, Karina's shotgun cut loose with two blasts, and the Indians assaulting the barracks made a hasty retreat, helping the wounded limp away but abandoning the dead. Anja knelt beside Will, her heart racing and her hands trembling. She placed her fingers to his neck, seeking his pulse.

"Is he dead?" Karina asked.

"No. He's alive. For now, anyway. We would never find Doctor Muller in this chaos. We must get him inside." Dr. Alfred Muller was the post's surgeon, who now not only had responsibility for wounded combatants but for whatever ailed the civilian population as well. With the assistance of Alexis Nilsson and several other women, he had delivered a dozen babies, half premature and stillborn, since the war began only days earlier.

As if replying, a woman's voice called through the window. "We'll open the door. Can you get him in here?" It was Alexis Nilsson, Will's mother.

"We'll try." She picked up Will's rifle and leaned it against the building with her own. It was then she noticed the side of his shirt, which was blood-soaked. She had assumed the ugly wound inflicted by the axe was the sole threat to his life. Thankfully, Billy arrived at that moment, and she waved him to her side. "In the barracks. We've got to move him inside."

Billy was not a big man compared to Will, but his sinewy frame seemed comprised of pure muscle, Anja thought. He grabbed Will underneath his arms and raised him effortlessly, and Anja and Karina each lifted a leg, and they carried him awkwardly through the door, lowering him to a blanket just inside that Alexis had spread out on the floor.

"Fix him," Billy said. "He can't die. He owes me. Anja, you stay with him. Karina and I better get back to the big gun. Things are still lively outside. I'll keep an eye over this way and bring help if I see any Dakotas sneaking in. But I think you did enough damage, they'll think twice."

Alexis seemed amazingly calm, considering it was her son who lay pale as whitewash on the floor in front of her. She was cutting away Will's shirt with the small skinning knife she had removed from the leather sheath on his belt. Anja knelt to help tear away the fabric.

"Water," Alexis called. A plumpish, young woman appeared from the mass of people crammed into the barracks carrying a half-full cooking pot of water with an armload of cloth strips. She placed the water and homemade bandages on the blanket. "Anything else I can get, Mrs. Nilsson?"

"Thank you, Lucy. Whiskey. Could you see if any of the ladies know where their men stash their whiskey? I need a bottle. Also, a heavy needle and thread."

"Reggie's got a bottle. He doesn't think I know, but it's in his haversack—a special pocket. It's with our things. And I can bring my sewing basket. I'll be back."

Alexis handed Anja some of the cloth strips and said, "Maybe you can fold some of these into compresses. I need to see what we've got here. Bleeding has slowed to a trickle on its own."

She dipped a strip of cloth in the water and began to wash away the blood, revealing a shallow furrow running along the rib cage. "This won't kill him. Bullet just travelled along his ribs and went on its way. He was bleeding like a stuck hog, but I don't think it even needs stitching. He'll have a pretty scar to brag on, but that's about it. Can you fashion me a compress about ten inches long? Then we'll wrap some of these strips about his chest to hold it to the wound. I need the whiskey, though."

On cue Lucy returned with the sewing basket and whiskey bottle. Alexis opened the bottle and took a healthy swig before offering it to Anja.

"Uh, no thanks," Anja said.

"I like a snort every week or two. Erik doesn't drink, so I have him pick up a bottle for cooking and medicinal purposes every so often. Probably not fooling him. Marriage works best sometimes if you know to keep your mouth shut. Of course he'd tell you that just goes one way at our house."

She took the bottle and poured whiskey in droplets over the wound, spreading it with one of the folded cloth strips. Will tossed his head and moaned, probably in response to the burning of the alcohol on his wound, Anja figured. She took his hand and squeezed it gently.

"That's good," Alexis said, "he feels something. Help me wrap the wound, and then I'll see about the damage to his head."

Anja helped turn Will's limp body so Alexis could push the ends of the cloth strips beneath his torso and pull them around to tie and anchor the compress to the wound. As she pressed her fingers to the flesh shrouding the taut muscular shoulders, back, and abdomen of the half-naked man, she could not help but notice and admire his physique. She wondered what it would feel like to be snuggled against him, his arms holding her close, his lips brushing her own before a deep, lingering kiss. She could feel herself blushing at the thought and tried to wipe the image from her mind, deciding she must be depraved to think such thoughts at a time like this.

"You can take his hand again, Anja, while I tend to the head wound. It is good for him to sense your presence."

Surely the woman had not read her mind. "Okay," she murmured and again claimed his hand, nearly certain she felt him squeezing hers in response.

Alexis cleaned the head wound. She found no cuts, but half his forehead was swollen with a melon-like mass. His head was tossing more now and his body beginning to squirm. Alexis said, "It may be a spell, but he will wake up. Just so his brain isn't addled. Could I impose on you to stay with him? I have some other things to tend to."

Impose? The woman could not chase her away. But she thought that Alexis, considering her own son lay unconscious on the floor, was not behaving in a very maternal way. "Yes, I'll stay with him."

She sat on the blanket, holding Will's hand for several hours, listening to the raging battle just outside. She had retrieved Will's Sharps and her own Henry and kept them within reach just in case the Dakotas launched an assault on the door again. But it seemed to her the cannons' roars were less frequent now and the rifle fire only sporadic. She took that as a good sign, although she knew the stockpile of ammunition for both cannons and rifles had to be dwindling. Will had told her they would be faced with hand to hand combat if the battle carried to a second day, and that would not bode well for the fort's occupants. Hopefully the Sioux were not aware of the dilemma.

"Is that you, Lisbeth?"

The feeble voice startled Anja, and she turned her gaze to Will's face. His lips quivered, and he seemed to be struggling to speak. "It's Anja." She placed a hand gently on his cheek, relieved just to hear his voice.

He mumbled. "I've missed you, Lisbeth. It's been so long."

She found herself irrationally angry at this Lisbeth, whoever she was.

"Will, wake up."

His eyes fluttered and then opened, looking at her with confusion. "You're Anja."

She thought he seemed disappointed, and she did not know whether to laugh or cry. "Yes, I'm Anja. At least you know me."

Alexis appeared, and Anja suspected she had never been very far away, that she was more concerned about her son's condition than she had let on. Alexis knelt by Will and traced her fingers over the lump on his forehead. It appeared to have shriveled a bit, leaving a slash of raw scarlet flesh in its wake, a prelude, Anja knew, to the blue, black, and purple hues that would replace it.

"Wilhelm," Alexis said, "how are you feeling?"

"Dizzy, sick. Like my head's going to explode. Otherwise just fine."

"Just stay here for now until we find a place where we can move you. I don't know if the infirmary will have space."

"I'll stay till I have some help getting up and moving, but this place stinks."

It did stink, Anja thought, of sweat and smoke and, worse, human waste. She had been oblivious to it earlier, so focused had she been on Will. The airy stable with its smell of horse dung was a bouquet of fresh prairie flowers compared to this.

Billy opened the door and entered with Karina. He grinned when he saw Will was conscious. "Knew your head was too damned hard to give in to an axe. This one's bigger than the one on the other side of your skull, but I'd say you've got enough decorations on your head for a spell. What about the side wound?"

"What side wound?"

"Guess that's an answer of sorts."

"What's happening outside?" Anja asked.

"It's winding down. Half of the Dakotas have called it good and are moving on. It might go on till after dark, but it's over. And we held the fort. Now, if they don't come back tomorrow."

"I need you to help me out of here."

"Where to?"

"The stable."

Alexis intervened. "You need to go to the infirmary and have Doc Muller look at you."

"Sorry, Mom. I guess that blow to my head took my hearing."

"You're worse than your father." She turned to Anja. "You're responsible for him."

Why not let Lisbeth do it? Anja thought. Then she realized she still had not released Will's hand.

Chapter 35

CUT NOSE STOOD gripping the reins of his horse on a bluff overlooking New Ulm. After the second aborted attack on Fort Ridgely, Little Crow had called for another attack on New Ulm. Again, the Dakotas had assembled to swarm in on the Germans, but the force that had attacked Ridgely had been reduced by nearly half. Other chiefs and other warrior groups had broken away to wage war on more settlers' homes and smaller communities. Many from the Upper Agency had ridden north to join a siege of Fort Abercrombie. Cut Nose, Beaver Tooth, and eight or nine other warriors, who had now cast their lots with the leader of the Soldiers Lodge, had joined the attack for a half day but had grown bored with what to Cut Nose appeared to be another standoff.

Thus, they had pulled away from the New Ulm attackers and loped their horses east. Cut Nose had been surprised to find there were still settlers ten miles out who had not heard of the uprising or had not taken warnings seriously. They had burned out at least five farmsteads that afternoon and killed fifteen whites, including four men and their wives and children. Yesterday had been a good day.

Little Crow had never taken New Ulm and had probably killed not many more whites than Cut Nose's band had that day. The town had burned down around the survivors, however, leaving a community of smoldering, smoking rubble. It could not be said whether Dakota flaming arrows had caused the destruction or if the damage had been self-inflicted as the whites torched their own homes and business structures to remove cover claimed by the attackers. It did not matter, Cut Nose thought, because very little of the town remained, and the whites were abandoning the town this morning. The barricades on the road had been torn out, and a seemingly endless line of wagons packed with people crawled like a giant snake up the road that led to Mankato. Still, he would have preferred to see the invaders dead.

Little Crow and the other chiefs had decided to permit the New Ulm occupants to depart without interference.

The whites were leaving. Why lose more Dakota lives in a battle already won? *Why?* Because the whites will return and breed more whites, he thought. The fools who claim to lead the Dakotas have no vision with which to pull the people together. He did not feel bound to follow these chiefs and did not. But he realized now that the Sioux were not pack animals like wolves that overpowered enemies by the united force of their numbers. He felt no joy as he saw the last wagon depart New Ulm. There were fifteen hundred fewer whites on the Minnesota River now, but he had already heard they would soon be replaced by that many soldiers.

He saw Beaver Tooth riding up the slope of the bluff's backside. He watched the young warrior's approach, certain the rider would bring him no pleasant news. Beaver Tooth relished the role as messenger of doom.

As Beaver Tooth came up to Cut Nose, he said, "I have news of Swims Like Otter."

Otter had disappeared two days earlier during the battle at Fort Ridgely. Cut Nose had been curious about the warrior's whereabouts but not especially concerned. He assumed that Otter had joined another war party for raids on settlers or other easier prey. He lacked the patience for a prolonged battle or siege and was easily distracted. He grunted, feigning disinterest, "And what is this news."

"He is dead."

This caught Cut Nose by surprise. He had never been fond of Swims Like Otter, but he had ridden with him for many years. His absence would leave a void but nothing like the hole in his heart left by the death of his friend, Round Bear. He replied, "He died during the battle at the fort?"

"Yes. He was killed by the woman."

"What woman?"

"The woman we encountered on the trail with the man you have called Stalking Wolf. The ones you would not let us kill." The statement was made with more than a hint of accusation. Perhaps it was not unfair. If Anja and Stalking Wolf had died, Otter might still live.

"How did this happen?"

"Otter and others escaped the anger of the big thunder-sticks and found an opening that took them behind the enemy's barriers. They went to the stone-walled soldiers' house where women and children hid but were stopped by Stalking Wolf and the mixed blood woman. Otter shot Stalking Wolf, but he did not fall. Then the woman shot Otter, and he charged the man and killed him with his war axe before the woman shot Otter again, and his spirit left his body. Other warriors died there, also. But those who escaped say Swims Like Otter died a warrior's death. That is what we all hope for, is it not?"

"Yes, of course." *Stalking Wolf dead?* This was an omen of good things to come. A huge burden was lifted from his shoulders. This war could yet be won. "Gather those warriors who wish to ride with us. There are many whites left to kill. We will go northward in the direction of the Upper Agency. I will find John Otherday there."

Chapter 36

NEARLY TWO WEEKS following the second battle of Fort Ridgely, Will sat on a bench outside the stable with a letter clasped in his fingers. An occasional recurring headache and a bruised forehead that had turned an ugly mix of yellow and fading purple reminded him of his confrontation with the Dakota war axe. He was hardly aware of the raw scar on the flesh sheathing his ribs, but he knew the bullet might have killed him had it struck an inch or two in the wrong direction.

The Dakotas were not going to attack Ridgely again. The fort was being smothered by "Sibley's Army," as some were calling the force of some sixteen hundred soldiers, mostly infantry, under the command of Colonel Sibley. The soldiers had set up camp around the outskirts of the fort proper while Sibley contemplated his next move. It seemed to Will that the man could do with a lot more action and less pondering. Some were grumbling that the colonel had moved his troops from Fort Snelling to Fort Ridgely like a sightseer on vacation. Others, especially civilians, suggested New Ulm might still be standing and occupied by its residents had Sibley marched his troops at a faster pace without stopping so often along the journey to procure reports and evaluations of the situation ahead of him. A local state legislator asserted that hundreds of civilian lives might have been saved with earlier arrival of the troops. Of course, it could be argued military lives were saved by the exercise of due caution, and second-guessing was an ingrained human habit, Will figured.

Sibley had received much public criticism for another tragic miscalculation. His troops had arrived at Ridgely on August 28. Several days later, he had dispatched a one hundred seventy man burial party under the command of Major Joseph Brown to search for survivors and to bury any dead found. The party searched mostly along the river from the fort to the Lower Agency. Most of the bodies had been exposed to scorching sun or torrential rains for nearly two weeks by this time. From his own experience, Will knew the soldiers had faced a grisly task. Despite what they were witnessing, the fresh troops and officers apparently were not taking the Sioux menace seriously, and on Monday, September 1 established a campsite some sixteen miles north of Fort Ridgely on low ground along the river.

Strategically, Will thought, they could not have chosen a more suicidal location, surrounded by high ground on three sides, and a ravine called Birch Coulee on the other. The Sioux had finally been handed a great victory. First they killed over ninety horses, thwarting any possible escape, and then, for several days, before relief arrived from Ridgely, rained gunfire and arrows onto the encampment. Lieutenant Gere had told Will that the Army's casualty rate at what was now being called the Battle of Birch Coulee was over eighty percent.

Armchair generals would have plenty to criticize here, Will figured, but it made no difference now. The challenge was to bring the killing to conclusion, and reports were that it was far from over. The Indians had moved northerly from the fort, fanning out into a territory that included the Upper Agency. The road between Fort Ridgely and Mankato and on to Fort Snelling seemed relatively secure now. The Lower Agency, with the few remaining buildings that had not been destroyed by the uprising, was under military control, although for what purpose remained to be seen.

Billy had just returned from Fort Snelling with the letter promised by Charles Hanscomb. He had departed

Ridgely the same day over one hundred fifty wagons and fifteen hundred people deserted New Ulm for their yet undetermined destinations. He had told Will about the pitiful sight of men, women, and children trudging along the sticky, mud-sucking road, devoid of nearly all but the clothes on their backs. The wagons had been filled with the wounded, infirm, and very young and had little space for any possessions that might otherwise have been salvaged. These folks had come to America with nothing, and, with hard work and ingenuity, had built lives of modest prosperity. And now they had nothing again.

Will turned to Hanscomb's letter and studied it again.

Dear Captain Nilsson:

You will remain at your station for the duration of the Dakota War. Continue to observe and report weekly by both telegram and letter. Conclusion of the fighting will be only the beginning of a new phase of the war, and the situation will be fraught with grave legal and political concerns. Be prepared for a summons to the Capitol to discuss this personally with President Lincoln and myself. Take care for your own safety.

Respectfully,

Charles Hanscomb

Counselor to the President

Not only did his assignment remain vague, Hanscomb had salted the letter with more mystery. The President? Why in God's name would Abraham Lincoln take his precious time to speak to a lowly Army captain who failed to understand what he was doing for the President in the first place? He folded the letter and stuffed it in his trouser pocket.

"You look very perturbed about something. May I sit down?"

He looked up, but Anja was already taking a place on the bench beside him. In a short time, she had adopted the familiarity of a sister to him, and he supposed the horrors they had seen and shared together had forged a special bond. He reciprocated the ease and comfort of their relationship, but if his caring for her was brotherly, his thoughts were becoming increasingly incestuous.

He did not think it appropriate to mention Hanscomb's reference to the President, so he simply replied, "I continue to receive rather indefinite orders and still am not certain what I am doing here, frankly."

"Why don't you ask your superior officer to clarify?"

"It's all very complicated." Especially, when your direct superior is Abraham Lincoln, he thought. "Anyway, I am to remain in the war vicinity indefinitely. It doesn't appear I head for the War of the Rebellion anytime soon."

"Well, I would think that would be a good thing. It should be a relief to your family and your lady friend."

"What lady friend?"

"Lisbeth."

Her speaking Lisbeth's name gave him a start. "How did you know about Lisbeth?"

"Well, I don't know anything about her. When you were unconscious, you called her name. You said you had missed her, and I think the words were 'It has been so long.'"

This was something Will never talked about. Never. But, for some reason, he wanted Anja to know. But he cast his eyes downward, focusing on a small stone on the ground as he spoke. "It's been nearly four years. Lisbeth was my wife."

"Wife? You've never mentioned a wife."

"We were married for six months. One of those West Point weddings, the day after I graduated. She was one reason I didn't apply for combat duty. I did not plan a military career, but I had a service obligation. JAG and law school presented the perfect opportunity. I probably would have joined her father's New York City law firm after my Army discharge."

"What happened?"

"She died. She was four months with child. Something went wrong. She miscarried. Died in my arms before the doctor arrived. He said he could not have helped her."

"I'm so sorry. That's terrible. I don't know what to say."

He lifted his head and faced her and saw the tears crawling down her cheeks. He plucked a handkerchief from his pocket, gently wiped the tears away, and pressed the cloth into her hand.

"I just don't mention it to anyone. Don't talk about it. My mother says that's not a good thing."

"Your mother is very wise. And very, very kind beneath that tough crust. But when you called for Lisbeth, you were dreaming? Hallucinating?"

"Most would say that, I know. But I will swear to my dying day, she was there at that moment, holding my hand."

"Like a ghost? There to take you with her?"

"Like a ghost? Yes. Taking me with her? No. She was telling me to live. She released my hand and told me it was time to let go." He took the handkerchief back from Anja's hand and daubed a few rolling tears from his own eyes.

Anja spoke so softly, he leaned nearer to hear. "I was engaged before I returned to my parents' home and the Redwood Agency teaching job. His name was Matthew, a second lieutenant. We planned to be married before he left for the war, but his unit was suddenly called out and he boarded the train in St. Paul with barely time for a good-bye kiss. His parents received the report of his death a few months later and notified me. We don't even know where he is buried. I don't know if we ever will. End of story. This conversation is turning maudlin. I just wanted you to know."

He took her hand, and they looked out over the parade ground, sitting in silence for some minutes. Death, he thought. He had seen so much of it these past days. Death lurking in the shadows could suffocate all the joys of living, if you let it. He guessed you had to fight back. Thumb your nose at it. Will abruptly switched subjects. "What do you do now? Where are you going from here?"

"Not back to the farm. Not yet. But I'm not letting it go. The folks are buried there, but I must let some memories fade. I hope I can just rent out the farm for now. Karina wants to keep her parents' place, too, but she's not of legal age. We'll find a good lawyer and work on the legal details. Too bad you have other plans."

"There will be plenty of legal work for lawyers to sort things out for another generation, but I refuse to think that far ahead. Not good luck in my current business."

"You asked where I was going from here, and I told you where I was not going. Karina and I are leaving for St. Paul tomorrow. There is a return supply wagon leaving for Fort Snelling in the morning and we've arranged with the wagoner to travel with him. Of course, Sniffer will ride with us. I consider him adopted now. I will tie Molly to the wagon and take her with me. I hope Warrior got his job done a few days ago."

Will was unexpectedly disturbed by her announcement, but he teased, "I can verify Warrior did his part, and Molly appeared ready enough for romance. I'm betting you'll have a foal by this time next year. As for the wagon, I've got a hunch the two of you cornered some young man who couldn't turn down two pretty ladies for company on a long journey."

"I don't know about that. We were persistent, but we both look like a couple of buffalo hunters just returned from the hunt right now. And in our ragged britches, and hair tucked in our hats, he probably didn't know we were women and certainly would hardly think of us as ladies."

"Sorry. You're not going to convince any male who still breathes and walks of that. But what do you do after you get to St. Paul?"

"Karina has grandparents there. They'll take her in while she gets more education. I'll look for employment, preferably a teaching job. Your mother said I should check out Mankato on the way. She pointed out that they will have a huge influx of refugees from the war, and with New Ulm having to start over, Mankato will likely become even more of a commercial center. She said it would keep me nearer the farm, too, so I could keep an eye on things. As I said, your mother is very wise."

And very devious, also. It seemed to Will she was showing an undue amount of interest in Anja's plans. "Would it be okay if I wrote once in a while?"

"I was hoping you would."

"How do I find your address?"

"As soon as I know where I will be living, your mother said I could send a letter to you in care of her at Fort Ridgley. They're heading back to their farm tomorrow, but mail service by coach will stop at Ridgely for the foreseeable future."

"You know more about what my folks are up to than I do."

"I've been helping Alexis for the better part of a week while you've been recuperating on your fanny. We've had a chance to get better acquainted, so I'm not so scared of her now."

"So you say outside of her presence."

Anja laughed. "Guilty." She hesitated a moment and then stood up. "Well, I promised to help your mother with supper, so I'd better get moving."

Will got up, too. "I'll see you tonight, if not before."

She bit her lip nervously before she replied. "I won't be in the stable tonight. Karina and I are planning to sleep under the freight wagon. Freddy wants to leave promptly at the first light of sunrise."

"I see." But he did not. "So this may be the last time we see each other."

"I hope not."

"I haven't kissed you since that evening at the boarding house."

"No, you have not."

He cast his eyes about the fort. Civilians and soldiers were thick as flies on fresh cow shit. He shrugged. "Would it be scandalous for me to kiss you now, Miss Lund?"

"Yes, Captain Nilsson. But please do anyway."

He took her in his arms, and his lips found hers. She pressed against him so firmly she stung his fragile ribs, but he did not complain or flinch. Instead he clung to her like a sinking swimmer to a life-saving rope. They separated only after a scattering of applause reminded him they had an audience. He hoped folks did not see him blushing. Anja turned toward the onlookers and smiled and waved.

"I won't forget you, Anja," Will said, when her attention shifted back to him.

"Nor I, you, Will. Be safe. Please, be safe." She wheeled and hurried away without looking back.

Chapter 37

"YOU TOLD ME a spell back that you owed me," Billy said, as he and Will saddled their horses.

Will wondered where this was leading. "Yes, I did. And I do."

"I told you I'm going to enlist in the Army when my work here is done."

"Yes, I remember."

"Well, I've been talking to one of the Renville's Rangers guys, and they're going to start four weeks' training at Fort Snelling when they are relieved from this mission, and I'd like to join them."

"I don't see why that would be a problem. Our work in the field should be finished up by then, or I'd be able to handle it. Curley's working on repairs here at the fort but would probably grab a chance to make his money in the saddle for a spell. With all the soldiers that have turned up now, Army's oversupplied with couriers."

"Not exactly what I'm getting at. Problem is the rangers are infantry. I ain't cut out for that. I want to go cavalry. I'd do my training with the rangers, but I want you to get me in the cavalry after I'm done. And I'd like to ride along with you."

He supposed he would be able to wangle a transfer for Billy from infantry to cavalry and, perhaps, to his own unit. That might depend some upon the extent of his own rank reduction when his transfer out of JAG was completed. "I'm not in a position to guarantee anything right now, Billy, but I promise I'll do my best to make the transfer happen. I'd be honored to have you ride with me."

Billy grinned, "That's all I can ask, Will. You won't be sorry. I don't suppose I can wear my coonskin hat?"

"You'll have to leave that at home."

"Figured as much. Of course, I got no home. Ain't had one for years."

"You can leave any personal belongings at my mom and dad's place. I know they'd be okay with that. Before we head up the river, I want to swing by the farm and see how they're making out and we'll ask if you can make that home base until you've got your own."

It was ten days into September now, and Will had not been out to the farm since his parents returned. As they rode up onto the knoll where he had nearly lost his life to Cut Nose, he looked down upon the farmstead and was surprised to see his father had already put upright poles in the ground for a lean-to building a short distance from the remains of the old barn. Both of his parents were at the former barn site, clearing rubble and loading it on a wagon for hauling to a wash or ravine to block erosion. He nudged Warrior ahead, and Billy followed. As they entered the yard, Erik and Alexis Nilsson looked up and hurried out to greet them.

They dismounted, and his mother rushed to him and gave him a tight hug, and then, to Billy's obvious surprise, he got one, too. The more reserved Erik settled for firm handshakes.

Alexis announced, "It's an hour short of noon. You'll both be staying for dinner. I've got fresh apple cobbler, and I can do fried potatoes and some ham slices in no time. Savages left my canning alone, so I'll open some green beans."

Will's mother headed for the house like she was on her way to a fire. "Does Mom ever just walk?" Will asked his father.

"I think I've seen her walk a time or two, but I can't remember when that was. Mostly goes after everything like she's killing snakes. I appreciate her help out here, but I don't move fast enough to suit her." Erik shrugged. "What are you two up to?"

"We're going to catch up with Sibley and stay within easy riding range of his troops while we try to collect a few more survivors. We also plan to check out what's going on at the Upper Agency and get a report back to my superiors about that. We'll stay to eat, but we need to be on our way after that. I would like to camp near Johnson Lake tonight."

"Twenty miles. That shouldn't be a problem. Dakotas cleared out from up that way?"

"I'm told so. But they have a way of coming back in small war parties, so we'll have to keep an eye out." He gestured toward the new construction. "I see you're putting up a lean-to."

"Yep. We'll rebuild the barn come spring but wanted some shelter for what livestock I've got left before the worst of winter hits."

"What stock have you recovered so far?"

"I got two mares bred to Warrior and a half dozen cows that will calve in March. Then I bought a new team that's hitched to the wagon that came with them. I'm luckier than most. Our house was untouched except for the windows that got busted out when I was holed up that night you two came along. I've got some money in the Mankato bank. Half the folks who survive this war will be pulling out if they haven't already. Livestock and equipment's going to sell for a dime on the dollar around here, so I'll be able to restock easy enough. Won't be the same quality for a few years, but we'll build it up again. Likely going to be some cheap land, too. You might want to think about that." His father, the natural-born entrepreneur. He had planted the seed though, and Will knew he would be thinking about it. Will told him about Billy's need for a place to leave his personal things, as well as a mare he had bought and been lodging at the Ridgely stable that Warrior had serviced.

Erik placed his hand on Billy's shoulder. "Son, from here on, you just think of the Double N as home."

Will had never heard the farm-ranch called the Double N before, but he didn't bite. Hopefully, the two "Ns" represented Erik and Alexis Nilsson. "Dad, when I leave Minnesota, I'm not taking Warrior with me. Nobody ever talks about it, but horses have a much higher casualty rate during war than soldiers. And he's not a youngster anyway. You can keep him busy here earning stud fees and building up the horse herd again. Billy might want to consider what he wants to do about Buster. I'm going to see about taking my spare horse, Red, off to war with me. That's where he'll end up if I turn him back anyway."

Billy said, "I hadn't thought about that. You could use Buster while I'm gone. He's a hell of a riding horse."

"They'll both be welcome here."

After dinner, Alexis declared at the table that she wanted Will to step outside and talk with her a bit. Will thought it a bit rude, but he stepped outside with her.

"When are you coming back, Wilhelm?" she asked.

"Mom, I have no way of knowing. I hope the end of the uprising is near and that I'll be back this way within a few weeks on my way to Fort Snelling."

"I expect to have a letter from Anja by then. I told her not to keep me waiting about her plans."

Will decided his mother was incapable of minding her own business. "Mom, isn't it a little presumptuous to expect Anja to do what you command?"

"It is not a command. I consider her a very good friend, and friends should be able to speak frankly with each other."

Anja was a woman with grit, but Will doubted she was ready to speak frankly with Alexis Nilsson yet. It occurred to him, though, that Anja, if it became necessary, would be capable of drawing a line and saying "enough" if his mother crossed it. He suspected his wily mother would know when to back off before that happened. Will replied, "I'm glad you are friends. She's faced horrors most folks cannot even imagine the past few weeks. She needs all the friends she can get."

"Are you her friend?"

"Of course. I like to think we're good friends."

"More than friends?"

"Just friends, Mom."

"I heard you kissed her in front of half the folks at Fort Ridgely. And it wasn't a peck-on-the-cheek kind of kiss."

Will shot his mother a look that said he was finished talking about Anja.

Chapter 38

WILL AND BILLY ranged the Minnesota River valley and surrounding farms for nearly twelve days, never straying more than a half day's ride from Sibley's forces. They had found several dozen survivors during that time and delivered them to troops that had been delegated to care for any refugees. Other than some roving war parties, most of the Sioux had moved northward, so this time out they took the time to bury the dead in shallow graves, sometimes interring entire families in a common grave. It was the best they could do. There were just too many.

Billy somehow located friendlies when Will sought information, and he learned that John Otherday was alive and well and had been using his influence to protect captives. A new group called the Peace Lodge was gathering captives near the Upper Agency, according to one of the friendlies. He reported there were nearly two hundred white captives, mostly women and children, being held in a village there. These Dakotas were committed to protecting the prisoners' lives. Other white women and children were dispersed among Dakota families who had claimed them, the women for additional wives and the children for adoption.

Estimates were that as many as one thousand white settlers and their family members had been killed by this time. Will did not doubt the numbers but thought that counts would be largely speculative in either direction, because many of the bodies would never be found or identified, and there was no accurate census of many who had occupied the war zone.

They had returned to Fort Ridgely twice during this period, and each time Will recruited Curley Riggs to deliver letters for Hanscomb to Fort Snelling for mailing and brief telegraph messages. Hanscomb's telegraph responses had simply acknowledged receipt of his reports and stated there would be no further letters from Washington until hostilities ceased.

Sibley's troops trudged slowly northward, veering east to pinch the fleeing Sioux toward the Upper Agency. The Dakotas still split off into raiding war parties, but there were fewer roaming the plains and woodlands as the last week of September approached. A fair number had already fled to Canada or westward to join other Sioux tribes in Dakota, Wyoming and Nebraska territories. The Dakotas were on the run. Sibley had dispatched troops north to Fort Abercrombie, but word was that the fort occupants had withstood the siege and the attackers were pulling out.

Will and Billy were two miles southwest of Sibley's column, but they could see the long line of dust being kicked up by the soldiers, both infantry and cavalry, as they marched across the dry prairie. Will thought the Army should have the resistance outnumbered by now, but numbers were not everything in war. Sibley commanded many soldiers who had little or no training, and very few with combat experience. An exception was the Third Minnesota Voluntary Infantry Regiment, and the Third Minnesota soldiers were seeking redemption.

The Third Minnesota had been ordered home from the Civil War with tails between their legs. In July they had been charged with guarding Union supplies at Murfreesboro, Tennessee when they were attacked and captured by Confederate cavalry under the command of General Nathan Bedford Forrest. The Third Minnesota's commanding officer had surrendered without being fired upon. Forrest insulted the soldiers by not even considering them worthy prisoners. They were released under an agreement with the Union Army that the Third Minnesota would not fight Confederates again. Thus, they had been sent home to Fort Snelling. They were looking for a fight.

Billy said, "Talked to a sergeant friend with Sibley. Says they're headed for Wood Lake. They're off course if that's what they're up to. That dip they're following will take them to Lone Tree Lake not far from the agency. That's most likely where they'll find Dakotas, but somebody's got the map mixed up. Do you want to join up with Sibley's bunch?"

"No. That's not part of my assignment. You say they're going to end up near the Upper Agency, anyway. I want to try to locate Otherday and see for myself what's happening there."

"I think that's where the end of this story's going to be."

"I have a hunch this is just the beginning of the story."

Chapter 39

CUT NOSE, BEAVER Tooth, and four other warriors were riding toward Lone Tree Lake, located at the juncture of the Minnesota and Chippewa rivers not far from the Upper Agency. They intended to rendezvous with other warriors of the Soldiers Lodge and join the Dakotas who were congregating for what could be the most important battle of the war. He knew Sibley, and he had nothing but contempt for the colonel, who was just another thieving trader as far as he was concerned. Sibley was not a true warrior, but the numbers of white soldiers marching toward Lone Tree Lake worried him.

He feared that the Battle of Birch Coulee was the last in which his people could claim victory. The faint-hearted were already departing the fight. He only hoped he could die a warrior's death and kill many whites before they took him down. As they came over a grassy hill, he was surprised to see a farmstead set in a shallow valley, apparently undisturbed by the war. The whites were like ants, there were so many of them. Stamp out one mound, and another appeared.

He signaled for the warriors to rein in, while he studied the lay of the enemy's lair. Nothing unusual. Barn. Chicken house. Two horses and a milk cow in a lot. The little house was made of stone and tucked back against a cliff, perhaps one reason it had animals in the pen? That did not make sense.

They rode their ponies at a walk down the rough slope toward the farmstead. When they were within fifty feet of the house, he called in English. "Hello. We come as friends. Want water and food. Then we go. Leave in peace."

A rifle cracked and one of the warriors toppled from his horse. Two of the warriors returned fire before they all whirled their horses around and raced half way back up the hill.

Cut Nose told his comrades, "We must leave the horses and spread out and rush the house."

Beaver Tooth asked, "But how many whites are in the house?"

Cut Nose replied, "We cannot know. Two, maybe. No more than three. Beaver Tooth and I shall go first and come from the sides of the house, while you shoot your rifles from a distance to draw their fire." He received silent nods in reply.

The others commenced firing their rifles, while Cut Nose and Beaver Tooth crept away in opposite directions, slipping outside any shooter's range of vision before sneaking cautiously into the farmyard. Then they rushed to the sides of the house. Cut Nose paused at the corner and listened. Someone was still shooting from inside the house. But then he heard more distant gunfire and looked back up the hill. Two men on horseback were moving down the hill, firing at his warriors. The Dakota horses had spooked and pulled free from the tiny branches of scattered brush that had held them steady.

He peered around the corner and saw that Beaver Tooth had crawled almost to the door. They must take the house now for the cover it would furnish against the new arrivals. He glanced up the hill again and saw that only one of his warriors stood now. There was hope, though, if he and Beaver Tooth gained the house. He turned and saw Beaver Tooth dart through the door with his rifle ready to fire. And then the distinctive sound of a shotgun's roar before Beaver Tooth backed out of the house and toppled backward to the earth, his naked chest a mass of scarlet.

In nearly the same instant, he saw the last warrior on the slope crumple to his knees and fall. Cut Nose was determined to die as a warrior. He tossed his rifle aside and pulled his favorite war club from the loop at his side, rushed the house, and leaped inside, stunned and hesitating a precious moment before a big woman slammed a frying pan against his face. He tripped backward before regaining his footing and moved toward her with warclub upraised. The woman backed away until she reached a table, where her fingers closed on a butcher knife, and she thrust it toward him, daring him to try to take it. He could find no fear in her eyes.

He readied for his kill when a muscular arm closed around his neck, and the hand of the other tore away his weapon. And then the young man he had seen near Anja defending Fort Ridgeway appeared in the doorway with a rifle leveled at Cut Nose's chest. He relaxed and surrendered.

The man behind him released his choking grip and pushed him aside. Cut Nose turned toward him. Stalking Wolf. Returned from the dead. The war was ended.

"It's Cut Nose," the younger man said. "We got us a prize."

Stalking Wolf spoke to the woman. "I'm Captain Will Nilsson, ma'am. You going to be okay?"

The woman was only three finger widths shorter than this man who called himself Captain, but wider. "I am Augusta Hochhausen. These sons-of-bitches butchered my husband and two sons out in the cornfield a few weeks back. I buried them here, and I was damned if I was going to leave them. One way or the other, this is where I'll die."

"We'll get him tied up and out of here, ma'am. Keep your eyes open if you plan to stay here, but the war's winding down. I'm terribly sorry for your losses. I'm sure there will be folks coming in to see if they can help."

"How do they bring back a good man and two boys not yet in their teens?"

Stalking Wolf did not reply. He and the younger man turned their attention to Cut Nose and soon he had his wrists bound with rawhide strips. He knew this was his first step along the trail to death.

Chapter 40

THE BATTLE OF Wood Lake, which took place near Lone Tree Lake, brought a final defeat to the Dakotas. On the final leg of their journey to the Upper Agency, Will and Billy came across an Army scouting patrol and surrendered Cut Nose to a young lieutenant, who was obviously pleased to be able to return to his superior with a notable captive in tow. Cut Nose, the notorious leader of the Soldiers Lodge, was more famous among white soldiers than many of the Dakota chiefs.

Billy had found a route to an encampment of friendlies and John Otherday, where Will and his young scout waited for Colonel Sibley to take control of the reservation. The Peace Lodge, as the friendlies were now being called, had now taken custody of most of the captives. They prepared for battle with their fellow tribesmen and Will marveled at their courage. Some would be fighting brothers and cousins and, in some instances, fathers. He hoped their selfless acts would be remembered when the inevitable retribution came. To many whites, the only good Indian was a dead one, and he feared that mentality might prevail in the minds of many Minnesotans in the aftermath of the uprising.

The Dakota war effort collapsed after the Battle of Wood Lake. It was reported that the Third Minnesota had performed beyond mere redemption and thwarted what could have been a disastrous ambush by the Dakotas. Little Crow retreated well ahead of Sibley's arrival and departed for Canada with some of his more devoted loyalists and their families.

Will and Billy were with Otherday at the Peace Lodge encampment mid-morning on September 26 when Colonel Sibley's column appeared on the horizon. They could hear the rapping of the military drums as the soldiers approached with bayonets fixed. Sibley promptly ordered his soldiers to set up an encampment adjacent to the Peace Lodge village. While soldiers worked on establishing a camp, Sibley and a few officers entered the Dakota village amid a flood of white flags, and within a few hours two hundred sixty-nine white and mixed-blood captives, mostly women and children, were surrendered to the Army. The next day the captives began a journey to Mankato under military escort.

It was time to report to Hanscomb again, and Will decided to accompany the escort as far as Fort Ridgely, where he would write his letter and prepare a telegram. Billy volunteered to deliver the letter and telegram to Fort Snelling, and they agreed Will would take the longer route that would permit a brief visit with his parents before they met up again at Snelling to await instructions from Washington. Will hoped he would finally receive some clarity regarding his mission.

Part II

Retribution

Chapter 41

WILL CHECKED IN at the Fort Snelling Headquarters early morning, where both a telegram and letter from Hanscomb were waiting for him to claim. These had been dated prior to the missives Billy had sent the previous day but had not been turned over to his courier because they had been labelled for personal delivery only.

Squinting when the rising sun struck his eyes as he stepped outside of the office, Will glanced at the telegram and saw that it simply acknowledged his most recent report and informed him of the detailed letter to follow. The letter, which he now held in his hand, did not appear unduly lengthy but was voluminous compared to previous correspondence. He strolled across the parade ground to read it in the privacy of the vacant sergeant's quarters in the barracks he had been offered for his lodging at the fort. Only a skeleton force presently occupied the fort, since every available soldier was in the field with Sibley.

Inside, he sat down on the cot, opened the letter and began to read:

Dear Captain Nilsson:

Based upon your latest report, I suspect the military conflict with the Dakotas will be substantially concluded by the time you receive this correspondence. The people of Minnesota are demanding severe punishment to those who committed the murders of the innocent farmers and townspeople of their state. Governor Alexander Ramsey is insisting that a military tribunal or commission be convened to try and punish the offenders. His unfortunate statements to the press and public do not create an environment for a more cautious and thoughtful approach. Such a commission is fraught with numerous legal and political implications.

At its beginning the Dakota War was under the technical jurisdiction of the state militia, commanded at Governor Ramsey's direction by now Brigadier General of Volunteers Henry Hastings Sibley. The war was federalized when President Lincoln on September 6 ordered Major General John Pope to assume command of the newly created Department of the Northwest. The General's arrival in St. Paul on September 17 effectively placed him in command of all state militia and federal troops engaged in the war. We are informed that Governor

Ramsey and General Pope are consulting regularly about the function of any commission.

The President has grave concerns about both the appropriateness of a commission and the procedures such a body might follow, as well as the ultimate verdicts. He must obviously devote his attention to the War of the Rebellion and cannot give this matter the attention it deserves.

You will remain on duty throughout any trials as an observer on behalf of Secretary of War Edwin Stanton. You will not participate directly in the trials but shall simply observe the proceedings and evaluate their validity and conduct under existing statutes, precedent, and the United States Constitution. Please send interim reports only by mail to my attention, as usual. When any proceedings are concluded, you will travel to the Capitol to make your personal report to the President, Secretary Stanton, and myself.

Henceforth, you will appear in full uniform. Your letters of credentials are included with this report. You will also find the commission evidencing your promotion to the rank of Major. This is not a brevet promotion, and this rank shall follow you upon transfer to an appropriate cavalry unit when your current assignment is completed. I extend my congratulations.

Respectfully.

Charles Hanscomb

Counselor to the President

Will placed the letter on the bed and sighed. He realized now that the work he had done to this point was intended to give him perspective and background to deal with what lay ahead. The possibility of war trials was why his legal background had led to the mission. His knowledge of the Dakota language would be valuable in performing the assigned task, but that qualification had been a secondary consideration.

During law school and while he served with the Army's Judge Advocate General's Corps, he had dropped a paper trail of articles and treatises raising concerns about the procedures followed by military tribunals in conducting court martials. He had questioned the military's authority to try enemy combatants and its jurisdiction over the Indian nations, which for many purposes had sovereign status. These were obscure topics in which few had any interest until an issue raised its ugly head. Yes, he had carved a niche of expertise there. And he was JAG until the President cut him loose, always mindful of the Corps' motto, "Soldier first, Lawyer always."

The promotion was nice. Will had never met an officer who was not hungry for promotion, and most nearly starved before one came their way in the peacetime Army. Of course, he had not earned it. But he assumed it was advance payment on services still expected of him, and the higher rank would increase his credibility should his presence be challenged. And if he botched the job, demotion could be implemented with the strike of a pen.

Sibley was still a colonel when Will had departed the Upper Agency, but the War Department must have been informed that promotion was forthcoming. Since Sibley commanded state militia, his promotion to brigadier general had likely required concurrence of both Major General Pope and Governor Ramsey.

General Pope worried Will some. Army gossip was no more reliable than any other kind, and fact and fiction would be soon separated, he supposed. An undeniable fact, however, was that Pope had been relieved of his command after his defeat at the Second Battle of Bull Run. It was not a huge step to conclude that his new command in the Department of the Northwest was, in a sense, a command in exile. He was said to be a pompous, bombastic man with a nasty temper, not hesitant to heap public humiliation upon those officers who displeased him. If these rumors were true, such a man, geographically detached from his superiors, might assume the role of God in the days ahead. He guessed he would learn soon enough.

His reverie was interrupted by a tapping on the door. "Come in," he called.

Billy opened the door and stepped in. He had bunked at the stable since his arrival, preferring that to a cot he had been offered in the barracks. "Checking to see if you got any orders. Me and Buster are getting restless."

"I do have instructions. It appears we are returning to the Upper Agency. I would like you to head out today. Stop at Ridgely and pick up Curley Coburn. Tell him we'll need him indefinitely. I may have to send letters to Snelling every few days, depending on developments."

"And when will you be coming?"

"I can't ride out till this afternoon sometime. I need to send a letter and telegram to my superiors, and I've been ordered to wear my uniform henceforth. I'll get my uniforms out of the storage locker, and I will likely require the assistance of the post tailor."

"Sounds like you're going to be all gussied up the next time I see you."

"I suppose so. It's a long story, but my job is changing now. Let me write a note so you can check out a spare horse. No need to run them into the ground, though. I'll camp along the road tonight and try to make Mankato tomorrow night. I'll check in at Ridgely the next day to see if there is any news there before I move on to the Upper Agency. You and Curley will have a good lead on me. If there is something you think I should know, maybe one of you can double back and intercept me. I will plan to check in with Lieutenant Gere at Ridgely along the way, so you could leave a message with him, also. Today is October 6, so I should be at the Upper Agency by the ninth, no later than the tenth."

"How do I know what's important enough for one of us to double back?"

"A good question. Shows you are thinking. I should have explained. I never said anything before because I didn't think it had much to do with my mission. I will become a cavalry officer, but I am presently assigned to the Judge Advocate General's Corps. Do you know what that is?"

"Nope. Sounds hellish important, though. You some kind of judge or something?"

"Let's say I am a military lawyer. I can tell you I report directly to the War Department, and I am to observe how any punishment of the Sioux is being handled and notify my superiors about any steps that are being taken. I have no authority, but the people who have power want to know what is happening. Does that help?"

"Yep. If something don't seem right, I just hope I know it when I see it—or smell it."

After Billy left, Will plucked a second letter from his shirt pocket. It was a single page that had been enclosed in a separate envelope tucked in another envelope that included a letter to his mother. When he had stopped briefly at the farm during his ride to Fort Snelling, his mother had handed him Anja's letter with the admonition that a prompt reply would be in order. The letter was a mite perfunctory, he thought:

Dear Will,

I hope this finds you well. I have explained in a letter to your mother that I have accepted a teaching position in Mankato to commence mid-January. In the meantime, I will be employed by Hank's General Store as a bookkeeper and clerk. If the arrangement works out well for both the proprietor and me, I may continue the bookkeeping duties after school commences.

I am residing in a cabin about one mile north and a half mile west of Mankato. The address is 120 Dakota Road, Mankato. The address is ironic, is it not?

It would be nice to hear from you, if you find time to write.
Sincerely,
Anja

Anja had told him nothing she had not already related to his mother in greater detail. His mother had informed him that the log cabin consisted of two bedrooms, a small kitchen and smaller parlor. It did have the uncommon luxury of a water line from the well to a small pump in the kitchen, if she could keep the line from freezing during bitter Minnesota winters. The property sat on 20 acres, which included some woodland that could be harvested for firewood. The house came with a little four-horse stable.

Anja had also advised his mother that Karina would be joining her in January to assist with teaching. Anja would continue to instruct her privately with the thought that Karina would qualify to enter high school in St. Paul at the eleventh or twelfth grade level the fall of the 1863 school term. Will was miffed just a bit that his mother had served as the conduit for any details. He missed Anja's constant presence more than he ever would have imagined. And the face of this dark, exotic beauty refused to be erased from his mind.

Chapter 42

ANJA WAS READING a book titled *Flower Fables*, written and published by an up and coming young author, Louisa May Alcott, a half dozen years earlier when the writer was only twenty-two years of age. She wore a pair of red men's long johns under a drab cotton robe and heavy wool socks. She sat in a chipped and scratched rocking chair near the crackling, sputtering fire that was due to be fed. The advantage of the tiny parlor was that the fireplace heated the room nicely, although she wished more of the warmth carried to the bedrooms. Since one bedroom was not in use, she kept the door to that one closed for now. The parlor had space for only two chairs, and the other was also an ancient rocker. A sturdy oak lamp table sat between the chairs, and she had only lighted the oil lamp a few minutes earlier when dusk started to set in.

Most of her books had disappeared in flames with the school at the Lower Agency. She was starting to rebuild her library and had been surprised to find she could do so cheaply, because books were not judged to be among the essentials for those settlers vacating the Western Minnesota River valley. Her employer, Henry Hellman, had been purchasing books from settlers who came to the store seeking to sell their personal belongings. He never paid more than a nickel for a book and allowed Anja to buy any title she selected at cost. If she had not needed the money to support herself, she thought she would have worked at the store simply for the book benefit. She loved her books, and she loved to write. She needed some time to pass, but she wondered if she might someday try to put down her own account of the Dakota War.

Sniffer lay on a buffalo hide rug in front of the fireplace when he caught her attention with a low growl and lifted his head. He got to his feet and ran to the door and commenced barking. Anja reached for the loaded shotgun that leaned against the wall next to the rocker. There had been few uprising atrocities that reached as far as the Mankato area, but there were still a few small war parties that had not surrendered and were raiding random farms. She thought it unlikely renegade Indians were outside. But Sniffer said somebody was. And there had been some no-goods ranging the area, scavenging what they could out of the chaos.

Her first instinct was to open the door to see who was in the yard. She thought better of it, however, and decided to wait. She placed her hand on Sniffer's head and scratched him behind the ears to calm him. "Quiet, boy."

A firm, but nonaggressive, rap sounded on the heavy door. She gently pushed Sniffer aside and leveled the shotgun toward the door. "Who is it?"

"Will," answered the familiar voice.

She lowered the shotgun, moved to the door and slid back the bolt that secured it. She opened the door and the light sifting through the opening from the parlor revealed a tall man in Army blues, with a dark wide-brimmed hat in hand. She hardly recognized him; she could not deny he cut a handsome specimen of a male.

"I see you've switched to scatter guns," he said, and smiled.

She had forgotten she still had the gun in her hands. "I'm sorry. You surprised me. Come in." She realized she was trembling for no reason she could explain. She moved aside and leaned the shotgun against the wall next to the doorway while Will stepped inside and closed the door behind him.

He cast his eyes about the room. "Cozy. Warm."

He turned to her, and his eyes fastened on hers. He extended his arms and moved toward her, and she slipped easily into his arms, relaxing as she found comfort there. They embraced for some moments before she stepped back, cocked her head to one side and studied him. "I've never seen you in uniform. It seems strange somehow. But you clean up quite nicely."

"Thank you. I've never seen you in long johns. Very fetching, I must say."

He smiled, and she was grateful her dark skin subdued most of her blushing. It occurred to her that smiles had been rare during their past days together. "I wasn't expecting company. I must look terrible."

"You could not look terrible if you tried. That's a fact. But I apologize for the surprise. I am passing through Mankato on my way to Fort Ridgely, then to the Upper Agency. This all came about rather suddenly. I didn't have time to write, and, on impulse, I decided to try to find your place." He hesitated. "I take that back. It wasn't impulse. I was anxious to see you, and I've been planning this since I left Snelling. I won't stay long, but I couldn't pass through without at least trying to see you."

"Where are you staying?"

"I'll find a room at the hotel or a boarding house in Mankato. That's why I'll be on my way soon."

"There's not a chance of finding a room in Mankato. With the refugee situation, there are ten people for each available room."

"I camped on the trail last night. I've got a pup tent and camping gear packed on Red. I'll just move on down the road a piece."

"That's ridiculous. You will stay here. I have an extra bedroom."

"That's kind of you. But that might cause some talk."

"You should have noticed that I don't have any neighbors nearby. But I don't think folks have much time for gossip these days."

"It's never so bad that folks don't make time for gossip."

"I suppose that sort of babble can sting, but it doesn't kill. And these past weeks, I've narrowed the list of things I intend to worry about in my life. And gossip failed to make the list. You're staying. I'll light another lantern for you, and you can put up Red and Warrior in the stable. Plenty of hay there. Grain in a few barrels. Buckets are hanging on the wall, and a water pump is just outside the stable door. Molly will be glad for the company."

While Will was putting up the horses, Anja opened the spare bedroom door, grateful that the bed was made up, and added a few split pieces of oak to the fire. She also confirmed that hot coals still heated the wood cookstove and put on a fresh pot of coffee. Confident Will would not have eaten, she warmed some bread, cooked some bacon slices, and placed the little sack of oatmeal cookies she had purchased from Maudie's Bake Shoppe on the table. Maudie's was a constant temptation because the bakery was attached to the general store, and the aroma of fresh-baked temptations drifted into the store throughout the day. Maudie happened to be the wife of Hank Hellman, Anja's employer, and Anja served as bookkeeper for the bakery side of the operation as well.

Anja was in the kitchen, just off the parlor, when Will returned with his Army haversack. "West bedroom," she called. "I've fixed a little supper for you. Come in here when you're ready."

When Will walked into the kitchen, she nodded for him to take a seat at the little table. She placed two mugs of steaming coffee on the table and a plate with two bacon sandwiches in front of Will. She sat down, facing him across the table.

He took a bite of his sandwich and closed his eyes as if savoring it. "Delicious. I hadn't realized I was so hungry. How did you know I hadn't eaten?"

"I spent some time with you. When I eat breakfast, I start thinking about dinner. It annoyed me sometimes that you never seemed to worry about when—or if—the next meal was going to take place."

"Well, I do appreciate this."

"You just eat but stop long enough to answer my questions."

"Teacher's going to give me a test?"

"Teacher's going to satisfy her curiosity. Last time I knew, you were a captain. Insignia on your uniform says 'major.'"

"Promotion."

"I'm sure you earned it, but it seems like you are climbing mighty fast."

"It's complicated. That's all I can say."

"And now you are wearing a uniform. Are you free to say what this is all about?"

"Most of it. Some is confidential. I hope you understand. It has nothing to do with my not trusting you."

"I understand that, and I wouldn't expect you to betray any secrets or confidences. I'm just a little puzzled by the sudden transformation."

"My orders come directly from Washington, and I report only to officials there." He continued, explaining his assignment to observe any trials or other proceedings regarding the Dakotas. "You might say that I am the eyes and ears for the folks in the Capitol. I have no authority here. I issue no orders."

"You are working for Abraham Lincoln, aren't you?"

"Well, he is my Commander in Chief, of course, as he is for all soldiers," he said evasively.

Anja smiled knowingly, "Spoken with the weasel words of a great lawyer. I will not press you further. You know, you did not tell me anything about your legal background until you told me about Lisbeth."

"I guess I had no cause."

"Of course, I knew by that time anyway."

"You did?"

"Your mother."

"Yes. My mother."

After they shared the cookies, Anja poured them each another cup of coffee and suggested they retreat to the warmth of the fireplace in the parlor. Will left his military coat and shirt in the bedroom and pulled on a wool sweater and dropped into the second rocker. They took up their conversation where they had left it.

"We were speaking of your mother. She recommended a lawyer in Mankato to assist Karina and me with our properties. Horace Meisenbach. Have you heard of him?"

"No, but I have been away from Minnesota for a long time and have been lucky if I got back to the farm twice in a year. And I have never had cause to use a lawyer here, or anywhere else for that matter."

"He's quite elderly but seems very knowledgeable about property. In fact, he owns this place. He and his wife lived here before they built a house in town. He has granted me a one-year lease and given me the option to buy it for eight hundred dollars when the lease runs out. After a two hundred dollar down payment, he would carry the balance for ten years. With interest, of course. What do you think?"

"I don't know what properties are selling for here, but this place is near enough to town, it could turn out to be a nice investment someday if you held on to it long enough. Dad's looking for a farm near his place for me to invest in. I've given him the go ahead and gave him power of attorney to negotiate terms while I'm away. I've got some money saved, and Dad doesn't think a bank loan would be a problem with land prices so low right now. Dad always says they won't make any more land. And, if I don't make it back, the land would still go to my folks."

His words left her feeling weak. "That's a terrible thing to say."

"What?"

"If you don't make it back."

"I'm sorry, but you of all people should be aware of that possibility."

"Let's not talk about it."

"Okay."

They sat silently for the better part of half an hour, staring into the fire. Anja found herself just savoring his presence. Finally, she asked, "When will you be back this way?"

"Difficult to say. I don't have a handle at all on where these Commission trials are headed."

"Will you stop here when you come through?"

"Of course. I'll be sending Billy or Curley with mail or telegraph messages to Fort Snelling to pass on to Washington. I'll see if they can swing past and drop off a letter on the return trip sometimes."

She brightened. "And I'll have one to send back." She hesitated to ask her next question but plunged ahead on the chance that Will might know something. "I wonder if Cut Nose was among those captured?"

He looked at her. "Why would you wonder about Cut Nose?"

She could not tell him the truth. She did not even know what the truth was. Or at least she was still denying it. "Well, we met him on the trail that day after he and his war party killed Karina's parents. I know Karina will want to know if he was among those captured."

"He was, I can promise you." Will told Anja about the incident that resulted in his and Billy's apprehending the Soldiers Lodge leader.

Anja felt conflicted at the news. By many accounts, Cut Nose had taken more white and mixed-blood lives than any other warriors. She could not wish him free or unpunished. But she had become convinced of her blood connection with this demon- man, as she was coming to think of him. Who was she? What was she, if this killer's blood ran in her veins? She tried to convince herself Cut Nose was just a soldier doing what he considered his duty. She found herself stopping just short of that conclusion, while conceding a valid argument could be made.

Will said, "There is something you're not telling me, but sometimes a little mystery makes a lady interesting."

The conversation shifted to more mundane subjects, childhood reminiscences, and the future, carefully avoiding the possibility that there might be no future. Anja was pleased to learn that Will hoped to return to Minnesota and carve out his life when the war was over, that a military career was not his destiny. She said nothing to discourage his plans. They talked until Will plucked a dented and battered watch from his trouser pocket and announced that midnight was closing in. She would have chatted through the night, but Will declared adjournment.

"I need to be riding out at sunrise. I suppose I should hit the hay."

"I understand. But you will let me fix a breakfast in the morning."

"That's not necessary."

"No. But it would make me feel like a good hostess. The room may be on the chilly side tonight, but there is goose-down quilt folded at the foot of the bed."

"I'll be fine. Remember, my other option was a wool army blanket on the hard ground."

Later, Anja lay in bed, sleep escaping her as she thought about her surprise visitor slumbering in the adjacent bedroom. It had seemed strange when they awkwardly said goodnight to each other and parted to go to their separate rooms. No embrace. No kiss. The behavior seemed unnatural to her. But would it have stopped with a kiss? What if he entered her room now, disrobed, and crawled between the sheets with her? What would she do? What a hussy she was, she thought. She had no doubt. She would have dealt with regrets later—if she, in fact, had regrets.

Chapter 43

WILL HAD DEPARTED Anja's house with a pleasantly full stomach after a breakfast of biscuits, eggs and ham, but he found himself nodding off in the saddle with the steady, rhythmic lope of his stallion as noon approached. He was paying now for that restless night when sleep had eluded him. The memory of his evening with Anja had been something he would savor in the days ahead, but he tried unsuccessfully to wipe away his recall of the awkwardness at bedtime when he wanted to take her in his arms but dared not. He had feared that his lust for her then might have triggered an unwelcome advance that would have spoiled the moment. He did not wish to risk losing something special he sensed might be growing between them.

This morning, though, they had kissed and embraced, albeit chastely, before he mounted Warrior and rode out.

Anja had told him she expected him to keep his promise to return as soon as he was able, and for his part, that time could not come soon enough.

As he neared what remained of New Ulm, he was surprised to find the frenzied activity there. Obviously, not all the Germans were abandoning the community. Dozens of men, and a scattering of women and children were clearing charred rubble away from the destroyed buildings and loading it onto wagons for hauling of anything that could not be salvaged to a dump site. The rapid echoes of hammers striking nails and the sawing of lumber told him that some had already started the task of putting the pieces of the town back together. He supposed it had always been true that some people were defeated by tragedy and adversity while others were made stronger by it and would rebuild their lives again.

When Will arrived at Fort Ridgely mid-afternoon, he found that the post was still a busy place, but uniformed soldiers had replaced sanctuary-seeking civilians. After leaving the horses at the stable, he notified headquarters of his presence at the fort in the event anyone should be trying to locate him. Then he tracked down Lieutenant Gere, who was supervising military crews in the reconstruction of buildings and other structures that had been destroyed or damaged outside the fort's perimeter. He liked Gere, and the young officer had unfailingly been a source of reliable information in the past.

Gere stood at attention and saluted when Will approached. Will returned the salute and said, "At ease, lieutenant." It felt foreign to him after his time out of uniform to stroll about the post being saluted and returning salutes when he encountered soldiers. He concluded he would adapt easily to the informality of civilian life when that time came.

"I didn't recognize the uniformed officer walking my way at first," the lieutenant said. "And I guess it's Major Nilsson now. Congratulations, sir."

"Thank you, Lieutenant. I just arrived less than an hour ago. I'm on my way to the Upper Agency. Whether I ride out tonight or in the morning depends upon what I can learn from you about what's happening up that way. It's been almost ten days since I left the Upper Agency." He explained his mission so the lieutenant might find it easier to sift out irrelevant information but remained vague as to the source of his authority.

Gere said, "May I speak frankly, sir?"

"Of course. Please do."

"Considering what you're looking at, I would be concerned about the way things are taking place up at Camp Release—that's what they call the village where they are confining prisoners and their families. They're holding several thousand Dakotas there. That includes women and kids, and the Army's rounding up more every day. Ridgely's coordinating food and supply shipments, but the Indians aren't allowed to forage on their own now, and we're just not getting enough supplies in to feed all the prisoners and fifteen hundred soldiers. Army gets fed first, of course. So the Indians are close to starving. There's talk that they might move all the Dakotas to the Redwood Agency, which would bring them closer to Ridgely."

"That makes a certain sense, I guess, since Ridgely is the Army's official headquarters and the central warehouse for food and other supplies."

"I don't know what that does to the trials."

"Tell me about the trials."

"Well, the rumor is that General Sibley and General Pope have been fussing about the trials. They've got about four hundred to five hundred Dakotas identified for trial. General Sibley first appointed a three-member commission to conduct trials of the prisoners. Then General Pope sent word there had to be five members, so that's where it ended up."

Will thought Sibley had no authority to appoint a commission, since the war had been federalized and he was commander of state militia. Pope, as a major general and federal officer was clearly in charge, although Will would argue the commissions were without power regardless. He also knew that politicians and the military would decide the fate of Dakotas adjudged guilty long before any court touched the issues.

Will said, "I heard that a commission would be established while I was at Fort Snelling. From what you say, it appears the commission is already in place."

"Yes, sir. It's been hearing cases for a week or better. I understand most, if not all, the cases they've heard have resulted in convictions and death sentences. At least a dozen or more. There's talk that the hangings will start soon."

Will decided he should not delay riding for Camp Release and the Upper Agency. He would procure fresh horses from the Army stable and leave immediately—ride all night, if necessary. The executions must be halted. He could not order the hangings halted, but he could point out to General Sibley legislation enacted by Congress and signed by the President in July that declared that the "judgment of every court martial shall be authenticated by the signature of the President." Hopefully, that would give him cause to defer any action until he corresponded further with General Pope in St. Paul.

"Thank you, lieutenant. As usual, you have been very helpful."

"Anytime, sir."

Will wheeled and headed for the stable to retrieve his saddlebags and pencil and paper for writing a letter and telegram. He had been instructed to communicate by letter, but he considered the possibility of executions an emergency. He was pondering the recruitment of a courier when he saw Billy Buck emerging from the stable and headed his way. He noticed Billy studying him as he approached.

When they met, Billy said, "Major, huh? I'll be damned."

"You got here just in time. I was going to be forced to dig up another courier."

"Got some stuff I figured you should know about. They got a commission up at the Upper Agency that's running Dakotas through trials like cattle through a chute. There's at least four hundred going to be tried. That might take a spell. But they're planning to start hangings in a day or two."

"I'm leaving for the Upper Agency tonight. Where do I find Curley Coburn?"

"We've been staying at John Otherday's place. Curley would be on a hay pile in John's stable if you show up before sun is up. Otherwise, he'll be snooping around the edges of Camp Release."

"I'll be there. I need to write some messages for you to carry to Snelling. Find fresh horses and pick up whatever rations you need for the trip. If anybody gives you a hassle, refer them to me."

"Won't be no hassle. Guy at the quartermaster's is a friend, and I'll just help myself to the horses. It's been so crazy here, nobody will even notice."

Chapter 44

WILL ARRIVED AT John Otherday's several hours before sunrise and went directly to the stables. He tied both Army mounts to the corral fence and hoisted his haversack and gear off the sorrel gelding that had served as a pack animal for the last leg of the journey. Both horses had shown strength and stamina, and he would see that they were well cared for.

He opened the stable door and stepped inside, but the darkness kept him from locating Curley. He had planned to just stretch out and nap a bit himself until sunrise. He started when a voice whispered from out of the gloom. "Identify yourself. I got a shotgun pointed at your gut."

"It's Will Nilsson, Curley."

Curley Coburn emerged from the black shroud of the night. "Sorry, Captain. Can't be too careful these days."

"I understand, Curley. It's reassuring that nobody's going to sneak up on you."

"Me, either," came a deep voice from behind him.

Will wheeled and saw the bear-like form of John Otherday outlined in the entryway by a backdrop of moonlight. Otherday smiled and stepped toward him with his hand extended. As they shook hands, he said, "Saw somebody in uniform dismount in the yard and head for the stable. That didn't concern me much, but it seemed strange, and I knew Curley was bedded down out here. Sleeping with one eye open has got to be a habit with me."

"I didn't intend to disturb everybody. I met up with Billy at Ridgely, and he said I might find a place in the stable to toss my bedroll. I've been riding all night, and I thought I'd grab a few hours' sleep. Then, I've got to locate General Sibley."

"That's easy enough," Curley said. "His command tent is at the encampment just off Camp Release. I can take you there. Why don't you catch some shuteye? I'll put the horses up."

"I'll take you up on that." Then he directed a question to Otherday. "I just learned yesterday that the military commission is already conducting trials. Tell me, have there been any executions yet?"

"No, but they're chomping at the bit to hang somebody. The public is screaming for it. I have nothing against General Sibley, but he's a politician and has an ear turned to the voters. Of course, General Pope is in St. Paul, and my guess is the newspapers up that way are hollering for revenge. Once Sibley gets official authorization from Pope, the hangings will start. The commission has sentenced at least twenty to die so far, and they probably have four hundred cases yet to take up. It makes me sick. Innocent men are bound to die, even some who helped the whites. I am even looking over my own shoulder."

"I hope I can at least delay the executions. But I don't know how much more I can accomplish. I will see Sibley in the morning."

Otherday said, "The general's been under a lot of pressure. He has been criticized for moving his troops like a parade of snails to New Ulm and Fort Ridgely. Now he cannot decide anything without being second-guessed by General Pope. I got a feeling your visit isn't going to make him feel any better."

Chapter 45

U P CLOSE, GENERAL Henry Sibley appeared a younger man than Will expected, not much beyond fifty years, if that, he estimated. His neatly-trimmed beard and receding hair were gray, but he had a young man's skin tone and appeared trim and fit. He had greeted Will with understandable suspicion and likely would have claimed he was too busy for a meeting had Will not presented his Presidential credentials. Will could hardly fault the man for that. He doubted any man enjoyed dealing with someone who was ostensibly a spy sent by his superiors.

They sat on two canvas folding chairs in the general's wall tent, a wobbly folding table between them. Sibley seemed ill at ease and chewed nervously on the tip of an unlit cigar. "I think I saw you at Fort Ridgley," Sibley said. "Out of uniform."

"Yes, sir. I was instructed not to wear a uniform on my previous assignment."

"And may I ask what that was?"

"It was non-military. I was directed to report on the seriousness of Dakota uprising rumors to an official in the administration. Of course, that question was answered as soon as hostilities broke out."

"An official? At what level?"

"I am sorry, but I cannot say, sir."

"Your credentials are signed by the Secretary of War. That is high enough up the chain of command to force my attention. The Secretary's letter states that you are to be an observer of any commission or tribunal proceedings. What does that mean?"

"It has been made clear to me that I am to observe and report. I have no authority to issue orders or directives, and I am not to participate. I am entitled to attend the trials."

"I see."

"I should make you aware I am presently attached to the Judge Advocate General's Corps. Although I am not to be a legal advisor to the military commission, I may occasionally express an opinion to you regarding legal issues raised by the conduct of the commission. You are free to disregard as you choose. In most instances, I will reserve my opinions for my immediate superiors."

"I will not pretend to welcome your presence, but I will see that Secretary Stanton's directive is complied with. I can assure you General Pope will not be pleased to hear of this development, and I suspect he will enter a protest to the department. There will be no trials today, pending word I am awaiting from General Pope, but I have scheduled twenty executions for tomorrow."

"That is why I felt it was urgent I contact you as soon as I arrived here."

"I don't understand."

Will decided this was a moment for diplomacy. "You have been a very busy man ever since the threat of an uprising appeared last summer, and then you have had to gather troops and lead them into battle. It would have been nothing short of a miracle for you to have received word of the bill passed by Congress and signed into law in July, so I felt duty-bound to make you aware of it."

"What are you talking about? What law?"

"A law that says every judgment of a court martial shall be authenticated by the President. I am suggesting that execution without the President's approval could be a violation of the law."

"I don't think this is technically a court martial. These are enemy combatants, not soldiers. Does the law apply here?"

"Only the courts can say, but do you want to be the man adjudged to have wrongfully killed dozens of Dakotas in violation of law?"

"I would still be a hero in the state of Minnesota."

"I don't know how much help that would be at your own court martial or in any decision by superiors to remove you from your command."

Sibley turned silent. He had obviously not considered the potential consequences. Finally, he said, "I never relished the hangings anyway. I had many friends among the Dakotas during my trading years. I will send a message to General Pope and will proceed with executions only upon receipt of his specific order."

Several days after Sibley's deferral of the executions, Will learned that the brigadier general had received an order to move all trials to the Lower Agency. That order would have crossed in the courier deliveries with Sibley's request for instructions regarding executions, but he figured implementation of the order gave Sibley another excuse to set aside plans for the hangings.

Within a matter of a few days, over four hundred Dakota prisoners, chained two by two, commenced the march to the Lower Agency. They were joined by families and other tribesmen interested in the trials, so that as many as two thousand Sioux flooded the rutted road that led to the new trial setting. The roadway was lined with surviving settlers who screamed epithets and tossed stones at the walking, stumbling Indians, many of whom lowered their heads or averted their eyes from the angry onlookers.

But Will, riding alongside the column but beyond the rim of guards, noticed some of the warriors, even though chained at their ankles, stood erect and held their heads high, defeated but defiant. He recognized one Dakota among the undaunted. Cut Nose. And he remembered Anja's puzzling curiosity about the warrior's whereabouts.

Chapter 46

THE TRIALS RECONVENED at the Lower Agency on October 15. A few were conducted in a tipi and a half dozen outdoors, but most were carried out in a small, square-shaped, log building known as Franqois LaBathe's Summer Kitchen. LaBathe had been a trader killed on the first day of the uprising, and the structure was one of the few not burned out at the Lower Agency. During the several days before reconvening of the trials and after arrival of the prisoners at the Lower Agency, General Sibley had warmed up a bit to Will and had started confiding some of his frustrations to the much younger major.

Will suspected that the new friendliness came from a strategy of self-preservation on the general's part. He was aware Will would be observing many of the commission trials and would be reporting to someone at the War

Department. On the other hand, he was duty bound to obey the orders of General Pope who had ordered that the trials be completed quickly. Sibley told Will that twenty-nine cases had been heard by the commission at the Upper Agency, resulting in twenty convictions. That left three-hundred-sixty-three trials which General Pope had ordered Sibley to complete by November 10, preferably sooner.

Will attended the first trial conducted in the summer kitchen. Sibley had provided him a list of the commission members. Colonel William Crooks, who was a West Point graduate and Regular Army officer, served as president of the commission. The other members consisted of state militia officers under Sibley's command: Lieutenant Colonel William R. Marshall, Captain Hiram S. Bailey, Captain Hiram P. Grant, and Lieutenant Rollin C. Olin, who was designated as Judge Advocate. Lieutenant Isaac Heard served as trial recorder. Will had been informed that the young recorder was an ambitious prosecutor in civilian life. Reverend Stephen Riggs acted as interpreter. With his own knowledge of Dakota, Will figured he would at least be able to evaluate the accuracy of the interpreter's translations.

He had always been troubled by the judge advocate's role in military tribunals. He had written articles for law journals contending that the procedure established by Article 69 of the Articles of War violated the due process clause of the Fifth Amendment to the United States Constitution. Article 69 provided that the judge advocate, who was also a commission member, would prosecute any alleged crime and would also act as counsel for the prisoner for the purpose of objecting to leading questions or inquiries made to the prisoner, the answer to which might tend to incriminate the defendant.

Will sat with several other officers and three reporters on benches located along the wall behind the commission members, who were placed at a long table facing a solitary chair on which each accused would sit. There was no need for a counsel table, since the defendants would have no attorney other than the judge advocate when he chose to change his prosecutorial hat to the defense hat. A guard stood on each side of the door at the opposite end of the room, where prisoners would enter and exit with armed escorts. The recorder, Isaac Heard, sat at the commission table and the interpreter off to one side.

The first trial involved Moon Eyes, a young, stocky warrior, who spoke no English. There were no witnesses for examination. Lieutenant Olin, as judge advocate, read the charges, which declared the warrior had personally murdered two children at one settler's farm and killed and mutilated a husband and wife at another. The Dakota was asked to enter a plea. The interpreter translated charges and explained what the plea met. Moon Eyes said he was not guilty. The judge advocate recited what other persons had related about the killings. Any eyewitnesses were dead, and the evidence would have been inadmissible as hearsay in a civilian court. The Dakota was determined guilty and sentenced to death after a forty-five minute trial.

After the first trial, the commission improved its efficiency, and a total of fifteen Indians were tried and found guilty. In two cases a witness appeared to testify. All other convictions were based upon what Will considered anecdotal evidence. In no instance had the judge advocate intervened on behalf of the accused or spoken on behalf of any defendant.

When the hearings were dismissed for the day, Will was notified by a young private that he was invited to General Sibley's tent to join him for supper in two hours. Will accepted and then went to his own tent and wrote a quick report to Hanscomb, informing the President's aide that trials had commenced at the Lower Agency and expressing his procedural misgivings. He then located Curley Coburn and dispatched him to Fort Snelling.

General Sibley was a congenial host as they dined on beefsteak and fried potatoes at a small table in the general's tent, but Will sensed that his mood was downcast. They discussed the weather and everything but the trials while they ate. Afterward, the general poured them each a small glass of whiskey and wasted no time getting down to business.

"What is your impression of the trials?" General Sibley asked.

Will decided to speak bluntly. "There is a name increasingly being applied to proceedings like these. Kangaroo courts. The defendant is presumed guilty, contrary to the presumption of innocence that is fundamental in the civilian court system. There are no rules to protect the accused, no lawyer to intercede on his behalf. I daresay most of the defendants have no real understanding of what is taking place."

"Do you think innocent people are being convicted?"

"There certainly could be, but most probably have killed whites. As far as justice is concerned, though, this is all pretense. The convictions are responses to public outcry for retribution, the innocent be damned."

"I share your concerns," Sibley said, "but General Pope has issued his orders. Any Dakota who had any complicity in the conflict, whether a witness can attest to his killing of a settler or any person or not, is to be subject to the death penalty. He is not backing away from expediting the trials. We must pick up the pace. Tomorrow, we will be sending six or more Dakotas at a time before the commission. We must average twenty-five trials daily to complete our goals."

"You cannot be serious?"

"I am serious. General Pope would like to proceed with executions within another week. I just want to make clear I am following orders. I am troubled by this. I know the Dakota people. As a trader and representative to Congress—and, finally, as governor, I had many friends among the Sioux and worked closely with them. Many Dakotas and mixed bloods had no part of this. Yet with only a few exceptions, neither the public nor the military makes distinctions."

It was clear to Will that Sibley was having second thoughts about the commission trials and the frantic rush to judgments. Again, he was using Will partially to cover his highly exposed ass. Will could not fault him for it.

When Will returned to his own tent, he found Billy Buck stretched out on the ground in front, his head, resting against his bedroll. "Got a room for the night?" he asked.

"Spread out your bedroll in the tent. Thanks to General Sibley I ended up with accommodations fit for a general."

Billy got up and tossed his bedroll in the tent. "It appears like you got room for three or more like me in here."

"Curley may show up, sometimes, but not tonight. He's on his way to Snelling. Surprised you didn't pass him, but I suppose you each have your own shortcuts. No cots here, but somebody rounded up a chair and a small table, which comes in handy for my notes and reports. Now, I assume you got the telegram and letter off?"

"Yep." He pulled an envelope from his jacket pocket and handed it to Will. "Got this back fast."

Will pulled the telegram from the envelope and read it. WELL DONE STOP ORDER TO POPE SOON STOP HANSCOMB.

The message told him little beyond Hanscomb's evident satisfaction with his report. It appeared some action would be forthcoming from President Lincoln, and Will assumed that would be made known to him in due course. Now he just wanted to grab a decent night's sleep, which he had been unable to claim for many days.

But sleep failed to arrive. Instead, he lay cocooned in his blankets ruminating about the trials. It troubled him that the interpreter for the commission, Reverend

Riggs, appeared to be working for the prosecution, gathering evidence and interrogating witnesses prior to the so-called trials, even assisting with the writing of the charges.

And, as was not uncommon in criminal cases, some of the accused had become witnesses for the prosecution, hoping to procure leniency for themselves. One of these, Joseph Godfrey, or Otakle, a mulatto married to a Dakota woman, had been among the first convicted. His memory was so perfect and rehearsed as to cause Will to question the man's credibility. Godfrey had a melodious voice, as Will had heard someone mention, and what some lawyers called an "affidavit face" that commanded belief. Will wondered how Godfrey could have so clearly recollected many of the atrocities without participating in them.

Chapter 47

ON OCTOBER 20, Will was on his way to the summer kitchen for another day of trials, when a seasoned, pot-bellied sergeant summoned him to General Sibley's command tent. Will promptly altered his course and walked briskly in the direction of the general's quarters. When he reached his destination, he found Sibley at the table in his tent, holding a mug of coffee and his coat snugged tightly about his shoulders and chest.

Will saluted, "Sir, you wished to speak with me?"

Sibley responded with a half salute and nodded for Will to sit in the other chair. "Coffee? I've got a pot. There is another cup on the bench just behind you."

"No. But thank you, sir."

Sibley pushed a sheet of parchment across the table. "Read this, Major. You will find it interesting."

The words were written on the letterhead of Major General John Pope. *To Brigadier General Henry Sibley: Be advised that by order dated October 17,1862, the President directs that no executions be made without his sanction. Major General John Pope.*

The message and its terseness suggested that Pope was making clear that the decision was not his doing, and Will suspected the general was boiling mad about the President's intervention. Will was confident Pope would not be taking the heat for the decision, and Lincoln's directive was likely being leaked to the press so that the predictable public uproar would be aimed at the President.

Will said, "This seems to remove any ambiguity from your position. I would think you welcome the President's assumption of responsibility."

"Absolutely. General Pope has been pressing for executions to commence, and I feared I would be determined insubordinate if I did not do something soon. Now we can proceed with the trials, render verdicts and impose sentences, and then throw it all in Lincoln's lap." Sibley added sarcastically, "Of course, he really needs this nasty bit of business with the war going on."

"Lincoln does not have an enviable job."

"No. I did not vote for him. And I thought of Lincoln as an imposter President early on. He received less than forty percent of the popular vote and a narrow majority in the electoral college, so it's hard to say he had a mandate to do anything. I am a Northern Democrat and was a Douglas man myself. But Lincoln's earned my grudging respect."

Will was not about to engage in a political discussion with a general. Will held a healthy suspicion of the political class but had voted for Lincoln as the lesser of evils, which, more often than not, was how he ended up making his political choices. He had not anticipated a civil war when he cast his ballot, however, and harbored misgivings about the necessity of the war and the rebellion that led to it. Personal doubts aside, Will saw himself as a soldier bound to do his duty, and, as the Commander in Chief's eyes and ears along the Minnesota River, he was determined to do just that. "General, I truly appreciate being informed about the President's order. It puts my mind at ease."

Sibley said, "I wonder who was responsible for this?"

Will replied with a nervous chuckle. "I cannot imagine. That is many steps above my pay grade."

"Seems like more than coincidence. We have our little chat about your concern with the executions, and in just about the time it would take for word to get to Washington and back, Lincoln sends his order."

"I have had no communication with Lincoln, I assure you." Will rationalized that his words fell somewhat short of a lie, but he did not wish to pursue the discussion. "Now, General, if you will excuse me, the first trial is likely underway." He did not add that in a half-hour's time, two trials had probably been completed.

Will had a special interest in this day's trials. At the present pace of adjudications, Case No. 96 should come up for trial by late morning. The defendant was an Indian listed on the trial roster as Mahpeokanaje, one of at least three spellings he had seen of the name that translated to Who Stands on a Cloud, but whose bearer was better known as Cut Nose.

As usual, the trials went quickly. In most cases, there were no witnesses, only allegations read by Lieutenant Olin, the judge advocate, a few questions asked and then interpreted by Reverend Riggs, denials by the accused, and a finding of guilt by the Commission. Cut Nose's trial was the last of a group of four Dakotas brought in chains before the commission.

Cut Nose, attired in buckskins, was an imposing figure standing before the commission, the tallest of any warrior who had so far been brought forth for trial, his muscular physique impressive, head held high, and his dark eyes unflinching. His eyes met Will's and held his gaze for several moments, leaving no doubt that the notorious Dakota recognized him.

The judge advocate read charges that alleged that on the first day of the uprising Cut Nose had participated in the murders of two men, four women, and eleven children. Will was surprised when a witness was called to testify to one of the incidents known as the Massacre at Beaver Creek.

Lieutenant Olin commenced examination of the witness. "Would you state your name?"

The witness replied, "Lewis Thiele."

"And have you seen the defendant who is seated before this commission on any prior date?"

"Yes, sir. On the first day of the uprising at Beaver Creek."

"Briefly, please explain the circumstances."

"This man and some other Indians attacked some wagons of folks trying to escape to Fort Ridgely. I couldn't miss him because of his size and the scar on his nose and face."

"And did you see him kill people?"

"I did. Including my wife and four-year-old little girl. He shot one man off the wagon seat. I saw him and others take their knives and kill children in the wagons. Four women and eleven children. All killed."

Cut Nose, when asked questions, began ranting in Dakota, speaking so rapidly that Will had difficulty understanding him. He was able to discern enough to know the Dakota was denying the charges. The commission chairman, Colonel Crooks, blurted out in anger, instructing the interpreter, "Tell him to shut up, or I will split his head open with my sword."

The interpreter replied, "I believe he understands English, Colonel, but I will inform him." Reverend Riggs spoke calmly to Cut Nose, who simply shrugged.

Will thought that the judicial temperament of the colonel left something to be desired, knowing that the remarks in a civilian court would have been considered seriously prejudicial. The judge advocate also recited other murders attributed to Cut Nose for which he was not being formally charged, obviously constituting hearsay and irrelevant to the case before the commission. No mention was made of Karina's parents' killings, but the identity of the attackers there, at best, was strongly circumstantial. Of course, Will and Billy had brought Cut Nose up short in his attempt to kill another white woman. Will could never assert the man's innocence. It was the process that troubled him.

The judge advocate in his dual role as defense counsel for the accused was consistent with his handling of the previous cases. He made no procedural objections and asked no questions that might elicit a response favorable to the defense.

The time that transpired for Cut Nose's trial was, perhaps, the longest of those held at the Lower Agency. It had taken the commission almost forty-five minutes to find him guilty and sentence him to death by hanging.

Chapter 48

WHEN CUT NOSE had seen Stalking Wolf in the room with the white chiefs, the shadow of death hovered over him. He did not understand this thing they called "trial," but the presence of Stalking Wolf told him it was just one more step on the trail to the end of his life's journey.

Now, as he sat chained with ten warriors in a tipi without fire to ward off the bitter chill that rode in with descending darkness, he felt nothing about the ruling of the white chiefs. What had angered him were the lies of the man they called "witness" and the boy bluecoat who asked questions and made accusations from words on a paper. Cut Nose had killed many whites, including women and children, and he would kill more given the opportunity. But he did not know of the place called Beaver Creek. He had not done the things they said. That was why he yelled at them, denied their lies, and called them fools.

He had understood the words spoken in the room where Stalking Wolf watched. He knew the white tongue but had refused then to speak their words. But nothing that was said there had made sense to him. Why had they not just killed him? That would have been the Dakota way. When the Sioux captured Chippewas there was no thing called "trial." They were enemies, and they were killed, perhaps tortured first if there was time. It was war, and women and children were not spared unless a warrior considered a woman suitable for wife or child worthy of adoption. And no different treatment was expected from a Chippewa enemy.

So now they were to hang. The whites had not even the decency to grant them warriors' deaths. Knife or thunder stick, even war axe, would bring an end with dignity. But to die like a rabbit caught in a snare?

Chapter 49

WILL KEPT BILLY Buck and Curley Coburn busy with courier duties as the trials continued, sending a report to Hanscomb every three days. Often his riders would meet on the road to Fort Snelling as one returned with a reply and the other carried new missives to Snelling for telegraphing and mailing. As the trials wound down and the first of November approached, Billy rode in after dark while Will sat at the table in his tent writing under the shimmering light of the oil lantern. The courier placed an envelope on the table.

"Thanks, Billy. Toss down your bedroll and put up your horse. I can smell grub cooking nearby. Find it and tell the Army cook that Major Nilsson sent you."

"Don't worry. I probably won't even have to pull rank. Never been turned down for a meal yet."

After Billy left, Will opened the envelope and removed the letter and what appeared to be a voucher or ticket. He assumed the dispatch was important since he rarely received a letter from Hanscomb. Correspondence from his superior was rare, except for an occasional brief obscure message. He spread the crisp sheets out on the table and read:

Dear Major Nilsson:

An order has been issued to General Pope that all notes, transcripts, or other documentation collected with respect to the Dakota trials shall be delivered to you at Fort Snelling on November 15. You are directed to procure an adjutant of your choosing to assist with the security of the documents and forthwith deliver same to the War Department in Washington, D.C. where you will receive further orders.

You will be an unofficial part of a team evaluating the trial evidence and proceedings. Since you attended most of the trials, your input will be most valuable. You should give some thought to identifying those defendants who were engaged in acts of war in contrast to those who participated in crimes and atrocities committed against civilians.

Lodging has been arranged at the Hotel Jefferson for you and your adjutant. Train tickets are enclosed with this letter.

If time allows following the trial, allow yourself a brief furlough to attend to any personal business prior to departing for the Capitol.

Respectfully,

Charles Hanscomb

Counselor to the President

Will pushed the letter aside and sighed, staring at the lantern on the table and momentarily mesmerized by its flickering flame. At least the curtain of mystery regarding his assignment had been lifted. President Lincoln was taking the Dakota War trials very seriously, and Will's role was more than a token mission. It was sobering to consider that he might be a significant part of life or death decisions regarding the fate of the Sioux warriors.

The obvious adjutant would be Billy, although customarily such a person would be an officer. However, Billy had effortlessly become his right hand. He planned to join the Army anyway. Will decided he would send him to Snelling to enlist along with a letter directing he be issued a uniform and insignia appropriate to the rank of private. He would specify that Billy Buck was being assigned until further notice to a special War Department

Ron Schwab

mission and that training would be deferred pending completion of his assignment.

Will was relieved to learn that the administration appeared to be recognizing the legal difference between enemy combatants and criminals. According to Sibley, General Pope was insisting no such distinction be made. Indians who faced the Army at the battles of Fort Ridgley, Abercrombie, Birch Coulee, Wood Lake, and others would not be treated as adversaries acting in a military capacity. Such acts were to be treated as capital crimes on the same level as attacks on civilian settlers and their families. As an avid student of military history, Will knew that it was unprecedented for a military commission to try enemy combatants for firing shots on a battlefield. And if the conflict was not considered a war, why was a military commission claiming jurisdiction over the uprising's consequences? It was a legal quagmire.

Will was grateful for the opportunity for furlough. It was time to return Warrior to his parents' farm and visit them for a few days. He hoped to see Anja in Mankato before he moved on to Fort Snelling to await delivery of the trial notes and transcripts. He could not wash the woman from his mind and did not want to. But war duties were likely no more than a few months ahead, and his fate seemed too uncertain to raise the subject of any fu-

{360}

ture they might share. With that thought, he got up and undressed and dropped onto his blankets. Sleep claimed him instantly, and he did not even hear Billy enter the tent a short while later.

A week later, on November 5, Will walked out of the summer kitchen after the last guilty verdict was entered. In thirty-seven days of sessions, the commission had conducted three hundred ninety-two trials, resulting in sixty-nine acquittals, twenty prison sentences and three hundred and three sentenced to death by hanging. In return for his testimony for the prosecution, Joseph Godfrey, the oft-performing witness who had ended up testifying in over fifty cases, had his death sentence commuted to ten years in prison.

Will encountered General Sibley outside the improvised courtroom and inquired about the disposition of the prisoners.

"I already have General Pope's orders in hand," Sibley said. "We are to march all the families—women, children, old folks, and non-convicted—to Fort Snelling. That's anywhere from fifteen hundred to two thousand people to walk one hundred twenty-five miles or more. And we'll take them past New Ulm, Henderson, St. Peters, and Mankato along the way. I'm concerned about the public's reaction to this. And it's starting to get damned cold. I don't know what kind of a calamity we'll have if a snow storm moves in while the move is in progress."

"Are you keeping the prisoners here?"

"No. We start moving the families out tomorrow. Two days later, we parade the condemned to South Bend near Mankato."

"Wouldn't it have made more sense to just allow the families to stay here or return to their villages?"

"Of course. But when have the military or the government made sense?"

"I would need to think about that for a spell. Anyway, I don't envy your job, General, and I wish you well. I'll be riding out tomorrow morning myself. I have new orders. I hope we meet up again."

Chapter 50

ANJA SAT AT an ancient, but sturdy, oak desk in the storeroom at Hank's General Store. She had been mildly surprised to discover she had a knack for keeping books, and, furthermore, found she enjoyed it. Her employer had taken a few accounting books in trade for foodstuffs from a New Ulm businessman who had decided to seek his fortune in a friendlier climate and given them to Anja. She had read both from cover to cover and was now studying them more carefully, setting up Henry Hellman's books systematically, so he could determine precisely where he was making money and where he was losing it. The boss was an unapologetic capitalist, and he loved her analysis of the numbers.

Already, Hellman was pressing her to work for him full-time when the teaching term ended. She did not discount the possibility. The man's entrepreneurial spirit was contagious, and she respected his integrity and work ethic, thinking she could learn much from him in what she thought of as the college of the real world. If not now, she was certain she would someday search out business ventures of her own. She had already nailed down the deal to buy her house and the twenty acres it sat on. She could always hold it as a rental property if she someday returned to her parents' farm.

As she was puzzling over some figures, Maudie Hellman entered the storage room. She was a petite auburn-haired woman in her late forties, who was often caught snacking on her own culinary delights, and her waist and rear seemingly never retained an ounce of the sinful stuff. So far, Anja had enjoyed the same immunity, but she feared the years ahead might not grant her the dietary luxury. "Looking for something, Maudie?" she asked.

"You."

"Me? What can I help you with?"

"Well, I hate to let him go, but there is a soldier out there—don't tell Hank I said this—who might be the most scrumptious man I've ever seen. And he's got the darkest bedroom eyes. His name's Will, and he's asking for you."

A surge of excitement raced through Anja, and she dropped her pencil on the table, scooted the chair back from the desk and stood up to go out and greet Will. But Maudie blocked her way and raised her hand and smiled. "Don't seem so anxious. Keep the man guessing a bit. I'll send him back here, where you can have a bit of privacy."

"You would do that?"

"Honey, Hank first kissed me in our boss's storeroom in Ohio, and he still traps me back here on occasion. Don't let his mild, business-like demeanor fool you. Those five kids didn't show up from our shaking hands. The man can be a stallion."

Maudie let loose an outburst of laughter that somehow didn't fit the refined, pleasant grandmother Anja had come to know. Once again, she thanked her dark skin for covering her blush. She did not think she could ever look at ample-girthed Henry Hellman again without remembering this conversation and conjuring up a naked image of Maudie's stallion.

After stifling her laughter, Maudie disappeared through the curtained doorway, leaving Anja to wait while she became increasingly nervous. It was all so confusing. She had still not sorted out just what Will was to her or, for that matter, what she was to him. It seemed interminably long, but she knew only seconds had passed before Will pulled the curtain aside and stepped into the room with hat in hand.

"Anja," he called.

She stepped from behind a stack of crates that blocked his vision. "Will, what a wonderful surprise."

He opened his arms and stepped toward her. She did not hesitate and moved naturally into his embrace, and she did not resist when his lips pressed against hers, at first softly, and then hungrily. Her body clung to his like a saddle to a horse's back, and she thought she should be thankful for the barrier afforded by the puffy skirt of her dress and undergarments. But she was not. Finally, he released her and stepped back.

"I guess I was a bit exuberant," he said, smiling sheepishly.

"You did take my breath away. In a nice way. I didn't know if you would get here. The Dakota families passed through yesterday on their journey to Fort Snelling. I saw them. It was a pitiful sight. At least they had most of the old and decrepit on wagons. And the children who were too small to walk. But they looked weak and hungry. Some folks screamed at them and threw things. The prisoners should arrive at South Bend today, but I hear they won't be there long. There is talk they will be moved to some buildings in town being leased by the Army for temporary prisons. The Army is putting up some log structures, too, it appears." She felt her mood sinking. "The executions will be here in Mankato."

"I visited my folks for several days and dropped Warrior off there. I'm not assigned to the troops that are moving the Dakotas, so you probably know more about what's going on than I do."

"It's terrible. But let's not talk about that now. How long will you be in Mankato?"

"That depends."

"On what?"

"If you can make time to see me. I have orders to report to Fort Snelling by noon on the fifteenth. This is the tenth. I will need to leave by the morning of the thirteenth to cushion my time a bit."

"I can take a day off, and there will be evenings. You will stay with me, of course."

Will was silent a moment. "I'm not sure that is a good idea."

She knew what he meant but feigned ignorance. "It will give us more time together. And I doubt if you can find a hotel or boarding house in town that's not full. What the Army has not claimed, the newspaper people have. They're like ants swarming in here. Besides, you will offend me if you don't lodge at my house."

He still seemed hesitant. "If you put it that way. I don't want to offend you."

"That settles it. I won't be off work for two hours. I'll give you my key, and you can ride out to the house and put up your horse and make yourself at home. It would be nice to have a fire started and come home to a warm house for a change. I'll bring along some baked goods from Maudie's Bake Shoppe and see what else I can rustle up when I get home."

"That should work out fine. When you aren't home during the next few days, I'll do some checking on the prison arrangements and write up what reports I can on the military situation here."

She stepped to him and they kissed again, more chastely this time. After Will departed, she sat back down at the desk. She knew Maudie would be anticipating a report, but she would be damned if she was going to give her friend an opportunity to interrogate her just now. She had work to finish up and things to ponder. Like the agenda for a serious conversation with Wilhelm Erik Nilsson.

Chapter 51

WILL REINED IN the blood bay when they turned off the roadway and into the yard of Anja's little house. He tugged the collars of his wool Army coat around his neck to thwart the chill of a biting wind that had started to whip up. He hoped it did not carry snow on its tail. He surveyed the building site, taking note of the stream that tumbled over its rocky bed some fifty feet from the house. No farm ground here, but the trees and undergrowth near the house could be cleared to make a decent garden spot, and a perpetual supply of firewood lurked nearby waiting for harvest by saw or axe. About ten acres of thick grass lay beyond the stable, enough to graze no more than a horse or two during pasture season.

Sniffer's bark pulled his eyes to the stable, where the dog had just emerged from a canvas-covered hole in the front wall. Evidently, this was where the big redbone spent his days when the weather turned disagreeable, which was most days during Minnesota's long winters.

He dismounted and led Red to the stable, and Sniffer ran out to greet him. The dog was gentle as a sleeping pussycat most of the time, but he would turn fierce in an instant if he sensed that Anja was threatened. It gave Will some comfort to know that her adopted canine friend lived with her in this isolated spot.

After he put up his horse with fresh water and hay and a bit of grain, he entered the house, followed by Sniffer. He suspected the coonhound smelled the meat in the packages he carried. He had passed a butcher shop after leaving Hank's General Store and picked up some steaks and smoked sausages. He sliced off a bit of sausage and tossed it to the dog, who caught it in his mouth and devoured the meat in a few gulps, before lobbying for more.

A few red-hot coals still smoldered in the fireplace, so the house was not yet unpleasantly cool. After locating the iron grate that fit on a frame in the fireplace for cooking, he fed some tinder and sticks to the coals, not wanting to build the fire up too much until after he had grilled the steaks.

After he started a fire in the cookstove, Will entered the bedroom he had occupied on his earlier visit and dropped his haversack and gear on the bed. After changing into some faded denims and a plaid wool shirt, he headed back outside to the woodpile. He found that Anja had an ample supply of cut logs but few that were split. He wondered if she was cutting and splitting her own wood. Probably. He grasped the handle of the big axe and pulled the blade free of the chopping block in which it was buried. Then he began the splitting, which he knew would render his arms, shoulders and back stiff and sore in the morning.

Will thought he had amassed an impressive stack of split wood by the time Anja rode in on her mare, Molly, more than an hour later. He waved and plunged the axe blade into the block and strolled out to meet her. She looked more like the Anja he was familiar with this time, wearing mackinaw and britches with knee-length moccasins. He concluded that she must change into a dress at work, keeping her office and clerking wardrobe there someplace. He could not begin to imagine Anja riding sidesaddle.

When they met, Anja handed him a sack she had been balancing on her lap. "Careful, Maudie insisted on sending along a small cake with the breads and sweet rolls."

"I'll put Molly up," he said, taking the mare's reins and returning the bakery sack after Anja dismounted. "Go on to the house. I've got some steaks I'll grill when I come in. Maybe you can figure out the rest."

"That sounds wonderful," she said. She cast her eyes toward the wood stacks. "You've split a mountain of wood. You can't imagine how long it would take me to do that."

"I'll try to do more before I leave for Snelling." No sooner had the words escaped his mouth than a scattering of fluffy flakes of snow started to drift from the sky. "I'd better see to the horses."

By the time Will returned to the house, a white glaze frosted the yard and the edges of the house roof's shakes, and a heavier snowfall was threatening a prolonged visit. When he entered the house, he told Anja, who was busy at the stove, "The snow's getting serious. It's going to be more than a flurry."

"I'm glad you split the wood. I brought in a few armloads while you were in the stable. We should have enough to last through at least noon tomorrow. And I'm off work for two days."

"Two days. How did you wangle that?"

"Maudie insisted. She said she would take care of Hank. He's my boss and her husband. I told her you were staying with me and had to leave on the thirteenth."

"You told her a man was staying in your house? With a single woman? Wasn't she scandalized?"

"Not Maudie. On her part, you might call this living vicariously. She thinks you are—what was the word? Scrumptious."

"Scrumptious? Sounds like food."

Anja shrugged, "Well, when I was selecting the baked goods, I think she did call you 'eye candy.'"

Will did not know what to make of Anja. He had never seen this playful, buoyant side of her before. "Can I go ahead and put the steaks on?"

"Sure. I'm warming up some canned beans, and I've got a pot of coffee on the stove. I've got butter in the cold box just outside the door, and a nice selection of breads." Many Minnesotans refrigerated foods with outdoor cold boxes during the winter. Summer food preservation was more challenging. Salting, smoking, pickling and canning were year-round tools.

Will built up the fire just enough to char and roast the meat. "I was surprised to find fresh meat in Mankato."

"Fred Carpenter has an ice house behind his market. Sells ice, too. Of course, nobody needs it now. Food production. There is money to be made there. Producing it is the easy part. Preserving and saving it for consumption is the challenge."

"You're serious, aren't you?"

"Somewhat. My job at Hank's has piqued my interest in commerce. Provide people with things they want and need and make a dollar profit in exchange to buy what you want and need. Why not? Buyer and seller both benefit."

"There is a man getting some attention in Germany right now who would not agree with your simple treatise on economics. His name is Karl Marx. He would say you are exploiting the masses with the practice of your ideas. He calls it capitalism."

"Never heard of him. Does he favor starvation for the masses?"

Later, as they finished a supper that left Will feeling stuffed, Anja placed on the table a white-frosted cake emblazoned with blue letters spelling out "Will & Anja" across the top. "I didn't ask her to put our names on it. She gave it to me that way. It's what she calls an apple cake, but it has nuts and raisins in it, too."

Anja seemed a bit embarrassed, and he spoke to reassure her. "I love it. I will have to stop by the store and thank her before I leave town."

He hesitated before slicing through the letters, but the taste washed away his guilt. "Now, this is the true meaning of scrumptious."

They washed the dishes and cleaned up the kitchen area together. Then Will built up the fire, and they retired to the parlor with mugs of coffee. Sniffer was stretched out on the buffalo robe in front of the fireplace, lost in canine dreamland. "It's the warmest spot in the house, and he will claim it for the night," Anja explained. "When the fire starts to burn out, he will come and wake me to put on some wood. If I don't, he'll jump in bed with me."

Lucky dog, Will thought. He said, "You seem happy here."

"I am not unhappy in Mankato. It's a nice enough stopping place. I am anxious to start the school term, and it will be fun working with Karina. It will give me an opportunity to decide if that is what I want to do with my life, now that I've found new interests. It seems I want to do everything, but that's not realistic, I guess. Why plan too far ahead? One thing I've learned since I got word of Matthew's death—and then, my parents—is that we can only count on this day, this minute. Everything we think we hold dear or consider important can be yanked from us in an instant."

"A reason to treasure what we do have."

"Yes. But let me hear about what you've been doing. You've attended the trials? I've read about them in the newspapers, but there is no objectivity. The news is all

Ron Schwab

one-sided. Hang the Indians and drive the others out of the state. I lost my parents during the war. I understand the anger. But this is so complicated, and I doubt my pain would be eased by seeing three hundred Dakota warriors hanging from the gallows in Mankato. Tell me what you can."

Will took the better part of an hour summarizing the trials and explaining his concerns about the procedures and the verdicts. "I have serious reservations about the legality of the trials and certainly about the constitutionality of the process. I fear that they are being used as an arm of a lynch mob comprised of a large majority of the people of Minnesota. The trials are more political than judicial."

"But you can see why retribution is a catharsis—a sort of cleansing—for the people?"

"Yes. But that is not what the law is about. The constitution is about protecting the individual. It is the last wall between the mob and the minority, keeping in mind that the smallest minority of all is the individual."

"So, will three hundred Dakotas hang?"

"That is up to President Lincoln. His advisors seem to be trying to draw a distinction between those who engaged in acts of war and those who committed atrocities against individuals. At least there is a rationale to this.

Of course, we know that many Dakotas who participated in slaughter of the settlers were not caught and are in hiding or departed the state. Most of the witnesses are dead. Those who hang will be largely symbols. Sacrifices for satisfying bloodthirst."

"You have been ordered to report to Fort Snelling by the fifteenth. It has something to do with this, doesn't it? You are not leaving for the war?"

"I am going to Washington to report my observations. It's not really a secret mission. I am to deliver transcripts and other documents pertaining to the trial. Billy is going with me as my adjutant."

"You're going to see the President?"

Will chuckled, "Not likely. I will be talking with people several levels removed from the White House."

"It's still quite impressive to a country girl."

"Then I won't play down its importance. I do like to impress beautiful ladies."

She rolled her eyes. "Will you be returning to Mankato?"

"I assume so. My immediate superior appears determined that I see this war through to the bitter end. And, of course, the bitterest will be the executions in Mankato, however many there might be."

"You will stay with me when you return?"

"If that is your wish."

"It is. I have a few more questions, and then we'll put the Dakota War aside for now."

"Go ahead."

"I haven't seen the list of the Dakotas sentenced to death. Is Cut Nose on that list?"

There he was again. Cut Nose. "Yes. He is on the list."

She did not seem surprised. "Will the prisoners be allowed visitors? I would like to speak with him."

"I don't know, but I assume so. Under guard. You would have no privacy."

"That would be no concern. I speak fluent Dakota, as you know."

"I will speak with the officer in command of the prison detail. I will need to ride in the day after tomorrow to get information for at least a cursory report on prisoner status. Perhaps I can blaze a path for you."

"I would appreciate that. And when you return from Washington, I promise I will explain what this is all about. I'm not sure myself just yet."

They talked until almost midnight about trivial things, often exchanging anecdotes from their childhoods and school days. Finally, Will said, "Could I heat some water to wash up in? And I'd like to step out and use the privy."

"Go ahead. I have a big kettle and a wash basin for each room. I'll heat enough water for both of us to use. I've got a bar of lye soap under the sink. Also, there is a chamber pot in each bedroom, so you won't need to go out during the night if nature calls."

They had been dealing with bodily functions on the trail for some weeks, so they were comfortable talking casually about such things. When Will returned from the outhouse, he said, "Snow is piling up. You can follow my steps now, but I'll dig a path out in the morning."

"Water should be hot enough soon. The basins are on the counter. Help yourself."

While Anja was gone, Will poured some hot water in a basin and then pumped some cold water from the little sink pump to cool it a bit. He peeled off his shirt and took the lye bar and soaped down his underarms and torso, washing and rinsing with a cotton cloth Anja had placed on the counter. He had started to dry off when Anja returned. He thought nothing of it, because she had seen him shirtless on other occasions and nearly naked after his battle injuries. She brushed his back with the tip of her fingers when she squeezed past him to fill her own basin. He did not know if her touch was intentional or not, but the tingling raced directly to his loins. He knew that his stay here had been ill-advised.

She stood beside him but turned her back to him while she removed her shirt. He brushed his teeth with the brush and baking soda he traveled with, trying in vain to avert his eyes from her perfect small breasts when she turned toward the sink to finish washing. Finished, he started to return to the parlor area, when she spoke huskily, "In the morning we'll bathe each other."

He stopped abruptly, thinking he must have misheard. He did not turn around. "I don't think I heard you."

"You heard me."

She left him speechless, struggling for a response he failed to call up.

Anja slipped up behind him and wrapped her arms about his waist. She had slipped back into her shirt, but he felt her breasts pressed against his back. "If we sleep together tonight, we can forget about the silly modesty, don't you think?"

"We're sleeping together?"

"A few things you should know. One. I am not a virgin, so wipe away any guilt about taking that from me. Virginity is highly overrated, anyway. Two. We cannot use the 'L' word."

"The 'L' word?"

"You will figure it out. As I said earlier, all we know for sure that we'll ever have is now. All you have to say is 'yes.'"

He eased from the embrace of her arms and turned to face her. "Yes. Yes."

Her impish grin told him she was having great fun with this. He kissed Anja's smile away and swept her into his arms and carried her into her bedroom. There, they spent the night extinguishing their modesty, ignoring the wind that howled outside and shook the cottage walls. He remembered sleeping some, spooned against her lithe, warm body. He could not bring himself to move away until he felt Sniffer's cold, wet nose against his bare butt, summoning him to feed the dying fireplace flames. He complied, and when he returned and crawled beneath the covers, Anja moved to him yet again. The woman was insatiable this night, and, although he was forbidden from speaking the "L" word, he knew he loved her.

Chapter 52

THE CLICKETY-CLACK OF steel against steel as the railroad cars trailed the engine down the tracks almost lulled Will to sleep. Billy had surrendered without resistance and was slumped chin on chest in the seat beside him. Of course, Billy could sleep on a bed of nails. Will could not shut down his brain long enough, however, to block the thoughts that refused to release their hold. Like his mission in Washington. Like Anja. Especially Anja.

Their few days together had seemed to pass in mere minutes. After that first crazed night when they could not get enough of each other, he and Anja had calmed some, although they had taken turns bathing each other in the tin tub and been too occupied to get out of bed for their noon meal. They had cared for the horses, though, and Will had scooped paths through cottony snow to the privy and the stable. The snow had ceased mid-morning, but a foot of the white stuff on the ground had provided the perfect excuse to stay holed up with a crackling fire most of the day.

The next day, however, had been less idyllic. Duty had called Will to Mankato to confirm the status of the Dakota prisoners. His report would be a gloomy one. He had heard again of the mobs that assaulted the innocent Indians on their long, cold journey to Fort Snelling. On one occasion an enraged white woman had snatched a baby from a Dakota mother's breast and dashed it repeatedly against the ground. The baby had died along with unnumbered other Sioux, who were attacked and beaten by mobs charging past the soldiers with clubs, axes, and pitchforks. Countless captives had been injured by stones and other objects launched from the crowds that gathered along the road as the pathetic caravan of Dakota families passed. A wave of guilt swept through Will when he compared his cozy haven the night of the snow, wind, and frigid temperatures to the unsheltered trek of that procession trudging up the road toward Fort Snelling, which would have been several days distant at that time.

And the condemned had no better accommodations for escaping the elements. They were presently held near a bend in the river a few miles distant from Mankato. The Army was rapidly constructing a shed in which to incarcerate the prisoners at that location, which was now being called Camp Lincoln. Mobs had already descended on the encampment with the objective of taking and killing the sentenced warriors, but cavalry units had been called in to reinforce the guard detail, and the assaults had been driven back. Before the shed had even been completed, however, several log prisons were ordered constructed within the town limits of Mankato to lodge the prisoners. They would be incarcerated there pending President Lincoln's decision and what a majority of Minnesota citizens probably hoped would be the condemned warriors' mass public execution.

They had boarded the train at St. Paul, and, after nearly three days on and off trains, expected to arrive at the station in Washington in a few hours, which would be about five o'clock in the afternoon. He worried about the baggage. They had loaded two trunks filled with transcripts and documentary evidence submitted at the trials. He and Billy had each carried on bulky canvas warbags, and Will had brought a valise with uniform changes. According to his instructions, the trunks were to be delivered directly to the War Department, but it would be an inconvenient time of day. And where in that maze was the delivery point? He had been stationed in the Capitol during most of his tour with JAG, and he knew that with the outbreak of the rebellion, the War Department had become cluttered with desks and makeshift offices and that its tentacles now reached into multiple buildings.

Will might just as well have given in to a nap, because, looking out the window as the train pulled into the depot, he caught sight of a young corporal standing on the wooden exit platform holding up a sign imprinted with the words "Major Nilsson." Will sent Billy to recruit the corporal's help in unloading their cargo. The corporal promptly appeared with two privates in tow, and the luggage was quickly moved to a wagon with a double row of seats in front of the cargo area. An impeccably-dressed man, a Robert E. Lee lookalike, stepped out from behind the wagon, his face revealing twinkling blue eyes and a congenial smile.

He extended his hand, offering a firm grip. "Welcome, Major Nilsson. You had a pleasant trip, I trust?" said Charles Hanscomb.

"Yes, we did, sir. An uneventful trip, which suited me fine."

"Travelling across the country in a bouncing ice house is not my cup of tea, but it beats the hell out of a stagecoach or, worse yet, riding horseback." He paused and sighed. "Well, the day is getting on. You may consider your merchandise delivered. He gestured toward a shiny, black carriage some twenty paces ahead of the wagon. "I would like to have you join me in the buggy up there for a few private words on the way to your hotel. Perhaps, your adjutant can hop in the wagon with the other soldiers, and the wagon team will follow."

Will and Hanscomb sat in the comfortable, upholstered rear seat of an elegant two-horse carriage during the brief trip to the hotel. Even during wartime, he thought, the upper bureaucracy did not forego certain luxuries. America did not recognize kings or noblemen, but in the higher echelons of government some royal amenities were not difficult to find.

As soon as they were seated, Hanscomb spoke, turning grim and businesslike now. "Major, I cannot overstate the importance of what you will be doing here. The President has read all your reports—delights in the simplicity of your language and your insight. He insisted that you be an anonymous part of the team that will be working together the next few weeks."

"I'm flattered."

"Don't be. You are about to step into the fires of hell. Understand that if I had my way, the savages would have been strung up and buried by now, and this would be ended. Justice be damned. The President's got a war to run, and it is not going well. On balance the Rebs are whipping us right now. The Republicans took terrible losses in Congress during the election a few weeks ago. The voters are fickle, and I am sorry to say, few understand the workings of their government. The President is visible so the blame for unpleasant news is cast upon him. Abraham Lincoln is not a popular man. You have heard of this Emancipation Proclamation he is planning to issue?"

"Yes. I was reading about it on my trip to Washington."

"Well, it is going to happen. On January 1, 1863. Less than six weeks from now. This will outrage the South— eliminate any possibility of truce or negotiated reconciliation. And for the same reasons, many in the North will become even more disgruntled. My point is that the President must dispose of the Dakota crisis quickly. It's another albatross clawing at his back."

"But he is unhappy with the outcome of the trials?"

"Yes. You must understand that with the President the law was his first religion. I would not be surprised to learn that the law is his only religion. He cannot abide a whimsical approach to the law. He sees it as the only barrier between free men and tyrants."

"I agree."

"He probably found that in your written words and that is how you came to be his pet."

"A strange feeling. Being termed the 'President's pet.'"

"You can take it as a backhanded compliment. But your words did nothing to steer him away from his conscience. More likely they reinforced it. I think it appropriate that you have been summoned to help sort this out, keeping in mind that even the President recognizes that political realities dictate rationally imposed executions."

Will found himself too overwhelmed with the man's words to respond.

Hanscomb continued. "A carriage will be in front of your hotel in the morning at seven o'clock to take you and your adjutant to the private rooms at the War Department, where you will meet the other members of your unofficial advisory council. You may use your adjutant as a clerk."

Billy's reading skills were rudimentary at best, so his clerical skills would be dubious. Still, his company would be welcome in what promised to be a tense environment.

Chapter 53

ANJA WAS DELIGHTED to find a letter from Will when she stopped at the Mankato post office to see if any mail was being held for her. There was no delivery to her farmstead, so her mail was sorted and held at the post office until claimed. She had few correspondents, so ordinarily she stopped by to check weekly. Lately, she had shifted to a daily routine and found herself walking away disappointed. Today, her perseverance was rewarded.

She did not open the letter, which she had retrieved mid-morning, until she settled in at home following her workday at the general store. She did not know why, but her hands trembled when she opened the envelope. She was surprised to find three precisely handwritten pages inside. The date indicated the letter had been written the day of his arrival in Washington, just a week ago. Very

fast mail service, she thought, wondering if he had pro-
cured special privileges to receive such attention. But,
knowing Will, that seemed unlikely. The letter furnished
his mailing address in care of the Hotel Jefferson but assured her that given delivery time he did not expect her
to write. He anticipated returning after the first week
in December and hoped she might join him to celebrate
Christmas with his parents if military duties did not interfere. She thought that would be fun. With the holidays
approaching, it already had occurred to her she had no
family anymore. Well, with perhaps a single exception.

Mostly the letter covered mundane matters such as
the railroad trip and the hotel accommodations, which
sounded quite nice and made her wish she was with him.
She learned that he and Billy would be working at the
War Department daily, but he had provided no other
details. The best news, though, was that he would be returning to Mankato to remain until the "sentences are
carried out." The joy of his returning was dampened
some by the purpose. It was the conclusion of the letter
that touched her soul.

*I think often of the furlough time we shared at your home.
After we first met at the Lower Agency, we started a journey
through Hades together and battled through it all and learned*

to trust and care. I thought later that we had unknowingly fashioned ourselves into a matched team, like spirited horses sharing a terrible and challenging burden, if you will forgive the equine comparison. But during those few days before I departed Mankato, we also found our way to Nirvana together. You forbid me to use the word, but I discovered something else there.

Please know that I shall return as soon as possible, because I left something very important with you—my heart.

Missing you always,

Will

Tears glistened in her eyes, and she felt a droplet rolling down her cheek. His words could have been her own. She had not intended for this to happen. Not now. She had stupidly thought it could stop at satisfying their mutual lust, but she had deluded herself. The other had come first as she supposed it should. It had already been too late to ward off love. But they still could not utter the forbidden word. She was a superstitious sort about some things, a trait likely passed on from her half-Dakota mother. She could not forget she had professed her love for another soldier, whose last words before he went off to war were, "I love you, Anja." And he never came back. They never found him. If they did not speak of love, perhaps the spirits of destiny would not hear. She supposed the notion was silly, but why risk it? They each knew what the other felt. There was no need to speak of it.

She found paper, pen, and ink bottle and placed them on the kitchen table to write a reply. She would not tell him yet, however, about the plans she had made for tomorrow. Yesterday she had approached the commander of the dayshift guards of those Dakota prisoners who had already been moved to one of the uncompleted log structures in Mankato and learned that Cut Nose was now incarcerated there.

Young Lieutenant Frederick Anderson had been nervous about her request, but she had assured him that Major Nilsson had obtained approval of some unnamed superior. Will had at least mentioned her wishes to someone whose name she could not remember, but he had received a non-committal "such arrangements will be addressed later." She had flirted shamelessly but pled a prior commitment when invited by the lieutenant to join him for supper. She had been shameless and disgusting, she thought, and she had found Lieutenant Anderson interesting and handsome. Another time she might well have accepted his invitation, but, strangely, she felt married now.

Chapter 54

C UT NOSE WAS sitting on the dirt floor, his back against the wall and a blanket wrapped about his shoulders when he saw the two soldiers walking among the prisoners. One held a lantern, while the other was grabbing the chins of chained warriors and harshly pulling them upward to examine their faces. They were obviously searching for someone. He watched, thinking he could easily trip a single soldier and strangle him with the slack in the chain between Crippled Horse and himself. Two he would be unable to take down alone, and Crippled Horse would not help. His warrior spirit had fled like a tiny field mouse from an overturned nest. Life was more precious to him than a warrior's death.

He tugged the blanket tighter, knowing it was a futile act given the unchinked cracks between the logs that welcomed entry to the bitter winds. The sun had started creeping through three barred windows and the wall cracks only a short time earlier, and the interior of the building was dusky, making the soldiers shadowy forms, and they would have been nearly invisible if one had not carried the glowing lantern that illuminated their faces and those of the Dakotas they were inspecting.

Cut Nose had slept well enough despite the endless chill. He wore his buckskins, although many had accepted white man's clothes, perhaps thinking they could make the white men treat them differently. Fools. He had acceded to acceptance of a sheepskin-lined coat when he learned there would be no fires in the prison. At least Camp Lincoln had permitted fires to warm cold bones. Unfortunately, for many Dakota prisoners that had been insufficient to prevent the icy attack on toes, fingers, and other tender parts that burned and then numbed and, finally, caused the flesh to die and blacken.

He waited and watched as the soldiers worked their ways through his fellow tribesman. He heard the words "Cut Nose" spoken by one of the soldiers and guessed they might be seeking him. They were apparently receiving no assistance from the other prisoners, and he would not reveal his place. It did not alarm him because he felt more an observer than a participant in all that happened here. As he waited, he pondered the visions and dreams that had sneaked upon him since his capture.

His thoughts turned to Stalking Wolf, who had invaded his sleep again in the hours before he awakened. The soldier's spirit haunted him but never brought violence to his dreams. The tall white man just watched him, always lurking in the shadows, and Cut Nose did not like it. During the war, he had seen the tall soldier many times, too often for coincidence. And often he had been paired with Anja. He had encountered them together on the trail that first day of the war and again standing side by side during the first attack on Fort Ridgley. She had fought like a fearless Dakota warrior. But why not? It was to be expected. Others had told him that Anja had fought at Stalking Wolf's side during the second attack and killed Swims Like Otter that day. The spirits of Stalking Wolf and Anja were intertwined, and he was uncertain how he felt about that. Stalking Wolf was a fine warrior and would make a worthy mate for Anja, and their breeding would not produce cowards or weaklings. But regardless of the hue of skin, they would be white warriors, not Dakota.

The soldiers looked his way now and were walking toward him. He feigned disinterest. As they neared, he saw that one was a mere boy, who treated the prisoners with kindness. The older soldier brought scorn and anger with him and was quick to use his boot or rifle butt on any who did not obey as quickly as he desired. He was a big man, as tall as Cut Nose, but carried a huge belly. With knife in hand Cut Nose would have taken great satisfaction in spilling the man's guts on the floor.

Cut Nose did not look up when the soldiers reached him. The big soldier kicked his hip sharply with his boot toe. "Hey, Injun, look at me."

Cut Nose chose deafness until the soldier grabbed his chin and yanked it upward to expose his face. The boy-soldier lifted the lamp above him, its blinding glare forcing Cut Nose's eyes to squint.

"That's him," the older soldier declared. "The chopped-up nose and scar. Ugly bastard, ain't he? This is Cut Nose." He knelt with a key to unlock the padlock that held his chains to those of Crippled Horse, who looked on silently. When the chains were free, he pulled Cut Nose to his feet and clutched the chain that anchored each wrist to the other to lead him away.

The boy-soldier stepped ahead with the lantern. "Where are we taking him, Herb?"

"Lieutenant Anderson says he's got a visitor, of all things. We're to take him to the sentries' nest."

Cut Nose was certain the soldiers were unaware that he understood the white man's tongue, as did many prisoners. Almost all played dumb, for they learned much by masking this knowledge and keeping ears alert. A visitor. This made him curious, and he was pleased to anticipate something—anything—that might break up the boredom of incarceration.

At the far end of the building they came to a door that the boy-soldier opened. The soldier called Herb jerked roughly on the wrist chain and drug him into a small room furnished only with a small table and four chairs—and a potbellied stove that tossed off heat like a summer breeze. He observed that the cracks between the logs in this room had been chinked and plastered over. He guessed this was a place where the guards came to get warm when the conditions in the prisoners' area became intolerable.

One of the chairs was occupied by a woman with sable hair braided Dakota style and whose back was to the door. He instantly suspected the identity of the visitor. It was confirmed when he was led around the table and pushed down in a chair facing her. He gazed at Anja Lund impassively while both wrist and ankle chains were anchored to a table leg. The soldiers stepped back, each taking a position in separate corners of the room on each side of the stove.

The Herb-soldier said, "Lieutenant says thirty minutes should do. No more than forty-five."

"Thank you, Private," Anja said. "That should be adequate."

Cut Nose studied the young woman. She was even more beautiful than her mother, Calling Dove, the loveliest he had ever lain with. Her skin was dark as some full-bloods, but her softer features, like her mother's, favored her white lineage. She wore doeskin shirt and pants and knee-high winter moccasins today, and he suspected this was by design. Anja was no fool. She thought he would speak more easily with a Dakota, and she was right.

Anja finally broke the silence between them. "I will speak Dakota to escape big ears."

He nodded, pleased with the perfect rhythm of her words. Her mother had taught her well.

"I asked to see you today because I wanted to talk about my mother and you . . . and me."

Again, he responded only with a nod.

Anja said. "Do you know that my mother is dead?"

"I know this."

"Did you kill her?"

"No. This I would never do. I saw her after your white father was killed and she sent me away. She said she was no longer Dakota."

"You call him my white father. That implies I have another."

"I think you are of my blood."

"I asked my mother. She was unsure."

"She said that to spare you. My seed was planted before she married Lund. I wanted Calling Dove for my woman, but I was young and had too few horses. Lund offered many horses and other goods in trade. Your mother was half-blood and not so prized among the other Dakota warriors. Your mother told Lund you came two moons early. He was no fool, but he wanted your mother and seemed happy enough to live the lie. He must have been a good man. He was glad enough to claim you as his own. Your mother cared for him and gave him two sons who shared his blood."

"But after they died, he was left with another man's child."

"I think he did not look upon you that way. Did he ever make you feel he was not your father?"

"No. Never."

"Then, he became your father. That is much more difficult than the mating that spills the seed, do you not think?" He surrendered a rare trace of a smile at what he considered a small joke, and it pleased him when she nodded and returned it.

"This is very strange to me," she said. "I believe what you tell me. I have long suspected, and my mother could not fully deny it. But you have removed any lingering doubt. And I did want to know."

"I have answered your question. I would ask one of you."

"Of course, what is it?"

"The tall soldier who was with you on the trail the first day of our attacks? Only he was not a soldier that day."

"Yes? That was Will Nilsson. Major Nilsson."

"I gave him a Sioux name. Stalking Wolf. Is he your mate?" He could see he had surprised her with the question. She hesitated as she struggled for her answer, which told him the truth, whatever her reply.

"We are not married. But, yes, he is my mate. But why did you name him? Why do you call him Stalking Wolf?"

"I have had visions that our lives were intertwined and that he would be my downfall. He was like the death wind coming for me, even though he did not know it. And I have come to realize it was more than that. He was sent to breed with one of my blood so I would disappear into the world of the whites. The medicine between you is powerful, and for you, Anja, my heart sings. But I know now that the whites have truly won, and my time is ended."

"I thank you for speaking with me," Anja said. "I must think about the things you have told me. Would you like me to visit again?"

"No. I think that would not be a good thing. I would not speak with you again. Too many tongues would wag, white and Dakota. I have nothing else to say and wish to hear no more."

"Very well." Anja pushed her chair back from the table, stood up, and stepped around it, startling Cut Nose when she bent over and pressed her lips softly to his forehead and said, "Good-bye, Father."

Chapter 55

WILL'S POSITION IN Washington was an unofficial one as a military consultant to President Lincoln's appointed three-member review team, all of whom he came to respect as capable lawyers and men dedicated to the Constitution and rule of law. While he did not share all the team's conclusions, he appreciated that decisions were made based upon court precedent and reasonable interpretations of statutes and the Constitution in the many instances where there were no precedents to guide deliberations.

John Palmer Usher was a former railroad lawyer and current Assistant Interior Secretary. George C. Whiting and Francis Ruggles were both experienced lawyers serving with Usher in the Interior Department. Thus, they did not have to waste time getting acquainted and adjusting to different styles and personalities.

The other lawyers treated Will respectfully, though they were all a generation his senior. The President sought recommendations by early December, so Will and the team worked twelve to fourteen-hour days, including Saturdays and Sundays, over a two-week period to review the trial proceedings and evaluate the involvement of the defendants. Will was troubled that the frantic rush to "justice" still prevailed, but he was consoled by the team's effort to seek as much of the truth that could be found. Several times during the deliberations Lincoln dispatched messages emphasizing his objective to distinguish between acts of war and crimes against innocent civilians, and team members sought to ferret out the distinctions among the defendants.

The files were divided by the team members, and Will circulated among the three to respond to questions concerning his personal observations at the trials. The transcripts were essentially handwritten and often sketchy. They were not near to verbatim accounts, and Will thought sometimes they were closer to fiction. Will referred to his own notes to supplement the information and was pleased to find that Billy read with greater literacy than he had let on and made himself very useful in the sorting and filing that was required.

Some decisions were quickly made by a single team member. Those that were in doubt were discussed and decided upon at the end of the day by the collective team after tossing questions to Will for comment. Increasingly, the "beyond a reasonable doubt" standard came into play among team members—a standard alien to the original trials. Near the end of November, another message was delivered by Charles Hanscomb on behalf of the President. This time Lincoln specifically admonished the team that they were to scour the trial transcripts with the purposes of identifying all cases of rape, murders of women and children, and unarmed men in the settlements.

Hanscomb pulled Will aside and said, "Grab your coat, Major, you will join me for a stroll."

Outside, facing the icy breath of a north wind, the two men started walking up the street that led to the White House. Will was puzzled by the destination but said nothing. When they reached the grounds, they were admitted by a salute from an Army guard. The salute was repeated by another soldier when they entered the building. Will was struck by the thin security on the premises. The quiet entry contrasted sharply to the chaos that reigned in the interior hallways. The halls were jammed with what seemed a horde of men, sprinkled with a few women, racing frantically up and down the hallway with at least one hand clutching either a stack of papers or a leather briefcase. Will knew from his own experience with JAG that paper was the lifeblood of the bureaucratic class, and the place was obviously drowning in the stuff.

Hanscomb made an abrupt turn and led Will down a calmer corridor past open doorways revealing men hunched over at desks, some shuffling the paper some assistant had just dropped on their desks. They came to a closed door with yet another armed soldier standing outside. The private tendered the familiar nod and Hanscomb gave the door three quick raps before taking out a key and unlocking it. He opened the door and signaled Will to enter ahead of him. Will stepped in, and, as the door closed behind them, he saw the gangly, bearded and bespectacled man behind the desk. Abraham Lincoln looked up and removed the wire-rimmed reading glasses and dropped them on the cluttered desk.

Will, unsure of protocol, stood at attention and saluted. The President waved him at ease and got up and stepped around the desk with his hand extended. The long, bony fingers engulfed Will's hand, and Will faced one of the few men he had encountered who exceeded his own height by several inches.

"Major Nilsson, I told Charles I would like to meet you and thank you for your fine work. Be seated, please."

Will and Hanscomb took chairs in front of the desk, and Lincoln returned to his own. The President continued, "The advisory team chairman, Mr. Usher, has been reporting progress to me with some regularity. He informs me that your input has been invaluable to expediting the decision-making. Of course, that is why we called you to Washington."

"Thank you, Mr. President."

"But your reports from the war and the kangaroo trials are what led me out of the forest."

"I don't understand, sir."

"You consistently took note of the differences between acts of violence against the innocent and those committed in combat. Your words struck a responsive chord in my mind. I am still troubled by the decision I must make, but I can live with what I expect to do. Sometimes that is the best we can do."

"I do not envy you, Mr. President. If some of the prisoners escape execution, there will be an uproar in Minnesota. Your Republicans will not be welcome there. The people are calling for retribution—and to most that means death or worse. They are not concerned about the niceties of constitutional rights these days."

"But the Constitution is in vain if we do not have the courage to defend it."

"I agree, Mr. President. I fear for our country if a day arrives when our leaders lack such courage or find it convenient to disregard its supremacy."

"Well spoken, Major. Thank you for coming by to see me. I will be thinking of you during the dark days ahead."

Will took the President's words as a signal to depart. He turned to Hanscomb, who was already getting up from his chair, so he followed suit, and they quickly exited.

As they stood in the hallway, Hanscomb explained, "This is the President's private office, where he slips away to do work without interruption. You could see from the mess it is a working office."

Will could not have missed noticing the stacks of books and papers lined on the floor along the walls. The hideaway was obviously not a reception area for dignitaries. "Yes, I could see the room is a serious workspace."

"The President also receives occasional guests outside the eyes of the hostile press and gossipy staff. No record is made of the people who visit here. He insisted he wanted to meet you, but he wished to protect you from the political storm that will be coming on."

"That was thoughtful of him, and I am grateful for that. I am not a politician and have no aspirations."

"Perhaps you will see it differently someday. We need more like Lincoln but will not realize it until he disappears into history."

"Somehow, I don't think Lincoln will disappear."

Hanscomb sighed, "Let's hope not. Now, I leave you to return to your work. Decisions are coming on quickly. When the report is submitted, you will return to Minnesota, where you are to monitor the execution proceedings and continue to send reports. Approximately two weeks after the executions, you may pick up orders at Fort Snelling for your assignment to a cavalry unit. As requested, there will also be orders sending your adjutant with you and promoting him to sergeant. You should be accompanied by a soldier with respectable rank. With the casualty list rising, this rank business is becoming very muddled anyway. I would not be surprised to learn we now have more brevet than regular officers. You may find yourself a general by the time the war is ended."

On the morning of December 5, the review team submitted its report. Lincoln had already reviewed preliminary recommendations and was prepared to act. Of the three hundred and three death sentences, only forty were considered for confirmation by the President. One of these was John Godfrey, a former slave, whose testimony throughout the hearings had been considered vital by the commission. Lincoln reduced his sentence to ten years imprisonment. That afternoon, the President sat at his desk and wrote out an order dated for the next day, which he directed to General Sibley confirming the remaining thirty-nine sentences:

Ordered that of the Indians and Half-breeds sentenced to be hanged by the Military Commission of Colonel Crooks, Lt. Colonel Marshall, Captain Grant, Captain Bailey, and Lieutenant Olin, and lately sitting in Minnesota, you cause to be executed on Friday the nineteenth day of December, instant, the following names to wit.

Lincoln wrote in his own hand with phonetic spellings the names of all thirty-nine Dakotas to be hanged and the trial numbers as set forth in the record. Number 17 on the list was Marpiya-te-najin (Who Stands on a Cloud) [Cut Nose]. Case No. 96. The last paragraph of the order directed that the remaining prisoners be held subject to further orders.

Chapter 56

A WEEK AFTER PRESIDENT Abraham Lincoln ordered the Dakota executions, Will and Billy arrived in St. Paul. When they disembarked the train, Will immediately purchased a copy of the St. Paul Daily Press. He learned that Generals Sibley and Pope were pressing for delay of the executions in order to complete preparations. It was anticipated that the President would be issuing a supplemental order postponing the execution date one week to Friday, December 26. *Merry Christmas*, Will thought. The newspaper was packed with Dakota war stories, and the articles reflected the predictable public outrage over Lincoln's commutation of most of the death sentences. Will stuffed the newspaper in his bag for future perusal.

Billy asked, "What are my chances of a short furlough, Major?" He had become accustomed to addressing Will by his rank in Washington and had vowed to stick with it, knowing first names would be inappropriate once they were attached to a cavalry unit. Since he had not officially received the orders yet, Will had not informed his friend that he would be going on active duty as a sergeant, not that Billy was likely to get full of himself over it.

"Unless the trial isn't postponed, I need you in Mankato by the eighteenth. I will want you to make a run to Fort Snelling before the executions and another after. Then, I can give you some time after the executions before our orders come through."

"That will be terrific. I want to spend some time with Karina before we go."

They started walking to the nearby livery where they had stabled their horses. "Karina? I didn't know you were seeing Karina."

"Meaning no disrespect, Major, but there's a few things that get past you."

And might rather not know about, Will told himself. My God, Karina was a child.

"When you get to Mankato, you will find me at Anja's house, or you can check at Hank's General Store. She would be there during work hours and would know where I am at. I can give you directions to Anja's."

"No need, sir. Been there. Stayed overnight a few times. All decent and proper, of course. Well, more or less."

Will was confident Billy had never paid for a meal or a room in his lifetime. He was not concerned about Anja's fidelity in the least, but he wondered what "more or less" meant. The two men saddled their horses and separated. Will decided to head his big blood bay down river to Shakopee and bypass Snelling. It was closing in on noon and the sun shone brightly in an azure sky. By Minnesota standards in December, the day was downright balmy. He figured he could find a place to sleep in Shakopee. If a room at a boarding house was not available, a pile of straw in a barn or stable would do. It would require another night on the road before he reached Mankato, but he figured he should be able to ride in at a decent hour day after next. Then he could plant himself there till he and Billy left for their war assignment.

Chapter 57

ANJA WAS SURPRISED when she reined Molly into the yard and saw healthy plumes of smoke rising from the chimney. When she found Red in the stable, her curiosity was satisfied. Will was home. She took her time unsaddling and caring for Molly, since the mare was carrying a precious foal and deserved special attention. When she was finished, she rushed to the house. She opened the door and stepped directly into Will's open arms. She pushed the open door shut with her toe, as her lips melted into his.

When she pulled back to catch her breath, she said, "I'm glad I gave you a key."

"You should be. I baked biscuits and chopped up bacon to put in some scrambled eggs. Coffee is hot. I'm ready to start the eggs right now."

"Can't we wait?"

"For what?"

"You know what."

"You are a lustful woman."

"I am where you're concerned. There. I've admitted it. Don't get a swelled head."

"That's not what's swelling."

"Oh, you vulgar man. Just for that, we will eat first." She slipped around him and headed for the kitchen. "But we'll eat fast," she added.

Later, they sat on the buffalo robe in front of the parlor fireplace, Sniffer wedged snugly between them. Will said, "We've barely spoken since you got home."

"I didn't need conversation."

"If you don't mind a long-term guest, it appears I can be here for nearly a month. I might want to talk some, though."

"You can talk now. Till bedtime. Then you will have to shut up. I don't like to talk when we're making love."

"Fair enough. I will have duties here until the execution. I have been ordered to check on the condition of the prisoners and report to Washington. I am to witness the hangings, which I do not look forward to."

"The conditions are deplorable. There are huge cracks between the logs that let the wind and snow whip into the buildings. The only stoves are for the guard nests.

Fires are not allowed. The Dakotas are living in virtual ice houses."

"You have been there?"

It was time to tell him. "Yes. I visited Cut Nose."

"I see."

"Aren't you going to ask why?"

"No. I cannot tell you everything about my missions. There are probably things I will never tell you. I don't think couples need confessionals. A secret you carry that does not affect me doesn't come between us, as far as I'm concerned. Tell me anything that makes you feel better. Otherwise, don't worry about it."

"It will make me feel better to tell you. I don't want to carry this secret alone."

"Then we can carry it together."

Anja took a deep breath and spoke with a shaky voice. "Cut Nose is my father."

Will turned his head and looked at her, and she could see astonishment in his eyes. He did not speak, so she continued. "I have suspected this for several years, but he confirmed it several weeks ago, and things he told me made me ninety-nine per cent certain." She could not dam up the flow of words now, and she found herself telling him about her conversation with Cut Nose and the visits the warrior made to her mother over the years.

Will said, "That's quite a load to carry by yourself."

"The man I still consider my true father was a fair-complexioned Norwegian, and I wondered about that. My skin was darker than my mother's, and she was half-blood. I should have been quarter-blood."

"You have beautiful skin, incidentally. Flawless."

"But I am three-quarters blood. I ought to be living in a tipi on the reservation. And I am the daughter of possibly the most fierce, despicable warrior of the uprising." She brushed away the tears that were starting to seep from her eyes with the back of her hand. She felt Will's hand close over the other.

"You're making too much of this Anja. I'm mixed blood—"

"Quarter-blood."

"I don't care if you are full-blood. I don't care if your skin's green. I know who you are, and you are the woman I—"

"Stop."

He looked exasperated. "Okay, I won't say it. But if you think Cut Nose comes between us some way, you should know that I played a role in determining which of the Dakotas would be spared and which would hang. He received no help from me. But I am glad I didn't know your relationship at the time."

"You were doing your job. If any deserve to die, it is Cut Nose. I would never fault you for that."

"And I would never fault you for being the daughter of, perhaps, the greatest Dakota warrior ever. The moral complexities are more than we can ever sort out. Somehow, in Cut Nose's mind, his actions were justified and necessary. But neither of us will ever be able to grasp that."

"He said you were sent by a spirit to breed with me. He believes you are a great white warrior. He even gave you a name. Stalking Wolf. But that's a story for another day."

"You can be cruel."

Anja decided it was time to depart the maudlin topic. "Tell me about Washington. Did you enjoy your visit with President Lincoln?"

"How did you know about that?"

"I did not till now. You just told me."

"You have a very devious side I must learn to watch out for. But to answer your question, no one knows about that meeting. Officially, it never happened."

"Two of us do—plus the President. And you know your little secret is safe with me. I don't care to know what was said there. That can be one of those little secrets we talked about. I just want to know how it felt."

"He seemed very tired and terribly sad. His voice was more high-pitched than I would have expected for a man whose speeches will probably endure for the ages. He spoke very deliberately, and I found myself hanging on every word. He struck me as very humble, yet I sensed I was in the presence of greatness. That, of course, does not render him infallible. I could not have been with him more than ten minutes. His time is precious, and I felt honored just to meet him."

"I can just see you sitting in front of a massive desk in a huge office with towering book cases, and the President sitting erect in his high-backed chair as he spoke."

"Actually, it was a grubby little room with a single window and no bookcases. The desk and floor were nearly covered with stacks of paper. He sat in a wooden, straight-backed chair and was mostly hunched over his desk. Sorry to destroy your illusions. There was nothing kingly about the surroundings."

She shrugged. "Well, that's interesting, too. I'm just glad you're here. I thought Billy might be with you. He is welcome to stay here, you know. He has overnighted here on several occasions—once with Karina."

"Karina? That's where he was going in St. Paul—to visit Karina."

"They're very enamored with each other. He has pro-posed marriage, but she wants to finish her schooling first."

"Marriage? She's a child. I thought they were friends, but I had no idea anything serious was going on."

"You must have a blind spot where some things are concerned. They were taken with each other instantly. Billy is not one to waste time, like some men I know. They are sleeping together. They shared a bed for one night here when Karina was visiting. You were at the trials, and Billy came through Mankato on his way back from a mission and stayed over." She giggled. "They were rather noisy and got Sniffer barking. I had to bring him into my bedroom for the night."

"I'm just afraid he's taking advantage of her."

"She's sixteen. She'll be seventeen in April. Many fron-tier women are married by that time. My mother was not yet seventeen when I was born. A woman is an old maid if she reaches twenty and is still unmarried. Did you real-ize you are sleeping with an old maid?"

"That could be easily changed." He paused. "As early as tomorrow."

Now that was a sneaky proposal. It would be so easy to snatch it. But the war barricaded that step. And the fear of loss and—no small part—superstition. "I wish,

Will. But not now. Don't give up on me. Please. I do want what you want. Don't doubt it."

"I have more persistence than brains. Our story is just in the first chapter. Let's go back to bed."

They did, and Anja promptly dropped off to sleep, her arm flung across his bare chest and her head nestled against his shoulder.

Chapter 58

OVER THE NEXT several weeks, Anja and Will separated each morning, she to work at the general store and he to monitor preparations for the executions and arrangements for the prisoners. The first day, Will called upon Colonel Stephen Miller, who had fashioned a headquarters from a leaning, log structure that he said was an abandoned tavern. Miller was charged with carrying out the executions and administering the incarceration for the yet to be sentenced prisoners. He was relieved to find that Miller, a tough, but conscientious professional, seemed not to resent his presence, and, in fact, welcomed it. The fit, mustached soldier appeared to be in his early forties, but Will thought the man had aged a dozen years since they last met two months earlier. He looked at Will with limpid, blue eyes that betrayed fatigue and frustration.

"The executions had to be postponed," Miller said, "because construction of the scaffolding for almost forty condemned is a gargantuan task, and we could not find the 600 to 800 feet of strong rope required for the hangings. I would wager that carpenters will be working Christmas day to finish the project."

"Where are the prisoners located?"

The colonel stood. "The sun is shining, and we are enjoying unseasonably decent weather. Allow me to give you a tour." Miller slipped into his coat and led Will in the direction of the gallows construction.

Will noted that the gallows would be within sight of Hank's General Store, where Anja was working. As they approached the construction, he said, "They are forming a square."

"Yes, each side will be about thirty feet long. Ten Indians on each side. There will be a single trap platform for each side, so the Indians in one row will drop simultaneously. Ideally, all thirty-nine would drop at the same time, because the ropes from the traps anchor to a huge single rope that will be cut and theoretically trigger all the trap platforms to swing open."

"Theoretically?"

"I am assured by the carpenters it will work. I am just a bit nervous. I have never supervised the execution of one man, let alone thirty-nine."

"There will be a crowd. I assume control measures are in place?"

"There could be several thousand people. God knows how many. I daresay local businesses are enthused about the event. I expect to have sixteen hundred troops in columns surrounding the gallows."

"So where are the prisoners?"

"They have been separated." He pointed to a three-story stone building not far from the gallows. "The condemned are housed on the main floor of that warehouse building now. They are in ankle chains riveted to the floor. But my guards have orders to keep them supplied with water and to tend to their needs. They are fed three times daily. They eat as well as the soldiers, but I suppose that's nothing to brag about. Also, they are accustomed to different food than the whites and have been known to dump the offerings on the floor or toss the food at the guards. We can walk through the prison, if you wish, but first I will show you where the unsentenced are housed."

They walked in the direction of the river, where Will saw a log stockade within which lay several log buildings. The gallows would still be within sight of the crude facilities. As they neared, he saw smoke rising from pipe chimneys protruding from the roofs of the structures. Inside the stockade, he observed that the gaps between the logs in the building walls had been freshly chinked and filled. It appeared that Anja's concerns had at least been minimally addressed. "I am impressed, Colonel, and will say so in my report."

"Thank you, Major. It would be appreciated."

He caught sight of a dozen or so prisoners huddled in a far corner of the stockade. "They are not in chains."

"Most are not, although some are belligerent and judged to be dangerous, so they are kept in ankle irons. We rotate them outside in the stockade when weather permits. Fresh air. That sort of thing. I am not certain they appreciate it. Their eyes say it all. They don't trust us. They know they are not going to hang, but they have no notion what is going to be done with them. Neither do I."

After a cursory examination of the confinement quarters, they headed for the warehouse prison for the condemned. When they were admitted by the guards, Will immediately sensed a change in atmosphere. In the log prison they had been stared at as curiosities, and the quarters were cramped with over one hundred twenty-five Dakotas in each building. Here the warriors gathered in silent clusters, and he saw sheer hatred in their stares. Will did not relish seeing any man in chains, but he would despise guard duty that sent him among these men unchained. It occurred to him that regardless of his concerns about the legal niceties, the President's evaluation team had chosen the right men for the ultimate punishment.

As the two officers strolled along a cleared pathway among the prisoners, Will felt the man's gaze before their eyes met. Cut Nose looked at him, his expression stoic, his face revealing nothing. But the warrior recognized Will. He had no doubt.

Colonel Miller interrupted the stare down. "Do you know that warrior? He's called Cut Nose. He led the Soldiers Lodge. Meanest bastard of them all."

"I have seen him before."

Chapter 59

WILL DECIDED NO officer, given the trying circumstances, could second-guess Colonel Miller's handling of prison and execution arrangements. He determined that a courtesy visit every few days would suffice, although he informed the Colonel that Anja could be contacted at the general store if a sooner meeting was desired.

He spent several days at Anja's farmstead cutting and harvesting firewood and then splitting it. He prepared supper most days, well worth the rewards when nightfall came. He also wrote a detailed report for Hanscomb and the President setting forth his findings about the Mankato situation, realizing it might not be read until after the executions had taken place. He also prepared a telegram: ALL PROCEEDING SATISFACTORILY. LETTER FOLLOWS.

Billy rode in a week before the executions, the day they were originally scheduled. He stayed the night and headed back to Fort Snelling the next morning. Will informed him he could claim whatever time he wanted on that end for his personal business, as long he was in Mankato the day of the executions. Will would prepare another letter and telegram to send back that day, and then Billy would be free until they picked up their orders at Snelling a few weeks later.

Several days before the executions, word arrived of commutation of the death sentence for one of the Dakotas named Tatemina. White settlers had petitioned on his behalf on the basis that he had helped them to escape raging war parties. Thirty-eight now remained to climb the steps to the gallows.

Because of the execution schedule, Will and Anja had to abandon Christmas plans with his parents. Weather permitting, they agreed to make the long day's ride to visit Alexis and Erik for several days over the New Year's holiday. It hurt to surrender the time alone with her, but Anja seemed excited about it, and he reminded himself he should be grateful his mother and father still lived.

Anja was working almost exclusively with bookkeeping at the general store now, so she had the flexibility to take off both Christmas Eve day and Christmas and took advantage of it. Will was grateful because their dwindling days together were precious. On Christmas Eve, he was surprised to find she had a gift for him, and he caught her off guard when he produced a small package for her. When he tore the paper off his ribbon-tied box and opened it, he found a silver-plated pocket watch with the letters "W.E.N." engraved on the back. It was made by the Timex Company, a relatively new watchmaker that was rapidly gaining a loyal following for its durable and reliable timepieces. It would be a welcome replacement for the battered watch with fading and peeling numbers he presently carried.

While in Washington, he had purchased a cameo pendant carved in mother of pearl. The carving was an opalescent blue-gray, set in silver and suspended on a silver chain. Anja squealed with delight when she plucked it from the package, and he could not recall when he had seen her emotions so out of control. She insisted he assist her with hooking the chain about her neck. She rushed to a mirror and inspected the result and then returned and kissed him warmly. "I will never take it off while you are away," she vowed.

"And the watch shall ride with me wherever I go."

He would never forget their first Christmas together. Only for a moment did it cross his mind that it could also be their last.

On Christmas morning, Anja's mood turned black. Not since they had found her parents' bodies in the yard at their farmstead had he seen her like this. He had awakened well after sunrise, having frolicked a bit too long and vigorously with the woman whose bed he shared. And it had not been the single glass of celebratory wine that triggered the dead sleep. He had reached for her instinctively when his eyes opened and found her missing. Warmth had been drifting through the bedroom door, and he realized Anja must have built up the fire already. He had dressed and gone into the parlor, where he found her sitting in her rocking chair staring hypnotically at the dancing flames of the revived fire. Sniffer sat in front of her, head resting in her lap.

Will walked over, bent and kissed her on the forehead, but she seemed to barely notice. She had started the coffee heating, so he asked. "Would you like a cup of coffee? I can heat up some of yesterday's biscuits."

"Coffee would be nice. No biscuit, thank you."

He placed two biscuits in a covered pan on top of the stove to warm them for himself and took Anja a cup of coffee. She nodded a silent "thank you." When his biscuits were warm enough, he spread some honey on the biscuits and took his plate and coffee cup into the parlor and sat down in the other rocker. He said nothing while he sipped at the steaming coffee and ate his biscuits. She would speak when she was ready.

"We've never talked about it," she said. "Are you religious?"

"Not especially. My mother has enough religion for the whole family. Of course, my sister, Annette, is married to a preacher."

"But you believe in God?"

"Yes, although I am something of a skeptic when it comes to all the doctrines claiming to be the one true religion. I wonder if the Dakotas' Great Spirit isn't just as valid for them as the Christian God is to my mother, for instance. I don't have it all figured out yet, but I'm working on it. Faith can be tough. It is something you believe but cannot prove. But a non-believer cannot prove his disbelief. It seems to me we are left to sort it out for ourselves. Some lawyers might say we must decide based upon a preponderance of the evidence rather than beyond a reasonable doubt."

"I didn't have much religious training growing up. My father had a Bible, but my mother never left the Dakota beliefs behind. I'm going to get my own Bible and read it and see what I think. Maybe your mom would talk with me about it sometime."

"She'll talk your ear off about it if you let her. And, if it works for you, that's fine. My dad is pretty much a heathen, but that hasn't seemed to interfere with what seems to be a damned good marriage. I think tolerance is the answer."

"I prayed this morning."

"Did it help?"

"No."

"You probably have to believe first."

"I want to believe."

"This is all about the executions, isn't it?"

"Yes."

"Colonel Miller told me that priests and preachers have been visiting the condemned prisoners all week. They will be at the prison today, seeking out last-minute converts. A good number are converting to Christianity. Catholics are winning that race, the colonel said."

"Cut Nose won't convert."

"No. I would think not."

"I will keep praying for him."

"It can't hurt."

"I am also going to the hangings tomorrow morning. I had thought I would not, but now I must."

"Are you positive?"

"Yes."

"Then go with me. It is a part of my assignment to be there."

"I would like to have you with me. Yes, I will do that."

Chapter 60

MANKATO TEEMED WITH people. Hundreds? Thousands? Anja would not venture a guess. She found herself in a county fair atmosphere as people assembled for the executions. Many were laughing and joking. She was surprised at the number of children of all ages in attendance. The event had become a family outing for many, and the sunny, unseasonably warm day had encouraged the throngs of humanity that were quickly being crushed shoulder to shoulder as the onlookers assembled around the gallows.

Anja had stopped at the general store to change into a dress and veiled hat of mourning black before meeting Will outside to accompany him to the executions. He had met briefly with Colonel Miller, who informed him that the political dignitaries would be keeping their distances this day. Neither General Pope nor General Sibley would

attend, nor Governor Alexander Ramsey, who had lob-
bied for the execution of all the Dakotas originally convicted. All members of the Congressional delegation had
conveniently been detained by business in Washington.

The gallows were surrounded on the perimeter of the
grounds by a line of cavalry. Between the mounted soldiers and the gallows were rows of infantry standing at
attention with bayonets fixed. Anja clutched Will's arm
as he wedged his way through the crowd, both his size
and uniform helping to open a narrow path. She recognized a few of the observers but most were strangers.
She was surprised to see Dr. William Mayo of Le Sueur
in attendance amidst a cluster of other professionally-at-
tired men. He was a respected physician, who had volunteered his services at New Ulm and other battles during
the uprising.

Will veered away when they reached the line of cavalry and escorted her along the row of mounted soldiers
a short distance and then made an abrupt turn and broke
through the ranks until they reached a spot no more than
twenty-five feet from one corner of the gallows. They
were joined in this open space by a scattering of officers
who strolled back and forth, eyeing the crowd and the
troops that surrounded them.

Will reached into his trouser pocket and plucked out his new watch. "Execution is at ten o'clock. Knowing Colonel Miller, they will be on schedule. We have twenty minutes. Cut Nose should be at this corner. I gather there was some fuss among the prisoners about who should go first. Cut Nose insisted that as leader of the Soldiers Lodge, he was entitled to be first, and his challengers backed off. Do you still want to do this?"

"Yes. I must be here. And I will not make a public scene." She was the daughter of Mapeokinijin, Who Stands on a Cloud. She would not shame the greatest Dakota warrior by displaying weakness.

They waited, and the minutes seemed like hours. The crowd grew noisy and restless, probably out of nervousness, she thought. There was a drum roll, and beyond the opposite side of the gallows, she saw the condemned emerge single-file from the warehouse, most dressed in buckskins, all with strange hats perched on the tops of their heads. Then she heard it, the Dakota death song, and silence descended over the crowd, save for a few scattered taunts and obscenities directed at the condemned.

Every warrior was joining in the death song as they neared the gallows. She knew it was a prayer to the Great Spirit. Conversions aside, they had not abandoned the religion of their forefathers. Perhaps, when faced with the reality of death, some had chosen to "hedge their bets" as her father had often said.

A second drum roll echoed across the prairie town as the prisoners climbed the steps to the platform. And, yes, Cut Nose was the first to step onto the gallows platform. She could see his face now, impassive, but his lips moving as the death song continued, casting an eerie pall over the scene. The onlookers' festivities ended.

Guided by one of the soldiers spread out on the platform, Cut Nose, hands hitched behind his back, walked in her direction. She saw that the trailing group of prisoners had split off and were walking down the opposite side of the square gallows, where the leader would turn and soon meet up with Cut Nose again. Cut Nose stopped just below the noose that hung from the thick beam above him. Anja saw that the "hat" she had seen on the prisoners' heads was a burlap bag. As the other Dakotas moved into position, Cut Nose looked straight ahead, his voice continuing with the death song. Her eyes were riveted upon his face, so she saw when his head turned almost imperceptibly, and his gaze met hers and locked briefly before averting. Was it her imagination that he surrendered a slight nod? She chose to believe that. Regardless, he knew she was there to bid farewell as he embarked upon his final journey.

Cut Nose

She watched as a soldier tugged the sack down over Cut Nose's face and fitted the noose about his neck. The death song stopped, and a chill raced down her spine. She steeled herself. Another drum roll broke the silence. The traps collapsed and the condemned Dakotas dropped.

But death was not instant for most. Legs kicked and spasmed in the air. Only a few went limp as the others struggled. Anja could see her blood-father's chest rising and falling, although, somehow, he resisted the reflexive kicking of his legs.

"My God," Will said, "the drop was too short. It didn't break their necks. They are strangling."

Anja was Cut Nose's daughter. She fought back the vomit that rose in her throat.

Chapter 61

THE NEXT DAY was Saturday, so Anja went to work. She had said it was much preferred to the brooding and moodiness Will would endure if she stayed home. Tomorrow would be better, she had promised. Will decided to pay a final call on Colonel Miller, before the officer returned to Fort Snelling.

Evidently, there was no escaping bad moods this day. Miller was beside himself. "The bodies are gone," he announced the instant Will stepped in the door.

"I don't understand. What bodies?"

"The Dakotas. The bodies were dug up and hauled away during the night."

"Where were they buried?"

"Along the river in a shallow common grave. They were laid out in two rows, feet to feet. There wasn't much cover, perhaps, two feet. The idea was that floods would come along, sooner or later, and wash out the grave and carry the remains down river. Those were orders. Army didn't want some burial site that would become a monument or sacred place and start more trouble for the folks here."

"You didn't have guards posted?"

"A lone private. The place wasn't that far from our main encampment. He was instructed to fire shots if grave robbers came around. I was worried about mutilation or other mischief by Indian haters. Soldier claims he was overpowered before he could get off a shot. I'm suspicious he was bribed."

"Do you have any idea who took the bodies?"

"Doctors mostly. A bunch of damned doctors. Can you believe that? Appears it was all planned out. They showed up with wagons and help to dig up the bodies. The private admits to knowing one of the doctors—Dr. William Mayo. Saw him when the doc was treating Army casualties. He wanted Cut Nose and claimed him and three or four others. A wagon load, I guess."

"Why would they want the corpses?"

"To study, I guess. Where else would you find such a collection of cadavers? I spoke with one of our surgeons. He said they shouldn't have trouble preserving the bodies outside in the winter—shed or barn or something like that. He said there is a market for these things, and some will likely be sold. Others will have the flesh and innards removed and the bones treated to form skeletons for display in offices, hospitals, and the like. Ghouls. That's what they are."

"What are you going to do about it?"

"Not a damned thing. I'll report it to Pope and catch hell and forget about promotion anytime soon. I'll be lucky if I don't get demoted. The general won't want to call attention to this fiasco. Rumors will get out, but my guess is everybody's going to deny any knowledge of it. I will if that's what I'm told to do. We probably couldn't locate most of the bodies by now. Mayo has got political connections, and my guess is that most Minnesotans would see this as a fitting end."

Will had sympathy for the colonel. He was a good man. Somebody had miscalculated on the gallows construction, but, all in all, he had administered the executions and incarcerations efficiently and conscientiously.

This news would require an addendum to the report he expected to send with Billy to Snelling for posting this noon. His next stop would be the general store. Anja should be informed of the latest chapter in the story of the Dakota War of 1862.

Epilogue

A MONTH FOLLOWING THE Mankato executions it was determined that Chaska, one of the condemned, had been hanged as a result of an identification error, resulting from multiple Dakotas bearing similar names. The executed Chaska had, in fact, rescued and provided refuge to several white settlers.

Less than two months following the hangings, on February 16, 1863, Congress enacted, and the President signed legislation abrogating and annulling all past treaties with the Dakotas. The delinquent annuity money that failed to arrive at the reservations prior to outbreak of the uprising was appropriated to a fund for reimbursement of victims of the war.

Land held by not only the Dakotas, but that occupied by the Winnebago Indians, who had not participated in the war, was made available for public sale. In excess of a million acres of prime farmland was included. The Indians were to be relocated outside the boundaries of the state of Minnesota.

The Dakota families that were sent to Fort Snelling remained there during a bitter winter that saw over three hundred die. In the spring they were shipped by steamboats to isolated, barren land in Dakota Territory. The prisoners convicted of crimes, but not executed, remained in Mankato until April 1863, when they were shipped by steamboat two hundred fifty miles south to be housed in military barracks at Camp McClellan near Davenport, Iowa. The departing Dakota prisoners were chained together and guarded by four companies of infantry to protect them from angry mobs. The prisoners received pardons when deemed deserving by some undetermined standard by the Army, and in five years' time, all who survived were permitted to rejoin their families in Dakota Territory or moved to the Santee Reservation in northeastern Nebraska.

With a few exceptions, the hangings brought an end to the attacks on the white settlers, but retribution was not ended. Public opinion and a raging press demanded that all Indians be exterminated or driven from the state. General Pope ordered Sibley into the field with three thousand infantry and four thousand cavalry soldiers to remove the Indians from lands that were no longer theirs. Any residents of the reservations were now trespassers to be evicted by force, if necessary. Countless villages burned and at least several hundred more Indians were killed, as most of the Indians were driven from the state. With a few exceptions, all that remained of the Dakotas and Winnebago were mixed-bloods and those full-bloods who had married whites or already accepted the white ways and secured immunity by their affiliations with newly adopted Christian religions.

Chiefs Shakopee (Little Six) and Medicine Bottle had settled in Canada, but, several years later, were lured back, captured, and tried by another military commission. They were both sentenced to death, although there was no evidence submitted of their personal participation in atrocities committed against civilians. The *St. Paul Pioneer* editorialized, *"No serious injustice will be done by the execution....but it would have been more credible if some tangible evidence of their guilt had been obtained....the general supposition that they are guilty, is very likely correct, but their execution will, nonetheless, establish the precedent of hanging without proving....About the only admirable element in the whole course of the cases was the serene and dignified behavior of the chiefs in their last hour."*

Chief Little Crow had also escaped to Canada but returned with a large war party in May of 1863. His followers scattered and most abandoned him upon seeing the overwhelming numbers of white soldiers engaged in the search for renegade Sioux. He was later shot by Nathan Lamson, a farmer who was hunting when he came upon Little Crow picking raspberries with his young son. He reported the killing, and a cavalry detachment was sent to retrieve the body. They scalped the chief and on July 4 the corpse was dropped in the middle of main street in Hutchison. Throughout the Independence Day celebration, boys stuffed firecrackers in the body's orifices and set them off. It was later left at a dump near town and recovered by a cavalry officer who sliced off the head with a saber. The town's doctor deposited the head in a kettle of lime to preserve it. The scalp lock and bones of both forearms found their ways to the State Historical Society in St. Paul and were put on display. Years later, skull and forearms were united there.

Cut Nose's body was taken by Dr. Mayo to his home and stored for display until he thawed it out and eventually dissected it in the presence of medical colleagues, Later the flesh was stripped, the organs disposed of, and the bones dried and deposited in a cast iron kettle for display in his office. The skull and bones were used for illustration to patients of their medical maladies and for education of his two young sons. The brothers, Will and Charlie, became physicians and were among the founders of the famous Mayo Clinic, which bears their name. Cut Nose's reconstituted skeleton was displayed in the hospital's lobby during the early years. Whether the skeleton ended up in a museum or was just ultimately stored and lost has never been verified. However, what was believed to be the skull was recovered and returned to Cut Nose's relatives more than a century after his death.

The Dakotas residing on the Santee Reservation harbored animosity toward the Mayo Clinic for some generations over the treatment of Cut Nose's remains. But a peace offering of sorts was made in August of 2018 when a representative of the hospital appeared before Cut Nose's descendants in Santee, Nebraska and issued a formal apology. At that time, it was announced that the Mayo Clinic would endow a perpetual scholarship in honor of Cut Nose allowing one Native American student annually to attend the Mayo Clinic's medical school without cost.

Anja Lund remained in her Mankato home after Will Nilsson and Billy Buck departed for the war. A pregnant Karina Johanns joined her in mid-January of 1863. Karina fretted her condition would scandalize parents at the school, where she was to assist Anja. Although Anja thought most frontier folks were not that concerned about a woman's marital status, she suggested Karina adopt Billy's surname and self-declare her marriage. Karina liked the notion and became Karina Buck. She was confident Billy would set things right when he returned. If he did not, God forbid, come back, she still wanted to claim his name for their child. At first, Anja had to shake off a bit of envy that Karina carried the child of the man she loved.

Anja corresponded with Will, but she could tell from his letters that he often did not receive hers. All she could do was post her letters and hope. The occasional letter of Will's that found its way to her was read until the paper wore thin. She would never say the word out loud, but she never doubted that what they shared was love, and if God delivered him home, she vowed the man would hear the word each day for as long as she lived. She would never allow him to doubt.

Will could not state his location in his letters, but she knew that Brevet Colonel Nilsson and Brevet Captain Buck were with Federal II Corps led by Major General Winfield Scott Hancock. The II Corps was a division of Grant's Army of the Potomac, and Will commanded a cavalry regiment.

She snatched up every newspaper she could find and devoured the accounts of the war, which had turned bloodier and longer than anyone had predicted, and the outcome was far from certain. She had figured out that Will had to be in Virginia or other adjacent states.

Mankato's Dr. Fletcher delivered Karina's healthy baby boy at their house on July 1, 1863, which told Anja that she and Billy had become lovers early on. Why had she and Will lost so much time? Gentlemen could be trying on occasion.

Anja visited Will's parents frequently and took on more debt to buy another 160 acres adjacent to the farm Erik had purchased on Will's behalf. Hank Hellman induced her to give up the teaching job for the 1863-1864 school term by offering her an opportunity to buy a one-fourth interest in the store, which would be paid from part of her profit share over a ten-year period. They planned to open a branch store at New Ulm and explore other opportunities.

She was also supporting Karina and the baby pending the younger woman's settlement of her parents' estates and payment of loss claims filed with the state settlement fund. Anja was confident she would be reimbursed, but, financial pressures dictated she devote full attention to her business interests.

Early May of 1864 a shroud of blackness dropped on Anja. She had not given in to such a mood since that Christmas day before the hangings. She tried to remain cheerful for Karina's sake, but her younger friend kept asking, "What's wrong? What's wrong?" Maudie had sensed it also and inquired whether something was troubling her. "Just tired, I guess," Anja had responded.

She truly was tired, for as the end of the month approached, she could not recall the last time she had enjoyed a good night's rest. Something had happened to Will. She just felt it. She was working at her books in the storage room when Maudie told her the St. Paul newspapers had come in with the stagecoach. She grabbed up the papers and took them to her desk. They were filled with headlines about something called the Battle of the Wilderness. As she read the first story, her fingers began to tremble when she read that the battle was a head-to-head confrontation between the troops of Grant and Lee in Virginia.

The battle at this reporting was apparently a standoff, with both armies suffering unprecedented troop losses. She felt weak when she read that Hancock's II Corps had suffered more casualties than the rest of the Army of the Potomac combined. She had three newspapers on her desk, and she read every story about the battle, trying to dig out a thread of hope, but found nothing to boost her sagging spirits. She put the newspapers away when she read a quote from Lieutenant Colonel Horace Porter: *"All circumstances seemed to combine to make the scene one of unutterable horror. It was as though Christian men had turned to fiends, and hell itself usurped the place of earth."*

She had held back her tears all these months, but the dam collapsed, and she could not stop the sobbing. The newspapers had confirmed all she had been feeling these past several weeks. Will was dead. Like Matthew, they would never find him. If they buried him, it would be in a forgotten grave in a forgotten place. In the wilderness, for God's sake. Maudie had heard her crying and came into the storeroom-office.

"I've been reading, too, dear," she said. "Will would have been at Wilderness?" She opened her arms.

Anja nodded and stood and spilled out her grief while Maudie held her.

Maudie said, "You don't know, Anja. Remember, you really don't know."

Anja pulled herself together. "I must go home and prepare Karina. I will not be able to keep this from her."

Will's letters stopped. So did Billy's, although he had been a sporadic writer. Late June, a uniformed Curley Coburn rode into the yard shortly after Anja returned home from work. Back in uniform, the sergeant had been assigned the unenviable duty of notifying families of the news of a loved one, often bringing the tragic message of death. He had become the Minnesota River valley's Grim Reaper. Nobody wanted to see him stopping by for a visit.

He carried separate telegrams addressed to Anja and Karina. "I won't keep you in suspense," he said. "They are both missing in action. You could have worse news. I guarantee it. Karina and little Anders are the only family Billy's got. I'll be taking the same telegram to Will's folks. Till I saw this, I had no idea Will was a brigadier general—brevet, of course."

Anja finally numbed herself to it all. She worked long hours, and Karina cared for the house and baby Anders, who by the spring of 1865 was approaching his second birthday and becoming a challenge to the young mother. Lee surrendered to Grant at Appomattox Court House on April 9 but still no word of Will's and Billy's fate. She feared they might never know for certain, only assume.

Then on the evening of May 7, Anja was on her knees weeding in the garden when she saw two men walking up the road toward the house. They were dressed in faded army britches, straw hats and clod hoppers, their faces hidden by ragged beards. The tall man with the black beard moved with a stiff-legged limp, and as they drew closer, she saw that he was pale and emaciated. And now she recognized him and got up. She began screaming for Karina to come out, as she raced toward Will. She almost knocked him over when she fell into his waiting arms.

"I love you, Will," she said. "I can say it now. I love you. Where on God's earth have you been?"

"Stagecoach dropped us off in Mankato. We've been on a little visit to Georgia, a place called Andersonville Prison. I love you, too, Anja. The dream of seeing you again was what kept me alive—that and a little help from a soldier named Billy Buck. But that is another story."

Author's Note

This novel is a work of fiction. Will Nilsson and Anja Lund, their families and closest friends, are creations of the author's imagination. Cut Nose and most of the major characters involved in the backdrop of historical events were real people, although historical accounts of their lives and actions sometimes conflict, leaving the author some room for literary license. Young Lieutenant Thomas Gere, for instance, did serve at Fort Ridgley during the uprising. He was later awarded the Medal of Honor for his heroism at the Battle of Nashville on December 16, 1864.

The Dakota hangings conducted on December 26, 1862 remain the largest mass execution in American history.

The author has tracked the story of the Dakota War of 1862 with an eye toward accuracy, realizing writers and historians have occasionally recorded conflicting versions of the same events. Even eyewitnesses to the same atrocities, perhaps because of perspective or fading memories, sometimes saw the stories unfold differently.

The following reference works were helpful in writing this novel:

Carl Sandburg, ABRAHAM LINCOLN, THE PRAIRIE YEARS AND THE WAR YEARS, Harcourt, Brace, Jovanovich, Inc., 1926

Duane Schultz, OVER THE EARTH I COME, THE GREAT SIOUX UPRISING OF 1862, Thomas Dunne Books, 1992

Loren Dean Boutin, CUT NOSE, WHO STANDS ON A CLOUD, North Star PRESS OF St. Cloud, Inc., 2006

John A. Haymond, THE INFAMOUS DAKOTA WAR TRIALS OF 1862, McFarland & Company, Inc., 2016

Kenneth Carley, THE DAKOTA WAR OF 1862, MINNESOTA'S OTHER CIVIL WAR, Minnesota Historical Society Press, 1961

Gregory F. Michno, DAKOTA DAWN, Savas Beatie, L.L C., 2011

Scott W.Berg, 38 NOOSES, LINCOLN, LITTLE CROW, AND THE BEGINNING OF THE FRONTIER'S END, Vintage Books-Random House, 2013

Cut Nose

Gary Clayton Anderson and Alan B. Woolworth (Editors) THROUGH DAKOTA EYES, Minnesota Historical Society Press, 1988

Acknowledgments

A special thanks to Ray Sarlin for his counsel of things military and historical. His efforts to rescue the author from embarrassment over occasional oversights or inconsistencies have been truly valued and appreciated. That is not to warrant that I have not made a few mistakes despite his insight.

My world keeper, Diane Garland has, again, helped straighten out timeline and character discrepancies with her usual skill and professionalism.

Leafcutter Publishing Group, Inc. via its Uplands Press imprint has done an unbelievable job of bringing my work to the reading public, and I am grateful for my publisher's expertise and attention to detail in the packaging and promotion of my novels.

Many of my stories feature lawyers and the courtroom. I have been fortunate to have Judge Linda Bauer available as an advisor on such matters, as well as her services as an important part of the editing team.

Bev Schwab works on editing at multiple stages and has been my sounding board and good right hand on all phases of producing this novel.

My editor, Mike Schwab, does the final edit and formatting of the manuscript and steers the book through the process that gets it to our readers. His input as the novel progresses is essential to producing a book that, hopefully, readers will enjoy.